When All Else Fails:

Ava's Story Part Two

Christian Cashelle

Copyright @ 2014 DYNAMIC IMAGE PUBLICATIONS

Cover design by: Christopher Howard of CKH Creative

ALL RIGHTS RESERVED

ISBN: 0989442314
ISBN-13: 978-0-9894423-1-2

To You
Don't ask others to forget the past when you keep showing them the old you. There comes a time when we all have to grow.

One

Ava's nose flared as she ran through the opening of the kitchen and tackled Bri to the ground. Bri yelled before turning on her back and trying to move Ava off of her. Ava grunted as she slipped her arms around Bri's back and tried to flip her over. Bri shuffled to plant her feet on the ground before pushing forward, knocking Ava on her back onto the gray and black peppered carpet. The action caused the twins to slide up against the cherry wood coffee table, inching it out of its place. Ava smirked, wrapped one of her legs around Bri's waist and used her lower body strength to roll them over. Bri huffed as Ava sat on top of her stomach.

"Ugh, get off of me, whale!" Bri yelled. Ava smiled down at her older sister by mere minutes and wiggled, causing more pain to her. "It was just cereal!"

"No, it was my cereal," Ava said, sticking her tongue out. She smiled as Bri struggled to get from under her weight. Over the last two years, Ava had gained a few pounds up on Bri so she knew she'd have a hard time getting out of the position Ava had her in.

"Still acting like kids," Rico said, walking into the living room. He pushed his arms under Ava's, wrapping them around her chest and pulling her off Bri. Instead of helping his youngest daughter to her feet, Rico unlaced his fingers and Ava fell with a soft thud on her bottom. She scooted next to Bri on the floor and they both laughed. Rico shook his head as he walked past his daughters and out of the room.

"I'll buy you some more," Bri said, turning on her belly, pushing her body up on her knees, and standing up. Ava shook her head. She could remember when they'd fight about the names Bri called her, how she'd conformed to the ways of the rest of her friends and labeled Ava a whore. They'd fight about how embarrassed Bri was to be Ava's twin; how embarrassed she was of Kita.

Now they fought over cereal.

It was amazing how different things could be just two years later. If the past events of Ava's life hadn't been so devastatingly relevant to the choices in her present, they would not seem real. Ava and Bri would be twenty-two soon. High school seemed like a lifetime away, but looking at the relationship she had with her twin now, Ava wasn't mad about it.

The fact that she didn't see Bri much because of her school schedule made Ava always pick on her when she did see her.

"Gelly is the one who's going to be mad at you."

"She could never be mad at Ti-Ti B!"

As if hearing her mother and aunt discuss her, three-year-old Angel came toddling through the living room with a dark pink feather duster glued to her hand. Ava watched attentively as her daughter sauntered over to the television stand and proceeded to swipe the duster across the bottom of it.

Bri walked towards the stairs as her cell phone rang and Ava sat up on her elbows and continued watching Angel.

Her face was less chubby than it had been during her first year of consuming Ava's life. Her eyes still sparkled in dark wonder and her sandy brown curls were beginning to somehow straighten themselves out. Ava loved the dimples that seemed to pop out of nowhere on her child, a trait she would have to attribute to the other half of Angel.

"Gelly, what you doing boo?" Ava asked after a few minutes. When Angel didn't answer, Ava rolled her eyes. "Angel D!"

"What mommy?"

"You heard me, I told you about ignoring Mommy."

Angel huffed before giving her mom a sympathetic eye and throwing her hands down. Ava shook her head again. Angel was so much like Ava it was scary.

"Clean."

"You cleaned enough," Ava said, stretching her arms out. Angel dropped the feather duster and walked over to her mom. She stopped at her feet and crawled on her legs to get up to her lap. Ava wrapped her up in her arms and kissed her forehead. Angel was tall for a three-year-old and Ava was almost looking up at her as she sat on her lap. She tried to smooth down the ponytail she'd just done the night before. Ava always joked that she would have hair like Romero's family.

"Go get your shoes and we can go," Ava said, patting Angel on her bottom. Ava's cell phone rang. Sliding it out of her pocket, she sighed when she saw Dre's name.

"Yo."

"Wow, you actually answered your phone," Dre said.

"I'm sorry. I've been busy," Ava said, pushing herself off the floor.

"I'm doing you a favor yo, I didn't ask you for this opportunity, you asked me." Ava rolled her eyes at the repetitive threat he gave her.

"I know, so who needs a hook?"

"It's a whole song this time, Ava. I need you in tomorrow to go over the idea of it." Ava swallowed the small lump in her throat that formed after 'whole song' left Dre's lips. "Ava, you're still there?"

"I'll be there," she said, before hanging up. Ava sighed before getting Angel and heading out the door to her car.

It had been two years since she stopped singing again, but she still wanted to be apart of the industry. She asked Dre to connect her with some upcoming singers who needed lyrics. The problem was that it didn't pay much at the moment so Ava had to get another job. Between that and taking care of her family, she had missed a lot of the appointments that Dre was setting up for her.

It was usually just a chorus or bridge, but now Dre wanted her to write full songs. She wondered if she was ready for it, but tomorrow was tomorrow and she didn't have time to think about it.

As Ava turned corners, she looked around in awe. At this point in her life she wasn't sure why she was still in Hamilton, Tennessee and how it could seem so different to her now. A few years before, when she was still in high school, it didn't seem like much. Now they had transformed everything around her. She was twenty-one now, things had definitely changed since high school.

Ava smiled as she pulled into her usual parking space next to Sunny's truck. Glancing into the back seat, she saw that Angel was sleeping and smiled harder. Today was Sunny's only day off this week and whenever they came over, he usual spent most of his time playing with Angel.

Ava loved Angel's relationship with Sunny, but it would be nice to have a few hours of alone time with him while Angel napped.

Sunny answered the door, running his hand down his head over his low cut fade and his eyes low.

"Get her please," Ava said, trying to shift Angel's weight. Sunny grunted a little before taking Angel and putting her in his bed. He soon joined Ava on the couch, falling on top of her as she laughed. She knew his job was taking a toll on him. His arms were more defined and the small gut he had was just about gone. His caramel skin had darkened from being out in the sun on different construction sites, but Ava fell in love with him all over again after he cut his braids off.

She ran her hand down his fade before he tipped his chin to kiss her lips. Sunny mumbled the words to a song about not knowing her name but loving how good she looked in heels. Ava giggled as she shifted around to get comfortable under his weight.

"I don't even have on heels."

"Don't even matter, baby," Sunny said, pecking her neck. Ava smiled before she closed her eyes. "You always go to sleep on me. I just woke up, I'm not tired anymore."

"Yes you are," Ava said with a sly grin. "Just close your eyes and think about it." She held in a laugh once she heard Sunny suck his teeth.

He was always her center, even before he knew it. Sunny was cool when Ava was anxious, he was collected when she panicked, and level headed when she was going crazy. Sunny was all those things when Ava was all the opposites. The one time she had to be strong for him had connected them for life. Ava never wanted to fall out of love with him.

His breathing evened and Ava smirked as her own slowed down just before she fell asleep.

"It just doesn't feel right today," Ava mumbled, pulling the large headphones off of her ears, allowing her dark curls to fall and frame her face. She tilted her head to the left and the right, waiting on some type of relief. Her eyes focused outside of the booth to see one of them glaring at her, one was giving her a disappointed head shake while the other was busy ignoring her.

"What's wrong?"

"Does it sound right?" she asked.

"It sounds a little off. Let's run through it again."

Ava nodded, swallowing a little saliva as her stomach twisted in knots. Quickly exhaling through her nose, she pulled the headphones back over her curls and stepped closer to the suspended microphone.

The walls of the recording booth didn't seem this close to her before. The dark grey padding was darker and the light was dim. Ava pulled at the neck of her shirt and cleared her throat.

She closed her eyes and tried to sing but none of the notes came out right. She wanted to push through it and get it over with but the track soon stopped, leaving her in silence.

"You're right, it doesn't sound right."

"You sound weird today. I know what you need."

Ava opened her eyes and panicked from not being able to move. She bucked her knees and tried to push what was holding her down. Sunny, jarred from his sleep, jumped up from the couch and looked down at her.

Ava sat up crying, looking around and blinking.

"Baby, look at me. You are in my apartment. You were having a nightmare again. You aren't there anymore. I'm here and Angel is in my bed sleeping," Sunny said, grabbing Ava's shoulders to try and calm her down.

"Angel's in your bed sleeping," she repeated as he nodded. Suddenly feeling a need to confirm his assurance, Ava got up from the couch and jogged into Sunny's bedroom. Her heart calmed as she saw Angel curled around one of the pillows. Ava wiped her face with the back of her hands before crawling into the bed and snuggling next to Angel.

Sunny came in minutes later and sighed at the sight of his woman and his little lady. He shook his head before he wiped his face with his hands. Ava had already fallen back to sleep, hugging Angel tightly. He slid in his bed behind her and wrapped his right arm around her waist, protectively.

Two

"So what's the deal? Why don't you want to do a whole song?" Trishelle asked. Ava's conversation with Dre was so heavy on her mind that as soon as she got to Trishelle and Kaylen's apartment, Ava asked her opinion.

Ever since she met Trishelle, they had been best friends, more like sisters. They had been through a lot in the short years they'd known each other and trusted the other with their lives. Ava knew that Trishelle would give her a one hundred percent real opinion on anything she asked her about. It was why Ava valued her so much.

"I don't know, it's not much of a difference but I'm just used to writing hooks," Ava said, pulling on her curls. Trishelle swatted her hand away before glancing at Jayla and Angel who were busy playing on the carpet in front of them. Trishelle rubbed her three-month pregnant belly and shook her head.

"I think you're tripping."

"I didn't say I wasn't going to do it," Ava said. Trishelle smiled.

"I'm going to check the food."

Ava huffed and pushed back into the couch, running her hand over her face. She hated having big decisions to make.

She looked around the living room at all the pictures on the wall. Ever since Jayla was born, Elle had gone picture crazy. Ava knew Kaylen was annoyed with taking pictures almost every month because most of the recent ones were just of Jayla by herself instead of them as a family. Angel and Jayla even had a picture together. Ava groaned remembering that day. The two toddlers were best friends but hated dressing alike.

The front door swung open and Ava, Angel, and Jayla all looked towards it at the two, loud men walking through it. Both toddlers took off towards them, Jayla scrambling to get to her dad and Angel hugging Sunny's leg.

Ava smiled watching Sunny pick Angel up and kiss her forehead. Every time they interacted Ava remembered Sunny telling her that Angel would like him better when Ava was pregnant. Ava thought that was really true.

"What's up, bro?" Kaylen greeted Ava while cuddling Jayla in his hands. Ava frowned as Sunny sat down next to her with Angel in his lap.

"I really wish you'd stop calling me that," she said. Sunny poked Ava's cheek before kissing her shoulder. She turned to him and kissed his lips.

"Wife is my dinner done?" Kaylen yelled towards the kitchen, ignoring Ava's irritation for her nickname. Trishelle yelled back for him not to rush her.

Ava shook her head and smiled. This was her chosen family. She didn't get to see Bri often because of her school schedule and Charity and Rico were always working. She loved being able to come over here and just fool around.

"Babe, Romero's outside," Sunny said, pushing back the tan curtains and peering out of the window. Ava sighed before reaching over to put on Angel's jacket and throwing her backpack over her shoulder. Sunny opened the door for her and Ava stalked down the stairs towards Romero's car. Once he saw them, he got out to help.

The sun was gone, but Ava navigated around his car with the help of his headlights that were reflecting on the side of the building. She shifted Angel's weight on her hip and handed Romero the bag with her free hand.

Romero's tall frame straightened up as he pulled the door handle of the back door behind the passenger. His other hand disappeared under his hood but came back down over his face as he licked his lips.

"I gotta be somewhere at three tomorrow," Romero said, his eyes shifting from Ava to the ground quickly. Ava caught on to his behavior and eyed him suspiciously. Ava never talked much so she could always pick up on when someone's usual behaviors changed.

"I get off at noon," she said after putting Angel in her seat. "What's up with you?" She asked, her open hands clapping down on her thighs as she stood back up.

"What? Nothing, I'm just, just tired that's all."

Ava nodded slowly before bending down to kiss Angel goodbye. Romero went back to the driver's side as Ava closed the back door and Angel waved at her. She jogged back up to Elle's apartment to see everyone eating.

"That's just rude," she said, walking past them all into the kitchen to fix her plate. She looked around at the new décor and shook her head. Since Kaylen was still against Elle having a job, she had a lot of hobbies to keep her busy. It seemed as if she changed the kitchen every few months. Ava was tired of helping her and prayed that since she was pregnant again she would slow down.

Her mind then switched to the meeting she'd had earlier with Dre and Solace, the singer looking for a song. The initial meeting hadn't been so scary. They discussed rates, ideas, and a general theme that she was looking for in the song. Ava felt like she could vibe with her but in the back of her mind pressure was becoming an unwanted issue. Dre had been betting his name on Ava's talents and although she'd delivered as far as hooks went, she wasn't too sure she'd have the guts to push out a whole song worthy of recording.

Ava shook her head, ridding it of thoughts of work, before fixing her plate. Elle had made a turkey meatloaf but looking at it Ava couldn't tell the difference from a regular one. She loaded her plate with mashed potatoes and fried corn before idly wondering if Angel would eat any of the food if she was there.

When Ava and Bri were younger, Kita would try and trick them into eating something healthy. Ava would usually fall for it, but Bri always figured it out and got Ava on her side in protest. They'd dance victoriously once Kita gave in and ordered pizza.

A sloppy kiss on her cheek delivered to her by the lips of her lover brought her back to the world. It seemed she zoned off like that often and it started around the same time her nightmares did. Only Sunny knew about the nightmares and it was only because she'd had one while spending the night with him. They were progressively getting worse and Ava couldn't figure out why.

That whole day was like a horror film. The nightmare always started relatively innocent as that day progressed into terror. She always knew though, what was coming.

She thought she'd put that horrible day behind her. She tried hard not to think about it; remembering the pain of hiding it all from the people she loved, dealing with being pregnant and making the decision to keep Angel, it was all too heavy for her.

Ava had gotten past it and moved on with her life, building relationships back up from destruction. Now that these nightmares had become routine, Ava felt like the 17-year-old that was gang raped in a homemade recording studio.

Maybe it would never end.

Later that day, Ava went back home since Sunny had to be at a new construction site early for work the next morning. It was past eleven when she pulled into the driveway behind her step mom, Charity's car.

Before she could get to the porch, the front door opened and her dad walked out.

It still took her a second to register that Rico had cut his braids off. He'd done it about a year ago, saying it was time he actually looked like a grown man and that he was tired of his girls joking about him nearing fifty with braids. Bri was upset about it but Charity and Ava were all for it. It was low cut; just enough for a short curl pattern to emerge.

It didn't matter to Ava if he had braids or not, Rico was still her hero.

"What's up?" Rico asked, looking past Ava to his car, pulling his snapback Chicago Bulls hat down over his head. Ava frowned before looking around and seeing nothing.

"Hold the door," Ava said. "Where you going this late?"

"I'm Rico, your dad, have we met?" he asked. Ava gave him a sarcastic smirk. "One of my boys needs a ride home."

Ava watched him step aside, holding the dark oak front door open. Using the indirect light from the kitchen that bounced out into the foyer, Ava stepped up into the house and turned back around. Rico reached in, kissed her forehead and closed the door behind him.

Ava shifted her weight to her left leg while she stood looking at the door for a moment. This wasn't the first time she'd caught Rico sneaking out late. Sure, he didn't have to sneak out since it was his house and he was her father, but something about the way he always had an excuse ready unnerved her.

While Ava walked to her room, she prayed that whatever her dad was doing, that he was careful. At any moment she felt like the law could come and take him away again. She felt herself getting angry just at the thought of Rico selling drugs again. She had forgiven him for being gone eleven years of her and Bri's life because he hadn't meant to do it. This time around, if it happened, she wouldn't be as nice.

He had a decent job with a wife who was also working, matter of fact, everyone who lived in the house had a job save for Angel. There was no need for him to risk his life for that anymore.

After taking a quick shower and setting her alarm, Ava looked around her room to make sure everything was ready for work. After a couple of years at the telemarketing company, Ava found another job as an assistant manager at an authorized third party vendor for several cell phone companies. Tomorrow was an early, but short day but after she got Angel from Romero she was supposed to meet Dre again. She'd only have about five hours of sleep so she was counting on being able to sleep in peace.

It was easier for her to stay in routine of her days when they were stable like this. She didn't have to worry about guys coming after her for what she could do for them or arguing with females over their man's infidelity. She didn't have to worry about coming home to a broken house full of distrust, animosity and spite. The only thing she missed from her past was her mother. The tranquility and contentment of her present life was something she wasn't ready to change.

Ava fell into her bed and attempted to pray the nightmares away.

The next day hadn't gone as planned. There was an issue with an order of phone accessories, so Ava ended up staying over an hour at work. Romero was blowing her phone up as she was clocking out and shutting down her computer.

"Where you at, yo?" Romero asked. Ava rolled her eyes at the attitude in his voice.

"I'm just now getting ready to leave work."

"I thought you got off at twelve?"

"Well, I didn't," Ava said, rolling her eyes in irritation.

"You out now?"

"I just said that, Romero."

"Well, I'll be pulling up behind your car in a minute."

Ava hung up without responding, now annoyed that Romero couldn't even wait until she got to his house. She grabbed her purse before pushing the backdoor of the building open and poking her lips out.

"What if I wasn't getting off?" Ava asked, as Romero stepped out of his car and went around to the side Angel was sitting on. "What's so freaking important?" Ava asked, remembering not to curse in front of Angel.

"You were supposed to be off an hour ago," Romero said, ignoring Ava's question and unbuckling Angel before grabbing her backpack. His car was parked sideways behind Ava's, so Angel ran around and hugged her mother's leg.

"Hey Gelly," she said, leaning down to kiss her. Romero put Angel's bag on top of Ava's trunk and picked Angel up to kiss her goodbye. "Why you acting all weird?"

"Weird, how am I acting weird? No, I'm good," Romero said, putting Angel down. "Just have somewhere to be."

Ava frowned but decided to leave it alone. She had to be at Dre's in the next twenty minutes and she already knew he'd have an attitude if she was late.

"Whatever Romero, bye," Ava said, opening her backdoor and securing Angel in her seat. She slung her backpack from sitting on the trunk and into the car before shutting the door.

Ava's job was in a small shopping plaza on George Hamilton Parkway. Since Hamilton, Tennessee was a small town, there were only a handful of highways and most of the restaurants, stores and the mall were off of the parkway. Ava loved working only five minutes from home so she didn't have to leave too early and it didn't take her a lot of time to get home after working a full day. If she wanted, she could go home on her lunch break but that was only if Angel was at home with her family instead of with Romero or Elle.

It would usually take Ava only fifteen minutes to get to Dre's house on East Bay Avenue but today it took an extra ten minutes.

She rushed out of the car and around to get Angel. Dre was sitting on his porch with his arms crossed.

"I know," Ava said, throwing one of her hands up while she grabbed Angel's hand. "Work was tripping."

"Whatever," Dre said, standing up to go into the house.

"We can leave the attitudes, Dre," Ava said. "I'm not even that late."

"Hey little momma," Dre said to Angel, but not before eyeing Ava for a second after her last comment. He held his palm up and Angel jumped to high-five him.

"'Sup Dre!" Angel yelled. Ava shook her head at her child's choice of words, but Dre smiled. Ava went ahead and put Angel's favorite toys on the carpet in front of the television while Dre went downstairs. She usually tried to get a sitter for Angel when she had to meet with Dre, especially if the artist was there. Since today was just the two of them, she knew he wouldn't mind Angel being there. Besides, Ava wouldn't hesitate to discipline her. Angel acted out at home, but she knew better than to do so at someone else's house.

Dre came back upstairs a few minutes later with his tablet and sat down on the couch next to Ava. He rubbed his right ear with his hand before looking towards the wall then back at her. Ava sighed heavily and sat back against the cushions of the couch.

"Solace likes what you have so far, as far as a concept, but we need to see some progress quick."

"How quick?"

"Like within the next few days," Dre said. Ava sunk her teeth down into her bottom lip and glanced at Angel to keep from cursing. "Just some progress, you need to stop spazzing out."

"I have no days off, Dre!" Ava said, through clenched teeth.

"You sit in front of a computer all day at work," Dre said, sarcastically. "How hard."

Ava placed the palm of her hand flat over her left eye and rubbed the back of her fingers into her eyebrow. Dre sucked his teeth.

"You in or you out? 'Cause we don't have time to waste, she wants to pay you so you have to be on her time."

"Is she paying that much?" Ava asked, crossing her arms under her chest and bending her right knee, relaxing her leg on the couch. Dre pushed it off and Ava rolled her eyes.

"She's paying."

Ava sighed, sinking down into the couch with her shoulders hunched.

"I don't know, Dre."

"What's your problem, yo?" Dre snapped. Ava frowned.

"Don't talk to me like that."

"You're pissing me off, Ava. I been riding for you for a while and you keep changing up. There ain't much more I can do for you."

"Would you just chill! I didn't say I wasn't in!"

"Well keep all the 'I don't know's,' and all that to yourself and get it done!"

Ava tapped her foot against the carpet as she watched Angel whose eyes were fixated on cartoons. She side eyed Dre and tried not to smile.

"Still though, don't talk to me like that."

"You can't tell me what to do," Dre said, before laughing. Ava grunted before shaking her head. "We're done."

'Thank God," she said, sarcastically. Dre waved her off before Ava packed up Angel and headed home.

Three

Sunny sat against a pile of cinder blocks and adjusted his construction helmet to block the sun. His day was almost over but it seemed to be dragging along minute by minute. He gripped his left shoulder and rotated it at the cuff, hoping he wouldn't be too sore. Having two days off of work really made a difference.

Sunny groaned when Kaylen came into view. Last year, Kaylen had been promoted to a site manager. He had somewhat of an office now at the construction base and only came to the sites a few times a week. They worked about thirty minutes outside of Hamilton.

He rolled his eyes at Kaylen's office attire as Kaylen walked up and smiled.

"You tired?" Kaylen asked.

"Shut up."

Kaylen laughed before sitting next to him. Sunny smirked.

"Be careful, we wouldn't want you go to back to the office dirty."

"Shut up."

"What's up?"

"Took an early lunch, trying to figure out what to get Elle for our anniversary," Kaylen said.

"She's pregnant, right?' Sunny joked.

"That's not a present."

Sunny laughed. He knew that Kaylen and Elle's anniversary was coming up soon. It seemed like it would be more years but that was because they had been together forever.

"Ask Ava to see if she's been hinting at something," Sunny suggested. Kaylen nodded.

"Speaking of bro," Kaylen said and Sunny laughed. They both knew Ava hated Kaylen calling her that. "When you thinking about proposing?"

"Proposing what?"

"Don't be stupid," Kaylen said. Sunny frowned.

"How did we get on this subject?"

"You ain't getting younger, you're almost 26."

"I'm not old."

"You trying to leave her?"

"No!" Sunny said, quickly. Kaylen smiled.

"Then what you waiting for?" he asked. Sunny narrowed his gaze and glared at Kaylen.

"What do you know?" Kaylen gave Sunny a knowing smirk, but shook his head. "Man I don't have to time for no guessing games,"

"You been with her for three years," Kaylen said. "Shouldn't be no guessing."

Kaylen left a little after their conversation, leaving Sunny to his lunch and his thoughts.

It wasn't as if he didn't think about marrying Ava, he just wasn't sure when the right time would be. They had been through so much in the past few years. He had to deal Romero being jealous of his relationship with Angel and him and Ava coming to common ground on how much time Romero spent with Angel. Issues with Sunny getting a legit job and Ava cutting back on singing and being at the studio so much had also come up. Ava's attitudes and mood swings weren't always the easiest to get over at times. Also having to deal with her dad treating her like **a child because** she still lived at home and then the debate on whether they should move in together after that. Sunny also had moods where he wanted to be left alone and a lot of times Ava didn't understand why.

But they were stable now, as stable as a relationship could be. He loved Ava and Angel so why wasn't now the right time to get married? Why hadn't he taken the necessary steps to make Ava his wife? Kaylen and Elle didn't make it seem too hard to do. Situations like this could always be better if Sunny had his mom to talk to. She'd know exactly what to say but at the same time, leading him to find his own answer. For a single mother, she'd done her best to make Sunny his own man. Over two years since her death and Sunny still wasn't sure how he was making it without her.

However, he did know part of the reason was the man who just left him confused. His friendship with Kaylen had been more than half of his life and somehow transformed into a brotherly bond in between middle school and high school. They had been a part of each others' lives, celebrating the good and getting through the bad together. Kaylen was his brother and even though Sunny was the eldest of the two, he looked up to Kaylen.

Kaylen never hesitated to go after what he wanted. From the first time Kaylen had seen Elle, he knew he wanted her and now they were married with a beautiful little girl and another baby on the way. When other guys their age were still clubbing and sleeping with multiple women and shying away from responsibility, Kaylen was just trying to take care of his family.

Sunny could respect that. He just wasn't sure if he was ready for it.

After work, while Sunny was driving down the highway towards his exit, he got a call from his cousin Shalena from back home.

"Santana, it's been too long," Shalena greeted him. Sunny rolled his eyes at the use of his government name.

"Well, that's what happens when you have a job," Sunny said.

"Funny," she said. "I miss you, cousin. I'm coming to visit tomorrow."

"Were you planning on telling me?"

"I just did," Shalena sang, in a teasing manner.

"What you do?"

"Huh?"

"You don't really miss me, so what did you do to my Auntie?" Sunny asked. When Shalena sucked her teeth, Sunny knew he had discovered the real reason for Shalena's impromptu visit.

"I did nothing! She's just losing her mind and irritating me. We need a break from each other."

"Um hum, how long you plan on staying?"

"It's just a few days, cousin! Thanks, I love you. See you when I get there," she said with no breaks in between her words before hanging up. Sunny shook his head before tossing his phone in the passenger seat and turning on his exit.

He hadn't seen Shalena since a few months after his mom's funeral. It wasn't as if he hadn't wanted to go home, time just got away from him. He kept in touch with only Shalena and her mom because everyone else was still upset with Sunny for selling his mom's house.

None of them understood why he couldn't stay there.

It took him a little while to make it down George Hamilton Parkway due to all the stop lights and traffic; listening to half of an old Jay-Z mixtape. Sunny still wasn't used to driving around Hamilton after living there for a few years. He couldn't understand how a town so small could have congestion like it did.

After hearing his stomach rumble over his radio, Sunny decided to stop and get food so he wouldn't have to bother Elle and Kaylen that night. Days like this made Sunny wish that Ava would just move in with him. She didn't cook often but he knew that if he asked she would have a meal waiting for him if she didn't have to work. That was something that Sunny could get used to.

Sunny got home by the time the sun began to set. He smiled once he saw Ava's car parked in her usual spot. Last year, she traded in the car Kita left her for a yellow 2008 Nissan Altima. Sunny didn't like the color at first but he was able to negotiate a good price for it being a year old. Ava didn't really care about the color then, but she loved it now.

Getting his things and his food out the car, Sunny hoped that Ava had used her key and was waiting for him and not goofing around with Elle at their apartment. He could see that Kaylen wasn't home yet and that usually meant Elle would talk Ava into bringing Angel over so that she and Jayla could play together. Those two little girls owned Sunny's heart, but they were terrible together. Angel was the loud, destructive one; you could always hear the mess she was getting into, while Jayla was the quiet, sneaky one. If Jayla was quiet, it was a problem.

Sunny hoped that Elle was having a boy because he wouldn't know what to do with another little girl running around.

When Sunny got into his apartment, it was quiet. He decided to eat before going to retrieve his woman from his best friend's house.

Ava and Elle glanced at each other when a loud crash came from Jayla's room. Elle sat back on the couch and looked at Ava, who sucked her teeth.

"What?" Elle asked, innocently. "I got up last time."

"You ain't worth nothing pregnant," Ava complained, getting up and walking around the corner to see what their girls were up to. Ava saw Jayla trying to push the basket of toys she'd knocked over back upright and Angel was just standing by and watching her. Biting her lip to keep from laughing, Ava cleared her throat to get both girls' attention.

"What are you two in here tearing up?" Ava asked.

"Toys fell, Ti-Ti!" Jayla said, pointing to the basket. Ava bent down to help her while Angel stood with her eyebrows pushed close together.

"What's your problem, Gelly?" Ava asked.

"I told her it would fall," Angel said. Jayla's head snapped around to glare at Angel. Ava laughed before telling them to be more careful and going back into the living room.

She sat back down across from Elle and continued to watch television. Every now and then, Elle would grunt or groan but when Ava looked at her, Elle would be looking directly at the television. After about ten minutes, Ava sighed heavily.

"You aren't *that* pregnant," Ava said. "Stop making all that noise."

"I have something to tell you," Elle blurted out. "I got a job."

"Kay is going to beat you up," Ava said, laughing. Elle sucked her teeth before flopping her open palms down on her thighs.

"Ugh, that's why I haven't told anybody. I started last week."

"You are really asking for it."

"I don't understand why he wants me to sit in this house all day! It's just home health care for a few hours while he's at work," Elle said, sticking her bottom lip out and stretching on the couch. "They pay out of pocket so I don't have to worry about check stubs and stuff." Ava laughed. "What?"

"You truly went all under cover to get a job, huh? I don't know why you want to work."

"Because I'm bored and there's no reason to start school when I'll have to stop in a few months again."

"Where you been taking Jay?" Ava asked.

"To my mom's house, you know she moved closer," Elle said, biting her lip. "Don't say anything G, not even to Sunny."

"Well, you shouldn't have told me," Ava said, looking around the room. Elle threw a pillow at her.

"I'm serious! If Kay finds out, I'm coming for your head."

"Just chill out, angry smurf! I won't tell your little secret," Ava said, smirking. Elle rolled her eyes before turning the volume on the television up. "I need to try and get the rest of this stuff for Gelly's birthday. I'm going to straight cry when she turns four."

"You cry over her all the time," Elle said, waving Ava's comment off. "What we doing?"

"Me and Romero rented out that new bounce house place for a couple hours on the Saturday before her birthday," Ava said, rolling her eyes. "He swears she's old enough for a big party now."

"I don't know which of you is worse," Elle said.

"Sunny!" Ava proclaimed. They both laughed. The house phone rang and Elle picked up the cordless that was lying face down on the end table next to the couch. After a few minutes she sucked her teeth and hung up.

"Speaking of Sunny," Elle said. "He just said tell his woman to come see him now."

"He swears he runs me," Ava said, pushing her back into the cushions of the couch in a silent protest. Elle laughed before shaking her head. About five minutes later, Sunny called Ava's cell phone. She groaned and Elle just laughed at her. "I'm going to fight him."

"You can leave Gelly here for a minute," Elle said.

"Cool, I be back down here after this dude falls asleep," Ava said. Elle waved her off and began to flip channels again. Ava slid her feet sluggishly across the carpet and went out the front door, somehow not wanting to go up the one flight of stairs to get to her man's apartment. It took her longer than expected.

Sunny was sprawled out across his couch with one leg over the arm and one bent at the knee. His head lay at the other end with his arm extending around the back of the couch and his right hand stuffing a mini chicken sandwich in his mouth. Ava sucked her teeth, seeing how small the bag on the coffee table was.

"You bugging me and didn't even buy me food, love?" Ava asked.

"Figured you would have eaten already," he said with his mouth full. Ava shook her head before snatching one of his cheese fries.

"I did, but you still could have asked," she said, smiling. It was Sunny's turn to suck his teeth and Ava laughed. She kicked her shoes off and stretched out on the floor between the couch and the coffee table. Sunny reached down and poked her hip before she swatted his hand away.

She pulled the dark maroon blanket off the arm of the couch from under his head and wrapped it around her body. The air vent under the couch was blowing directly on her and she knew she'd be sleep in no time.

"Can you go get Gelly from downstairs when you get done eating?" Ava asked, she looked up just in time to see Sunny nod his head.

"How'd your meeting with Dre go?" Sunny asked. Ava groaned.

"He pretty much snapped on me about my hesitation."

"Why you tripping though, baby? It's what you wanted to do right?"

"Yeah," Ava said. "Maybe I just never thought it would go as planned."

"Some things don't," Sunny said, as Ava turned on her side and brought her knees up to her chest. "But it don't work if you don't work."

"Um hum."

"It just doesn't feel right today," Ava mumbled, pulling the large headphones off of her ear, allowing her dark curls to fall and frame her face. She tilted her head to

the left and the right, waiting on some type of relief. Her eyes focused outside of the booth to see one of them glaring at her, one was giving her a disappointed head shake, while the other was busy ignoring her.

"What's wrong?"

"Does it sound right?" she asked.

"It sounds a little off. Let's run through it again."

Ava nodded, swallowing a little saliva as her stomach twisted in knots. Quickly exhaling through her nose, she pulled the headphones back over her curls and stepped closer to the suspended microphone.

The walls of the recording booth didn't seem this close to her before. The dark grey padding was darker and the light was dim. Ava pulled at the neck of her shirt and cleared her throat.

She closed her eyes and tried to sing but none of the notes came out right. She wanted to push through it and get it over with but the track soon stopped, leaving her in silence.

"You're right, it doesn't sound right."

"You sound weird today. I know what you need."

Ava looked up at Davion in disgust. He was eyeing her through the glass, occasionally licking his lips.

"That is definitely not what I need," Ava snapped. "From you anyway."

The other two laughed, pointing at Davion. He frowned before his nose flared.

"You ain't that good, don't flatter yourself."

"Good enough for you to be begging for it," Ava said with a smirk. "Don't even know why Bri still deals with you, must be for the popularity."

"You talking a lot right now," he said. "I might need to shut you up."

"Ava, you ready to go?"

Ava looked across the room to see Trishelle crossing it quickly, coming to stand next to the sound board as Tre stood next to her. Trishelle looked at Ava with concern before glaring at the other three.

"She's good," LaDanian finally spoke up. "Why don't we take a break? Tre, weren't you going to the store?"

"Yeah."

"Cool," he smiled. "Take Trishelle with you."

Ava grabbed her chest with her right hand and a hand full of her hair with her left as her eyes popped open. Her heart was pounding as she looked around and wondering why she was looking up at the coffee table and on the side of the couch. She closed her eyes as tears fell from them and she refused to open them again. She knew she was back in Sunny's living room on his floor but she cried anyway. Her head felt heavy against the carpet as sweat plastered a few of her dark curls to her face and rolled down her cheek, mixing with her tears. She sobbed loudly before covering her hand, hoping not to wake him. Ava knew she failed when something clicked and a light behind her came on.

She could hear Sunny sigh before he wrapped his arms around her and pulled her off the floor and into his lap on the couch. Ava's first instinct was to fight, something she hadn't done that day all those years ago. She pushed at his arms and kicked her legs, but Sunny was still able to wrap her up in his arms.

"It's okay baby," he mumbled, sleep still on his face and in his voice. Ava shook her head violently and held on to him tightly. "It's over."

"Why do I keep having these nightmares?" she cried. Sunny shook his head but pulled her closer. "I want them to stop!"

"I know you do," he said, rubbing her back, trying to calm her down. "I know, love."

Ava tried to sit up but Sunny's grip on her wouldn't allow it.

"Where is Angel?" she asked, almost panicking.

"She's sleep at Kay's," he said. "She was sleep when I went down so Elle just said get her in the morning."

"I need to go get her now!" Ava said, trying to sit up again. Sunny's grip tightened and he shook his head.

"You can't wake her up, she'll freak if she sees you like this," he said, pressing his lips against her cheek. The touch of his lips calmed Ava and she sunk into his embrace.

"God, I want this to stop," she repeated, pushing her face into Sunny's neck in an attempt to hide from her own pain. Sunny kissed her temple then cleared his throat a little before he began to pray aloud. Ava reached behind her back with her right hand and intertwined her fingers with his, sighing as she let herself relax with the words of his prayer.

"Lord, I pray that you release this terrible memory from Ava's mind, we pray that you bring peace to this situation, allowing her to move forward in the healing process that only you can control. God we thank you for allowing us to move past this valley and grow. Amen."

Ava sighed again, repeating the last line of Sunny's prayer in her head before closing her eyes.

For the next few nights, the nightmares didn't end. That day played over and over in her head with agonizing vividness. It always started at the same place, while she was recording, but it never got to the end. However, each night it played a little longer and each night was more than Ava wanted to bear. Whenever Elle left her dream, she felt her heart stop subconsciously. It wasn't fair that she had to relive that.

It was the day before Angel's birthday and she and Romero were at a party supply store getting the rest of the party essentials. Ava didn't really like spending long periods of time around Romero. It was almost as if he hadn't gone through puberty. He was a great dad to Angel, however, he often reminded Ava of why she hated him and all his friends in high school.

"Do we have to get all this purple and pink, man?" Romero groaned, looking around the isle as if it was contagious.

"You are aware that we have a little girl right?" Ava asked, cutting her eyes at him. Romero grunted before waving her off.

"That don't mean anything right now, I'm saying it could have been red or something."

"You say this the day before her party when everything else is already set just to annoy me right?"

Romero didn't respond. He only picked up a pack of purple napkins and slung them into the cart. Ava laughed before shaking her head, crossing napkins off of her list.

"So it's cool if my girlfriend comes right?" Romero asked. Ava frowned.

"Sunny will be there."

"Sunny is always there," Romero said, sarcastically. Ava smirked.

"I'm saying though, you asked like I give a crap who you lay down with. I don't want you."

"First of all, midget, don't flatter yourself and second of all, I don't just lay down with her."

Ava noted the seriousness in Romero's voice and studied his face. She slowly smiled. Romero looked up at her and shook his head.

"Nah, don't go there Ava."

"What? I didn't say anything!" Ava said, throwing her hands up in the air for a moment before gripping the cart again.

"Don't make this deeper than it is."

"You're the one who said you weren't just laying down with her," Ava said. "I think it's cute."

"Shut up."

Ava attempted to hold in her laugh as they got the rest of their things and confirmed the details for tomorrow.

"Tell your mom if she can watch Gelly while I'm at the studio tonight, I'll pick her up before I head home," Ava said to Romero as he put the things in the trunk of her car. He nodded, knowing that Angel was with his mom for the day anyhow. It was hard to get Angel away from her grandmother so getting her while she was sleep would be the easiest for all of them.

"Don't be up too late, you know how she is on her birthday," Romero said, joking. Ava nodded.

"I hope I can get some sleep tonight."

Ava pushed past the door of the smoky room as the walls closed in and her feet disobeyed her mind to stay still. Her mind felt empty of all but one memory as the soundboard buttons moved up and down, a few small lights glowing red and green against the top. The tall black speakers bumped in silence and all she heard was the low hum of her heartbeat.

The room was never what she expected. It had a way of encompassing her each time she'd come in before but this particular visit would fossilize its décor in her mind forever. It was modestly decorated with dark reds, grays and black. Most of the furniture was new and stuffy, not quite yet broken in. The horizontal lines through the plush pillows caught her attention and she tried to focus on that as long as possible.

She hadn't been in this room in over four years. She remembered it though. She remembered what happened here.

Stacks of blank CDs lay across the cluttered coffee table, a row of three computers on the other side and modems that had multiple burners. The air was cloudy almost. Ava blinked and the fog went away.

Her heart dropped as the dark, wooden door that led to the sound booth creaked open, stopping to allow only a small strip of light to come from it. She could hear scrambling against the wall, nails clawing trying to find a way out. Grunts and panting followed before a voice boomed.

"Hold her down!"

Ava tried to swallow the burning in her throat as the tears clouded her vision more.

"You ain't so bad now are you?"

"St...Stop!"

Ava shook her head. How can she be hearing this when that voice belonged to her?

"Just let me up...please, just stop!"

"Shut her up now!"

Ava's screams were muffled before someone cursed.

"She bit me!"

Smack!

Ava jumped back from the glass as blood splattered over it, tiny droplets in various places coming up the glass. Her heartbeat grew louder as she stepped back towards the glass.

She couldn't see anything but the microphone at first, and then their heads came into view. She could see her legs kicking from the sides of LaDanian's body. She could see her fists balling up and releasing under Romero's hands. She could see the torn pieces of her black tank top hanging around them.

She saw her legs freeze. Then she screamed.

Four

September 22, 2010

For Angel's forth birthday, they rented out a room in the bounce house in a small town outside of Hamilton. The party was set to start at three. Normally, someone would have to wake Ava up and she'd be rushing to get ready, but today was an exception. She hadn't slept at all.

Last night the nightmare had finally reached its climax and to Ava it was almost like being raped all over again. When she woke up, her stomach was in knots and she was sweating. Since she was at home, Sunny wasn't there to comfort her. She attempted to pray but even that hadn't been able to relax her.

When the sun rose, she tried to put on a smile. She woke Angel up and made her pancakes. Ava wanted to put the nightmare to rest and focus on her baby's birthday, but every time she blinked she could see it. Even for that mere second that her eyes were closed, it was something she dreaded since it happened.

"I wear my new shoes today?" Angel asked, while Ava was giving her a bath after breakfast.

"You promised not to get them too dirty, remember?" Ava asked, knowing it was no use in even mentioning it. The custom leopard print Nikes would probably be unrecognizable by the end of the day. "How old are you today?"

"Five!" Angel yelled. Ava laughed and tried to correct her but Angel shook her head. "Yes momma, I'm is five."

"I am five," Ava corrected her. "And no you aren't."

"Ti-ti B said I could be five if I want," she said, attempting to roll her neck. Ava sucked her teeth, knowing that was exactly what Bri had done when she told Angel she could be five.

"Well Mommy said you're four and that's what you are." Ava took Angel out of the tub and dried her off. "You can be five on your next birthday."

"Bet!" Angel said. Ava shook her head before wrapping Angel up in her towel and letting her run off to her room. Ava sighed before running both hands up her cheeks and into her mass of black curls. She closed her fist and tugged lightly hoping to energize herself. Her body wanted sleep but it was the last thing she wanted to do.

"Come on!" Angel yelled from her room. Ava frowned before jogging into Angel's bedroom to help her get dressed. Angel's birthday outfit, along with her new shoes, was a pair of light denim jeans with the same leopard print around the leg cuffs and a purple short sleeved shirt that had 'Cute & Awesome' in bold, leopard print letters. Ava moisturized Angel's hair and put her purple headband on.

Since she had been up, she was already dressed in a simple pair of shorts and an oversized, sleeveless blouse.

"Girl are y'all ready?" Charity said, coming around the corner of Angel's door. Ava smiled and nodded.

"I feel like I haven't seen you in weeks," Ava said. Charity laughed before grabbing Angel's hand.

"I was surprised my job finally gave me a day off," Charity said. "Papi was acting like we hadn't spent time together all month."

Charity and Rico had gotten married a year and a half ago although they had been together ever since before Angel was born and Rico was released from prison. Recently, Charity had picked up more hours at the hospital and often worked over night. Ava knew that Rico liked to act tough but it bothered him that Charity worked so much.

"I hope this goes quick," Ava mumbled. Almost instantly, Angel began to bounce up and down as she walked and sang some random song. Ava rolled her eyes and Charity laughed.

"Papi and Bri are meeting us at the place," Charity said. Ava nodded before sending a text message to Elle and Sunny that she was headed out the house.

The birthday party had been going on for about an hour and Ava couldn't seem to get out of her own thoughts. Although Romero had stepped up and kind of guided the party along, she didn't even want to be near him. To Ava, remembering that day so vividly in her nightmare made her remember when the three that hurt her tried to blame her for it. It was true that with much prayer she was able to forgive Romero and let him be a part of Angel's life, but she hadn't had to relive the rape before the way she did in her nightmares.

"You okay?" Romero asked, lightly touching her hand as they set up the food. Ava looked down at their touching hands and almost felt sick to her stomach.

"Something's not right," she mumbled.

"Go sit down, I'll get my sister to help."

Usually Ava would decline, but she walked over to where Sunny and Kaylen were sitting and sat as close to Sunny as she could without sitting on his lap.

"You get any sleep last night, babe?" Sunny whispered after turning his head to look at her. She shook her head no and he sighed, wrapping his arm around her shoulder.

Ava tried to relax, closing her eyes and taking a few deep breaths. She was able to get through cutting Angel's cake and opening her presents, but as soon as the kids took off to play for the last thirty minutes of the party, all of her anxiety came rushing back. Angel was still hyper and her birthday cake and ice cream hadn't helped at all. All the other kids were gone except for Jayla and Angel, who were running around the biggest bounce house. It was set up like an obstacle course with a small hill to climb up and a slide on the other side. Ava looked at Elle and she threw her hands up.

"Don't look at me," Elle said. "I'm pregnant."

"You good for nothing," Ava joked. She looked to see that Bri and Charity were cleaning up and Romero and Sunny were taking Angel's gifts to the car. Kaylen came around the opposite side of the bounce house with Jayla hanging sideways on his hip with his right arm wrapped around her body. She was giggling and kicking her feet.

"I grabbed this one but Angel slid into the tunnel before I could grab her," he said. Ava let her arms fall, her open palms hitting her thighs, as she looked to the tunnel that went around the bounce house. Ava stepped out of her shoes and climbed up into the bounce house. She almost slipped a few times but she made it to the tunnel without falling.

"Angel Na'mya Daniels!" Ava called into the tunnel.

"Come in, Mommy!' Angel yelled.

"No, you come out!" Ava yelled back. "It's time to go."

"Nooo!" Angel whined. Ava bent down to see if she could see her but she couldn't.

"Angel, if I have to come in after you there will be a butt whooping coming with me."

Angel went silent and Ava slid down on her belly and crawled into the tunnel. It was bright orange but since it was made for children, she could barely fit. Once she got all the way in, she felt as if she was trapped. Ava closed her eyes for a second but her nightmare popped in her head so she quickly opened her eyes.

Ava's heart rate quickened as she went as fast as she could. Once she rounded a corner, she saw Angel. She tried to crawl the other way but Ava reached out and grabbed her ankle, making Angel fall flat on the tunnel floor.

"Mommy, don't whoop me!" Angel yelled as Ava kept her grasp on Angel's leg and scooted backwards, dragging Angel with her.

"Too late for all that!"

Once Ava got out of the tunnel, she pulled Angel up by her arm and swatted her bottom with her open hand. Angel tried to move away but Ava hit her two more times before letting her go. Angel immediately started crying loud, causing most of the people in the building to look their way.

"Now do what I tell you to next time!" Ava said, pointing to wear Elle was standing. Angel pouted and ran over to her, hugging her leg. Elle tried not to laugh.

"This isn't funny," Ava said. "She's getting out of hand."

"You sound like something else is bothering you," Elle said. Ava pushed her hand through her curls and sighed. Leave it to Elle to know everything.

Ava couldn't talk to anyone except Sunny about the nightmares because he was the only one who knew that she was having them. It wasn't as if she didn't want to talk to Elle about it, Ava didn't want to talk to anyone about it.

She just wanted them to go away.

"I'll catch you tomorrow, girl," Ava said, kissing Jayla on her forehead before grabbing Angel's hand. Romero walked up to her before she got to her car.

"Let me take her tonight?" he asked. Ava quickly nodded before walking Angel over to Romero's car.

"You never say yes that quick," Romero said, searching Ava's face with his eyes. She shrugged.

"I'm tired and she's not."

Romero nodded as Ava strapped Angel in and stalked over to Sunny's car, waving bye to Charity and Bri as they pulled off.

"So I get my woman alone tonight?" Sunny asked. Ava nodded.

"Don't expect much," Ava said. Sunny laughed before starting his car. Sunny was about ten minutes from the apartments when Ava looked in the backseat to see Angel's backpack.

"Hell," Ava mumbled and Sunny frowned.

"What?"

"She's not going to sleep without that dang bear in her backpack," she said, pulling the bag up into her lap. Sunny shook his head before turning down Almond Avenue to get to Romero's house. He stayed on the outside of

Hamilton on Hinder Street with his mom. Sunny pulled onto Hinder and in front of Romero's house just as another car was pulling up. Romero's car was already in driveway.

Ava squinted, trying to see into the car. Once their headlights dimmed, she still couldn't see through the dark tint.

"That's a nice ride," Sunny said.

"What is it?" Ava asked, knowing Sunny's obsession with cars would give her a quick answer.

"C250 coupe," he said. Ava frowned in confusion. "Mercedes."

"Who would they know with that type of money?" Ava thought before pushing the passenger door open and jogging up to the door. She knocked on the door and Romero answered quickly.

"Um, Ava what's up?"

"I forgot to give you Angel's bag," she said. "Where is she?"

"My sister took her to Wal-mart to pick out a toy," he said. He looked over Ava's head and bit his lip.

"Is that your girl in that car?" Ava asked. "Why didn't she come to the party?"

"She had to work over and nah that's not her."

"Okay I'm gone," Ava said, turning on her heels. Just as she was making her way back to Sunny's car, the owner of the Mercedes got out and smiled at her.

That feeling of dread came running back into the pit of Ava's stomach with the urge to throw up. She stood frozen in Romero's yard and although her mind was screaming to move all she could do was stare at the source of her nightmares.

She knew then why she'd been having the nightmares. The younger version had been in her dreams but she hadn't seen him in person since the night he raped her with his friends.

    Sunny rolled his window down and asked her what was wrong. Ava's eyes couldn't look away as he walked around his car and had the audacity to smile at her.

    "What's up, Ava?" he asked. As if a fire had been ignited in her heart, Ava stumbled back, holding her chest.

    There in front of her, walking as cool as he could, was LaDanian Taylor.

Five

He was a little more built but still about the same size he was in high school. His long, black braids had been chopped off and a short curl sat on his head. He had a little facial hair around his upper lip and chin. Everything he wore had a name brand shining on it as usual, except instead of the popular ones from four years ago he now wore Roca Wear from head to toe with some type of expensive brand of sunglasses over his eyes, although it was night time.

He still eluded cockiness and arrogance as he had all those years ago. Paranoia and fear now mixed with the disgust Ava held for him. Nothing much had change.

It was as if seeing him put her back at 17, wishing the world away. The feelings of being raped by four men and having to deal with the pressure of no one believing her, attempting to end her life before she found out about her Angel and Sunny's feelings for her all came back. She didn't want to be there again, ever.

Ava looked from LaDanian to Romero and to Sunny, still frozen in the lawn. Romero jogged off the porch with both of his hands up in the air in a mock surrender.

"Ava, calm down."

"I don't want him around my child!" she yelled. She could hear Sunny's car cut off and his door open.

"That's why she's with my sister," Romero explained. "He's visiting his mom. He was just stopping by."

"You sound like a female right now," LaDanian said. Romero glared at him.

"Shut up!"

"No," Ava said, shaking her head violently. "I want Angel right now. She's not staying here!"

"Baby, what's going on?" Sunny asked, protectively wrapping his left arm around her waist. Ava stumbled into his chest but she was still shaking her head.

"Why are you here?" Ava asked, before turning to Romero. "Why is he here?"

"Sunny, can you take her home please?" Romero pleaded.

"No! I want Angel."

"She's still annoying," LaDanian said, snickering as if he'd told some type of joke.

"Aye, I don't know who you are," Sunny said. "But you need to watch what you say to my woman."

Ava grimaced as LaDanian smiled. "You didn't tell him about me?"

"Call your sister and tell her to bring me my child!" Ava said, ignoring LaDanian's question. She walked over to Sunny's car and got back in the passenger seat. She crossed her arms and told Sunny that she wasn't leaving without Angel.

Ava's leg began to shake violently. She could feel her eyes burning with the threat of tears, but she refused to cry. Sunny watched her for a moment before a light of recognition went off in his eyes.

"He's one of them?" Sunny asked, lowly. Ava bit her lip and nodded as a tear defied her and fell. Sunny's nose flared before he nodded. Ava quickly grabbed his arm just as he tried to get back out the car.

"No, Sunny!" she pleaded. "I just want Angel."

Ava could hear Romero ask LaDanian to go wait in the house. He walked over to the car but Ava rolled her window up. Romero sucked his teeth just as his sister's car pulled up. Ava jumped out of the car and ran over to it, pulling Angel from the car seat. She could hear Romero's sister ask what was wrong but she ignored them both before heading back to Sunny's car.

"Ava, don't do this," Romero said.

"As long as you're around him, you won't see my daughter!"

Before Romero could protest, Ava demanded that Sunny drive off.

"When's the last time you seen him?" Charity asked.

"The night I was raped."

"You didn't see him at all after that?"

"I didn't go to the trial. The only one I saw after the rape was Davion and then when school started and Angel was born I saw Romero. LaDanian's mom shipped him to New York with his dad. Kita still saw Kay because she didn't know what happened at first."

"So he's the only one you haven't seen?" Charity asked and Ava nodded.

"He's the one who started it," Ava said, glaring off at the wall in a trance. "It was all his idea."

It had been three days since Angel's birthday party. Romero had been calling trying to see Angel, but Ava was ignoring him. She had to figure out how she felt about LaDanian but she knew there was no way she'd allow Angel to be around him.

"How did you get over seeing Romero all the time?" Charity asked. Ava glared at her for a second before shaking her head.

"That's not going to work."

"What?" Charity asked, innocently.

"I'm not forgiving them just because I'm okay with Romero now," Ava said.

"I didn't say that," Charity said.

"It's what you're trying to say," Ava said. "Romero's different. Every time I look at Angel I can see him. He's a part of her and that's the only reason why I even gave him a chance but it was not easy at all."

Charity grew silent as tears fell from Ava's eyes.

"There were times when he would accidentally touch me and my whole body would cringe and sometimes I'd even want to throw up, but I had to move past it. I had to move on so that Angel wouldn't know how she came into this world. She didn't need to know what her Daddy did to her Mommy and in order for that to go down, I had to get over it. But not with them," Ava said. "Not with them."

Charity nodded and sat silently on the end of Ava's bed. Angel lay curled up against one of Ava's pillows, the burnt orange color of the pillow case almost matching Angel's pajamas.

"Have you prayed about it?" Charity asked.

"Nah," Ava said, honestly. Charity shook her head.

"Didn't God help you the last time?" Charity asked. Ava sighed heavily before nodding. "He'll do it again, Ava and you know it."

"It's hard to forgive," Ava said. "It's so hard."

Charity gently rubbed Ava's back to help her calm down.

"It feels good though doesn't it? After it's all said and done?"

Ava remembered how it felt that night at their New Year's Eve party years ago. How she'd come to the epiphany that she was happy with how her life had turned out. Even after being gang raped and losing her mother to AIDS. Ava had worked hard to get that peace and she missed it.

"You should probably let her sleep in her own bed," Charity said, standing up and walking towards the door. Ava knew that she was right. Angel had been sleeping in her own bed for awhile but the only way Ava seemed to get any sleep was if Sunny or Angel was next to her. She nodded her head before sniffling a little.

"I will," Ava said. "Tomorrow."

Ava kept the television on mute that night for a little light. She slid as close to Angel as she could without waking her, praying that sleep would overtake her soon. She lay there for about fifteen minutes before she gave up. Just as she was about to get out of bed, Ava felt her cell phone vibrate on the nightstand next to her. She smiled to see that Sunny was still up.

"You have to be at work in a few hours," Ava said.

"Can't sleep when I know my woman ain't sleep," he said, groggily. He sounded so good to Ava at the moment and all she wanted to do was be next to him.

"I'm trying, babe," Ava said, sighing heavily. It took Sunny a few minutes to respond.

"You remember when Elle was trying so hard to get us to hook up and you ended up agreeing to show me around town and we went to breakfast?" Sunny asked. Ava looked up at the ceiling of her bedroom and sighed.

"Yeah."

"We were chilling and I tried to make you sing for me but you said I wasn't Diddy."

Ava laughed, remember that she was already irritated that day because Sunny had woke her up but her eagerness to spend time with him had taken over within minutes.

"Back then I was only singing to get back at Bri and her friends," Ava said.

"I still wanted you to sing for me baby," he said, his drawl coming out in his term of endearment. Ava bit her lip.

"I sing for you now."

"I just want to make you smile."

It was just like Sunny to make Ava blush for no reason. Since the day she met him, Sunny had some type of effect on Ava and even though she didn't know how to deal with it all those years ago, she welcomed it. Sunny was genuinely interested in Ava, even when everyone in Hamilton had condemned her as being a confused and promiscuous little girl.

Sunny made up his own mind about her and she'd love him forever for that.

The lethargic feelings that ran through her body were a relief and she'd only been on the phone with Sunny for about twenty minutes.

"I sound mad corny right now," he said and Ava giggled. "But I wish I could erase your pain. I mean, you held me down when my moms died."

"And you did the same," Ava interrupted. "You've helped me get over every down point in my life since the day I met you, Sunny."

Ava hadn't known how this moment became so emotional for her, but Sunny's love always did it. He called just when she needed him.

"I got you," he said. Ava smiled and closed her eyes, hoping that Sunny wouldn't mind her falling asleep on him.

"I know you do," she thought.

And just like that, Ava was able to sleep.

The next few days, Ava was up before the sun, writing on the song for Solace. It was supposed to be a love song and although she had no intentions of being romanced at that time in her life, Sunny had once again proven to be inspiration. He'd taken her out on his off day and they played around in the park as if they were high school lovers. Once Ava was done with the draft of it, she emailed it to Solace and Dre. Only a few changes needed to be made but overall, they both loved it.

They weren't set to record for another couple of weeks, but Ava felt the weight of doing her first full song for someone gone and now she only had one other thing to deal with.

She'd heard from Bri that LaDanian was back in town only for a couple of weeks, visiting his family and taking a break from his New York life. Supposedly, he had been making moves in the producing world there, building a name for himself and working with some notable aspiring artists. Ava almost threw up when Dre had said he'd heard of him from a few associates. She wanted nothing to do with his return to Hamilton and it seemed as if everywhere she went, someone was excited for LaDanian to be home.

Ava had other things to focus on, like work. Rico didn't really ask for help with bills from her and Bri so her job paid enough for her to take care of Angel and save a little each month.

The retail store she worked out had its days where it was really busy and days when not one customer showed up. She often wondered how she ended up in customer service, knowing she wasn't exactly a people person. She'd been in her position for a little under two years and although it wasn't something she was passionate about, it was stable and that was exactly what she needed in her life.

With LaDanian's return home, her nightmares had ended but the paranoia stayed. Her performance at work was so disturbed that her manager asked if she needed to take the rest of the day off. She opted instead to take an early lunch. While Ava was walking out to her car, she noticed Romero's parked next to her. He opened his door and hopped out as he noticed she had turned around to go back inside.

"Ava, wait!"

She sighed, turning back around and stalking slowly over to where he stood.

"What are you doing at my job? I'd be the crazy baby momma if I came to your job with some mess!" Ava snapped.

"Well, right now you are the crazy baby momma for not letting me see my kid!" he snapped, right back. Ava's face fumed as she held her lips tightly against her teeth and huffed.

"You know how I feel about him. It's why you had been acting weird. Did you plan on letting him be around my baby?" Ava asked, calmly.

"No," Romero said. "But he's still my friend."

"He's still a rapist."
Romero stepped back and ran his hands down his face.
"I was there too," he mumbled. Ava frowned.
"What?"
"You heard what I said."
"Say what you mean, Romero!" Ava said. "You saying you want me to keep you away from my daughter, huh? Is that what you saying? Because you reminding me that you were a part of the crew that raped me is sounding like that right about now!"
"I'm not saying that, Ava! Dang, just…" Romero shook his head, trying to get his words together. "How can you forgive me and talk to me and not them?"
Ava was tired of this conversation already. She straightened her back before pulling at one of her curls.
"You know why."
Ava left him where he stood to think about the beautiful mixture they created, who stood a little less than three feet with a small gap and sandy brown curls. The small miracle in the harsh reality that Ava's past was not a happy one and Romero, no matter how redeeming he was as a father, was still a part of that.

Elle calmly navigated through traffic yet in her mind, she was panicking. She'd gotten off of work late. She couldn't leave until she finished her client's laundry and she had estimated the time wrong. She didn't have much time to get Jayla from her mom's and make it home before Kaylen.

"Get out of my way!" Elle yelled aimlessly at the cars in front of her. Her stomach turned a little, reminding her that she hadn't fed her son in the last few hours. Elle bit her lip in frustration as she pulled up to her mom's house.

Janet had moved to Jasper, the small college town outside of Hamilton, once she and Elle reunited. Elle was a little concerned after Janet popped up wanting to be in her life after Jayla was born. Since Janet kicked her out because of her relationship with Kaylen, it had been years since Elle had spoke to her mother.

Kaylen had been everything to her since she was 16. They'd been through rough patches but everything seemed to be okay after they got married and had Jayla. Now pregnant with their second child, Elle was bored out of her mind at home and Kaylen didn't want her to work.

It is why she was keeping her part time job from him.

Elle didn't get the job for the money; Kaylen had always been a great provider. Elle couldn't finish out the year in school because she'd miss most of it so working was her only option to not die of boredom.

Elle spoke to her mother in a rush while packing Jayla up and heading home. She silently cursed when she saw that Kaylen had beaten her home.

"Where you been, woman?" Kaylen asked, quickly kissing Elle and picking Jayla up to greet her as well. Elle smirked when Kaylen bent down and kissed the top of her belly.

"Um, at Mom's," Elle said, walking past Kaylen and into the back room. She was glad she didn't have to wear the usual scrubs that other home health care workers did, but she still smelled like her client's home and wanted to at least change her shirt. "Baby, can you put that meat loaf in the oven for me!" Elle yelled, as she pulled off her dark green tee. "I don't feel like cooking."

"Where you been?" Kaylen asked again, walking into their bedroom with Jayla on his heels a few minutes later.

"I told you, at my mom's," Elle said. "I be so bored at home, Kaylen."

"You need to chill and worry about getting my boy here safe," he said, wrapping his arms around Elle. She smiled before kissing him.

"We still got a little while before we find out what the baby is."

"It better be a boy!" Kaylen said. Elle giggled before pushing him away so that she could put a shirt on. "I got something planned for our anniversary."

"Oh yeah?"

"Yeah, I'll probably take off Friday for it. Ask your mom if she can watch Jayla for the weekend."

"Um, okay."

Elle sighed, hoping that she would be able to find someone to work for her on Friday. She wasn't ready to tell Kaylen that she went against his wishes and got a job anyway, so she'd just have to keep covering her tracks.

Ava sighed while looking at Bri and Angel cuddled up on the couch watching a movie.

"You sure you don't mind watching her?"

"Ti-ti B, got this!" Bri said, waving Ava off with her hand. Angel adjusted her head on Bri's chest but kept her focus on the television. Charity walked into the living room with a Bible in hand.

"You ready?" she asked. Ava nodded.

On the way to Charity's church, Ava ran her hands up and down her thighs repeatedly. She tapped her left foot against the floor mat a few times before slipping her foot out of her flip flop and pushing it into the worn fabric.

"Would you chill out?" Charity said. "We'll only be here for an hour and it's not like a regular service, more like a class."

Ava nodded, stilling her hands but still working her foot into the fabric of the mat. A few minutes later, Charity pulled up in front of Living Testament Baptist Church. Ava smirked as she read the sign in front of the doors.

"Seven days without prayer makes one weak."

Ava followed Charity from the small, uneven parking lot to a side door of the building. The steps under it must have been uneven as well because the dark gray metal door looked as if it had been held open but was only stuck on the concrete. Ava followed Charity in but stepped aside to allow Charity to wrap her arm around the metal, round pole connected to the door. Charity yanked it until the door scraped across the concrete step and closed shut.

"Nobody ever takes the time to close this door behind them," she mumbled. Ava looked around at the small building and admired the pictures on the wall. Although they were of people she didn't know, Ava could tell that people had confidence and poise. She read each of their names and their titles; chairman of the deacon board, chair of the trustees, mothers, a first lady and the pastor.

"The pastor's wife looks young," Ava mumbled. Charity chuckled.

"She acts young, too," Charity said. "She's cool though. Remind me of your Granny."

Ava nodded, not sure how to respond. She never had a real relationship with her grandmother. She always wondered why she stayed in the same town and never attempted to reach out to Ava and Bri. Everything they went through with Kita, it seemed as if someone should have tried to step up when Rico couldn't. Ava was cordial with her now, but she never made any real efforts to reconcile their relationship.

Charity waited for Ava to make it to the wooden double doors she was standing at before slowly opening them just enough for them to slide in. Ava gripped the back of Charity's shirt and clung to her as she maneuvered up the aisle and into a pew in the middle of the sanctuary. They were a few rows behind everyone else but a few people turned around and gave a warming smile; some just turned around to be nosy.

Ava rocked side to side to get comfortable on the stiff cushion as an elderly man turned and reached his hand out with paper in it. Charity reached for it and gave Ava one. It was the lesson plan for that evening. Ava looked at it, bewildered. It wasn't confusing like some of the bible scriptures she had tried to read before. It had a scripture at the very top, right under the date.

Jeremiah 29:11
"For I know the plans I have for you," declares the LORD, "plans to prosper you and not to harm you, plans to give you hope and a future."

Ava smiled, relaxing her shoulders and looking up at the man teaching. It wasn't the same man in the picture labeled, "Pastor Davidson" on the wall outside, but he resembled him slightly.

"The enemy of this world comes to kill, steal and destroy. He brings confusion and mess and all those type of things. He wants you to relive your past and stay there, but God has other plans."

A few people responded with, "Amen's," and "Yeah's."

"What God says is real," he continued. "He doesn't want you to suffer or hurt. He doesn't want you to be broke and he doesn't want you to be poor and brokenhearted. He wants you to have joy everyday of your life."

Joy everyday of your life, Ava thought.

She was tired of going up and down. Everything had been great in her life so why all of the sudden, just because one of the guys who raped her was visiting his home, was everything so hectic and frustrating?

She'd thought her life had been stable enough to where she could deal with things as they came. It made her shake with anger at how unstable her life really was. She felt like it was way past time for change.

"I want to get saved."

Ava could see that Charity had done a double take once the words left Ava's mouth.

"You serious?" Charity asked. Ava swallowed the saliva forming on her tongue. She slowly turned towards Charity and nodded her head. If Ava hadn't been so serious, she would have laughed at the expression on Charity's face. Charity was trying to hide the smile that was forming but couldn't. She nodded a few times before telling Ava that they would talk to the assistant pastor after he finished teaching and dismissed Bible study for the night.

"You sure you want to do it tonight?" Charity whispered.

"No time like now," Ava responded. Having joy everyday of her life sounded heavenly to her and she didn't want to wait for that feeling any more.

Ava's heart thumped against her chest after the closing prayer. Charity gave her one more questioning look and after Ava nodded, she grabbed her hand and led Ava up to the front of the sanctuary.

"Sis. Charity!" the man said, "Nice to see you tonight."

"You too," Charity said. "Deacon Davidson this is my daughter-in-law, Ava. She wants to be saved."

Ava inhaled and exhaled slowly as a smile spread across Dec. Davidson's face. He nodded before taking Ava's hands out of Charity's.

"You're ready child?" he asked. Ava narrowed her eyes and nodded. "Well come on, my brother's in his office."

The walk to the pastor's office was short and although Ava thought she would be nervous, she wasn't. The deacon knocked twice before a deep, comforting voice allowed them to come in.

Charity took a seat near the door and stayed quiet. Pastor Davidson stood up as the deacon walked Ava closer to his desk.

"Sorry I couldn't join you all tonight," he said. "I have a revival to prepare for. What can I do for you?"

"This is Charity's daughter-in-law, she wants to be saved, bro."

Ava wanted to giggle at the deacon's affectionate greeting of his brother. He smiled at her and took her hands as well.

"Now usually we do this on Sunday morning, but when someone says they want to join the kingdom we do it when they feel led," Pastor Davidson said.

Ava nodded, feeling comforted by his smooth tone and shuffling her feet to stand straight.

"We have new members' classes that you will probably want to look into if you have time. It will help you learn the ends and outs and just give you a better understanding of what it means to live a saved life."

Ava nodded as his words kept coming.

"Do you believe that Jesus Christ is Lord?"

"Yes."

"Do you believe that He died for our sins on the cross that we may have eternal life?"

"Yes."

"Lift your hands and repeat after me."

Six

When Ava got into Charity's car, she had two missed calls from Sunny. She'd almost forgotten that Shalena was in town and most likely getting on Sunny's nerves. He usually tried to push Shalena off on Ava whenever she came to visit.

Tonight she just wanted to chill with her daughter and think about how much her life would change from this point on. She was still a little confused at what exactly took place, but she knew that she was ready to change her life. It was amazing how one little incident can make you rethink everything you did every second of everyday. Thoughts of her previous life invaded her subconscious and what hurt the most was how much the old Ava disgusted her now.

Back then, she had no problem with the things she was doing until she got hurt physically. Thinking back on how many nights she'd spent with someone else's boyfriend or someone older than her made her stomach turn. Ava thought she had gotten over it but now, she wasn't so sure.

Before she could return Sunny's phone call, Romero's number flashed across her screen.

"Yes, father of my child."

"Can I see my kid?" he asked, annoyed.

"You can come to the house and see our child," Ava said in a condescending tone. Romero sucked his teeth and Ava fought the urge to laugh.

"Stop playing, Ava."

"I'm not going to argue with you," Ava said, interrupting him. "If you want to discuss how you broke my trust then you can come over. I'm on my way home now."

Romero sighed heavily before hanging up.

"He's mad?" Charity asked.

"Don't care."

"You can't shut him out now."

"I can do whatever I want," Ava said. Her eyes focused on the road ahead of Charity's car and she sighed. "But I won't."

"Good because Gelly loves him."

"I know she does and I don't really have a problem with that, but what I do have a problem with is thinking that LaDanian will be within ten feet of her," Ava said. Her nose flared and her cheeks felt hot at just the thought. "I can control that."

"Do you know how long he's staying in town?" Charity asked.

"No, but Romero will just have to deal with the fact that he'll have to visit Gelly at home until his friend leaves."

"Do you think that's fair?"

"Don't care," Ava repeated.

When Ava and Charity pulled into the driveway, Romero's car was already parked against the curb in front of the mailbox. He wasn't in his car so Ava assumed he was already inside. Sure enough, when they opened the door, Angel was screaming in laughter as Romero tickled her on the floor.

"How was church?" Bri asked.

"You went to church?" Romero asked, eyebrows high as he stopped tickling Angel for a moment to question Ava. She ignored him.

"It was good," Charity said, smiling. She obviously wanted to tell the whole story but Ava gave her a look as if to say, 'not now.'

"Why don't you get Angel ready for bed," Ava said, putting her purse down on the coffee table.

Angel rolled her eyes but one quick glance from Ava and her hesitation ended.

"It's only 8:30," Romero said, but stood to pick her up anyway.

"She's in bed by nine here," Ava said. Romero rolled his eyes in the same manner that Angel did before taking off towards the stairs.

"I guess you heard Danian's in town, huh?" Bri asked. Ava looked at her and nodded. "I just heard today. You saw him?"

"The night of Angel's party he showed up at Romero's house."

"What!" Bri said, her face turning red. "And he didn't tell you? That punk!"

"Calm down," Ava said, laughing at her twin. "That's why he's over here and Angel's not at his place."

"Cool," Bri said. Charity shook her head before Ava jogged upstairs to help Romero get Angel ready for bed. The quicker it was done the quicker they could get this conversation over.

When Ava got upstairs, Romero already had Angel in the tub. He was singing off key to some Disney show theme song and Ava could hear Angel suck her teeth.

"Daddy, Ma sings better."

"So what?" Romero said. Ava laughed before walking in and making her presence known.

"Don't be a hater," she said. Romero gave her a quick glimpse but did not respond. Ava decided to hang back and let him do the work since he hadn't seen Angel in almost a week. Watching them interact was making her feel guilty, so she went into Angel's room to put her pajamas out. She took out two pairs; a black pair with rainbow stars all over it and a princess nightgown. Angel always wanted to pick her own pajamas so Ava always gave her two options to pick from. It made Angel feel as if she'd made the decision on her own.

Ava put both sets of pajamas across Angel's bed before going to her underwear drawer. By the time she got her panties and socks, Romero came through the doorframe with Angel cradled in his arms, wrapped in a towel. Ava was glad to see her head dropped on his shoulder.

"Lotion up, kid," Ava said, handing Romero the Jergen's bottle. After Romero got Angel dressed, he kissed her cheek before she pulled Ava's arm. Ava bent down to her knees and repeated Angel's prayer with her before she hopped in bed.

Ava turned her television on, setting the timer to fifteen minutes and followed Romero out of the room. When they got downstairs, the living room was empty. Ava folded her legs under her body and pushed her back into the cushion of the couch. Romero stood near the other end, looking at her.

Ava raised an eyebrow before crossing her arms under her chest. Romero sighed heavily.

"Look Ava, I didn't tell you he was coming back in town because he wasn't planning on staying long. I knew you'd trip out but I didn't plan on having him around Angel."

"That day you came and picked her up from Sunny's, you knew he was coming?"

"What would have been the point of telling you though?" Romero asked, indirectly answering Ava's question. "I haven't given you any reason since you let me in Angel's life not to trust her with me."

"Which is why I can't understand how you would do this right now?" Ava said. "It made me question everything and I don't like feeling like I made the wrong decision letting you in Gelly's life."

"Keep talking slick, Ava," Romero said, nodding his head and licking his lips in anger. "Don't make this ugly."

"You say that like someone can force me to do anything with my own daughter that I don't want to."

"I'm not trying to get into no mess, I just want my daughter."

Ava sighed, battling within herself already. She wanted to punish Romero for not being honest and revealing the bane of her existence for the past few months in her nightmares. He was grimy, disrespectful and arrogant and just the thought of him even looking at Angel the wrong way made Ava want to kill him.

She didn't want to be that person.

Ava looked up at Romero, ready to tell him off, but the softness in his eyes stopped her.

"Look," she said, glancing at the blank television screen. "I'm not saying I don't totally distrust you but you have to see where I'm coming from."

"I know that but…"

"No, hear me out," Ava said. "It took me weeks to even think about letting you see Angel once I found out you were her father. It hurt me to no end but I knew it had to be done for her sake. I don't have to be around LaDanian nor do I want my child around him. I can't keep you from him, but I can control what happens to her. So I just need you to bear with me and come see her over here until he's back in New York."

Romero's back straightened as his nose flared but he nodded his head.

"I'm off tomorrow, so you can come see her anytime."

Ava knew that Romero wasn't happy with her decision but she'd explained it as nicely as she could without getting ignorant and saying, 'because I said so.' He had no other choice but to deal with it.

"You acting a little selfish."

"Excuse me?"

"You heard what I said."

Ava glared at her best friend, waiting for her to giggle and admit she was joking but that never came. Ava could feel her eyebrows move closer together and the tip of her tongue slap against the left corner of her upper lip.

"Don't look at me like that," Elle said. "You know I always keep it real with you, G."

"What about that was real?" Ava snapped. "I was raped! Or did you forget?"

"I was there."

"No, you weren't."

Ava immediately regretted her words, not because she didn't mean them, but because Elle's pregnancy had been an emotional one. Once Ava saw that Elle's eyes were glossed over she knew that she was on the verge of tears.

"My bad, G," Ava apologized. Elle waved her left hand in dismissal.

"Don't worry about me, I'm just a depressed, pregnant woman."

Ava sighed heavily as Elle got up and walked to the kitchen. She knew she would have to go in there and talk to her but she didn't want to apologize. It was true that Elle had been at the studio that night Ava was raped. The guys had sent Elle and a friend to the store before going along with their plan to teach Ava a lesson. Their torture ended when the two returned and fought them off.

But not soon enough.

All this made Ava wonder how she could possibly seem selfish.

"Elle!" Ava yelled but all she got in return was a few dishes clanking. Before she had time to get up, Ava's phone rang.

"Yo, Dre!"

"I still want to marry you."

"You been saying that for years," Ava said, laughing. "What I do this time?"

"Solace's camp loves the song and they want to do a video for it. Possibly looking at it for a single option."

"Great," Ava said, almost uninterested. Dre sighed.

"You were never invited to parties as a child, huh?"

"You're a jerk."

"The director wants to meet with you here tomorrow to see if you have any ideas for the video."

"I'm taking my cousin-in-law out tomorrow," Ava said. After a long pause, Dre sighed.

"See you at one."

Sunny rolled his eyes in irritation as Shalena kept talking. He couldn't wait for her to go home. She had been there close to a week and she hadn't made any plans to go home. Sunny had been trying to get Ava to make plans with Lena, but Ava seemed to always be busy.

"When are you going home?" Sunny asked. Shalena looked up from her personal conversation and frowned.

"Are you trying to kick me out?"

"You're getting on my nerves."

"I love you too, Santana."

"I need to find something for you to do."

"Where is Ava," she asked.

"She better be on her way."

"When are y'all getting married? You think she'll let me be in the wedding. She don't have too many friends, huh?"

Sunny frowned, wondering if Shalena and Kaylen had been talking. Knowing that Elle would try to kill both of them if that ever happened, he figured that was negative. However, it didn't feel like a coincidence that they'd both brought up marriage to him in the same week.

"I been thinking about it," Sunny admitted. Shalena's eyes grew wide as her mocha face lit up.

"Oh wee, wait until I tell Mommy!"

"Chill out, Lena," Sunny said. "I said I was thinking about it."

"What's there to think about?"

"I'll do it on my own time and I wish everyone would get off my back about it!"

Shalena smirked but said nothing. The lock on the door clicked and a few moments later, Ava walked through it smiling.

"You have a key?" Shalena asked. Ava's eyebrows closed in with confusion but the smile never wavered.

"Yeah, you ready? Nail appointment in like ten," she said, leaning over the couch to bite Sunny's bottom lip. Sunny swung his left arm around and tapped the side of her butt. Shalena rolled her eyes before grabbing her purse and following Ava out the door.

Sunny scratched at his fade, knowing he'd have to get a haircut soon. He glanced at the portrait of his mom's face tattooed on his upper arm and blinked a few times. He'd be able to talk to her about all these feelings of moving forward and marriage but since she wasn't here, he'd have to figure them out himself.

Ava spent a few hours that morning with Shalena before her meeting with Dre. After talking with the director of Solace's video and getting a good idea for the shoot, they put down a schedule to produce it and wanted Ava on site for her input. Not only did she have a meeting with them, but Dre also waited until everyone else was gone to give her another bit of information.

She wasn't able to process what he had done with her lyrics behind her back and she couldn't quite figure out what it all meant. He'd told her not to get her hopes up so she tried to push it to the back of her mind.

Once she made it through the front door and Angel came running towards her, everything else didn't matter.

"Was she good?" Ava asked Charity and Rico, who were cuddled up on the couch.

"You know she is with us," Charity said. Rico mumbled something but Ava ignored him. She still wasn't too happy about what she assumed he was doing but tried not to have an attitude since she had no real proof.

"I hope you're sleepy, lady," Ava said, kissing Angel's cheek.

"You in for the night already?" Rico asked.

"Yes, I think I want to read my Bible some before I go to sleep," Ava said. Charity smiled but Rico frowned in confusion.

"When you get a Bible?"

"I gave her one last week," Charity said, giving Rico a stern look. Ava let them keep talking while she snuck upstairs with Angel glued to her hip.

"You know since you're four now, I don't have to carry you like this," Ava said. Angel huffed before locking her legs around Ava's waist and almost chocking her around the neck. Ava giggled a little before kissing Angel on the side of her head.

"Sunny will carry me," Angel said, matter-of-factly. Ava laughed harder.

"Not if I tell him not too," Ava lied. Sunny still acted as if Angel was a baby and Angel loved being spoiled by him. She always wondered if Angel having two dads would confuse her but Angel was smart. She knew Romero and Sunny and played both of them against each other, usually leaving Ava to diffuse any issues. Angel usually got her way and even though Ava knew that would lead to larger issues for her in the future, she let it slide.

After putting Angel to bed, Ava went into her bedroom and closed the door. She looked around her room almost as if it was her first time in it. Stripping herself of the long sleeve thermal and jeans, she put on a pair of Sunny's plaid boxers and an oversized tee shirt. Lifting the Bible from her nightstand, her bed made a woofing sound as she plopped down onto it.

The Bible was a shiny, onyx peeking out from the gold edges of the pages that created a block all pressed together. There was a design on the left side in gold that looked like a stained glass window with the words 'Holy Bible' written in clean, gold letters near the top. After flipping the front cover over, Ava noticed Charity had written her name in it, under a line that asked who the bible belonged to and her own under the gifter. She had no idea where to start.

After reading the first chapter in Genesis, Ava knew she couldn't read it head on without falling asleep. She sighed in irritation before closing it. Pushing her back into her pillow and closing her eyes, she let the Bible fall to the bed at her side. The weight of it annoyed her hand so she put it back on her lap and tapped her nails against it.

She remembered the deacon reading from a book called Jeremiah during Bible study and flipped to the table of contents.

"Wow," she said, her eyes widening at how many books there were. Once she got to Jeremiah, she ran her finger over to the page number and read it twice in her head. She remembered the chapter but not the verse, so instead of trying to remember, Ava just read chapter twenty-nine entirely.

Jeremiah was a prophet that was sent from Jerusalem to Babylon. He warned of false prophets and how they weren't sent from God. Jeremiah went on to talk about how the Lord favored his people and had good thoughts and futures planned for them.

Ava remembered verse eleven perfectly.

"Thoughts of peace," she repeated. "And not of evil."

Ava read a little more before sending up a prayer. Something inside of her told her to go lay on the couch. It wasn't unusual for her to sleep there, so she grabbed a blanket and headed downstairs.

Rico appreciated the silence in his home. Living with four girls, there always seemed to be something going on. Even though he was sure Ava would move out before then, the thought of Angel being older and becoming as demanding as the other women in his life made him cringe. He wasn't looking forward to Angel growing up at all.

He made a mental note to call his own mother in the morning before turning his head to look at his wife's profile. Her sunflower colored skin was lighter than usual since winter was approaching. Her dark brown hair was routinely wrapped around her head and tied securely with a brown scarf, a few strands peeking through the sides. Charity's left hand pressed against her stomach while the other one curled around her pillow. Her bottom lip poked out as her mouth hung slightly open. She hadn't been sleeping long, Rico knew the snoring would begin soon.

He pressed his lips to her shoulder before sliding as smoothly from the bed as he could. Instead of trying to change, Rico kept his black sweats on and grabbed a hooded sweatshirt. He pulled his sneakers on and walked out of the room and downstairs. Rico went through the kitchen to get his wallet, keys and phone before heading to the front door. He punched his alarm code in a quickly as possible, grateful that it didn't beep loudly. When he opened the door, he turned around to lock it and caught a glimpse of Ava lying on the couch watching him. He hesitated but closed the door anyway, locked it, and then jogged to his car.

He knew Ava assumed she'd figured something out and Rico was pretty sure that she wasn't too far off. Obviously she was waiting to get more concrete evidence before telling Charity and Bri, but Rico hoped she wouldn't go to them before she came to him.

Rico didn't have time to worry about what his daughter was thinking. The fact of the matter was that she was grown and so was he. He didn't have to hide anything from her but he knew where her suspicion stemmed. Out of all the years he spent in prison, Ava was the only one to visit him. She would take him being sent back the hardest.

Rico drove to Jasper and parked near the late night diner that most of the college kids hung at. He was meeting his cousin there to discuss possible business. Rico wasn't selling drugs again, there was no way he would, he was just transporting money for his cousin. He made a few extra dollars and wasn't so pressed about bills. Since Charity began working, he had only done it a few times to get extra cash when it was needed.

His meeting lasted all of thirty minutes before he saw a known drug dealer walk in the diner with someone familiar. Rico hadn't seen him in a while but they both knew exactly who the other was. The guy noticed Rico and looked back at the door but before he could blink, another guy came through it Rico locked eyes with Sunny. They both watched each other for a moment.

It might have been an unspoken rule that a lot of deals went down in this diner. The employees didn't care and most of the college kids were customers. Rico didn't want to assume that Sunny was selling drugs just because he was at the diner with his boys, because then Sunny could assume the same thing about Rico.

He wanted to go find out for the sake of his daughter not having to go through what Kita went through, but how would he expose Sunny without exposing himself?

However, he couldn't just not speak.

Once his meeting was over, Rico walked over to the booth Sunny and his boys were at and nodded.

"What's up, Rico?" Sunny asked.

"You Ava's pops?" the familiar guy asked. Rico nodded. "I'm Kaylen, Elle's husband."

Rico nodded, instantly thinking of the little girl Elle always brought to play with Angel.

"How's Jayla?" he asked. A smile hit Kaylen's face instantly.

"Spoiled, definitely not trying to see how she acts when the new baby comes."

Everyone laughed a little as Rico and Sunny exchanged glances. Rico looked towards the glass window and smiled, patting Sunny on his shoulder before telling him that he'd see him later.

Elle woke up on her fifth anniversary to Jayla running around the apartment screaming, telling her father that she didn't want to put her clothes on. Elle rolled her eyes and sighed, wondering why her child loved to run around naked. She prayed it didn't transition into her adult years. Elle always had a fear of Jayla wanting to be something ridiculous like a half naked video girl or a stripper.

She knew that it was a silly fear, but the way some teenagers were turning up pregnant and running around with no home training, Elle made sure to keep an eye out for any suspicious behavior from Jayla at any age.

"Little girl don't make me spank your butt!" Kaylen's voice boomed through the house. Elle shook her head before running both her hands down the sides of her belly. She was only four months and she was ready to be big and bloated, hopefully with a boy. She smirked at the thought of Kaylen going crazy with another girl. He was already so protective of Elle and Jayla.

"Baby, you need help?" Elle yelled after clearing her throat. She heard Jayla squeal and giggle before she got quiet.

"Naw, baby relax, I got this."

Usually she would go against it and help him out with their wild child, but today she did as told.

She had gotten someone to cover for her at the last minute and was thankful that her cover hadn't been blown. Elle knew she'd have to tell Kaylen sooner or later, probably sooner since Ava now knew. That meant Sunny would know soon. Elle didn't doubt Ava's loyalty to her but when it came to Sunny, Ava couldn't be trusted to hold water.

Besides being bored, Elle really wanted to be able to help Kaylen with bills. Most of the money she got from her job was sitting in a bank account accruing interest. She started to tell him several times but either he was having a good day and she didn't want to mess it up, or he was having a bad day and she didn't want to make it worse.

Elle laid in her bed a little longer, listening to her husband struggle to get Jayla together. After he fed her, he said he was dropping her off at her mom's, telling Elle to be ready when he got back.

October was a tricky month. The weather was spontaneous and Elle never knew how to dress for her anniversary. Her second pregnancy also made her hate everything in her closet already. She thought about a pair of destroyed jeans and a light sweater with matching boots and knew she'd be comfortable at least. If she needed to dress up later, she'd change.

The other thing about October was Miss Angie's death. It had been four years since Sunny's mom died and it hadn't hurt any less. Her death is what caused Elle to forgive her own mother and rebuild their relationship. Miss Angie was like a mom to her and Kaylen and although she was sad, Elle still couldn't imagine how Sunny was feeling.

He'd usually go home that day and visit her grave, sometimes taking Ava with him and other times wanting to go alone. Ava always understood. They were made for each other like that.

Elle groaned before pushing her weight off of the bed by her fists and punching the sheets. Knowing that her mom's house was not that far away, she needed to get up and get ready. After adjusting to the elevation change, she made her way to the bathroom to get ready for the day. She smiled as she hummed a Tony Toni Tone song on the way.

After showering and pushing her curls back with cream colored headband to match her sweater, Elle got dressed and waited for Kaylen to return. When he came through the front door, Elle smiled at him. He had on a long sleeve polo, a pair of jeans and his Timberland boots. His dreads were twisted into a few braids she'd done the night before. Elle stretched her arms out to him as he bent over where she sat on the couch and kissed him.

"Happy anniversary," she squealed. Kaylen kissed her again before holding his hand out to pull her up. "We leaving already?"

"You ready aren't you?" he asked. Elle rolled her eyes before swatting him in the chest.

Kaylen ended up taking Elle out to the park for a picnic. He already had everything packed away in a basket with a few blankets for them to sit on. He even brought a pillow to support Elle's back.

Most of the dishes were finger foods, fruit, meat and cheese and a vegetable tray. Elle was more interested in the dessert.

"Aw, baby you got red velvet cupcakes?" Elle said, giggling as she picked icing off of one. She knew that Kaylen didn't like them too much so he'd gotten them for her only.

"Never again," he said.

"You know you want to taste it," she said, moaning as she bit into the actual cupcake. Kaylen licked his lips.

"I want to taste something else," he mumbled. Elle blushed but kept eating. "But we need to talk first."

"About what, baby?" she asked.

"About what you been doing while I'm at work."

Elle's heart dropped as she stared at the cupcake. She swallowed the food in her mouth before slowly looking up at Kaylen. The knowing look on his face told it all.

"How'd you find out?" Elle whispered. Kaylen chuckled.

"You act like I don't know nothing, Trishelle," he said. "That's what still amazes me after all this time."

"It wasn't like that," she started.

"Well, what was it like then?" he asked, letting his anger show. "Because sneaking and taking my child to her grandmother's everyday when I think you're taking care of home like I asked you to sounds like you think I don't know shit."

Kaylen hadn't cussed in a while. Elle knew that he was mad then.

"I'm sorry I kept it from you."

"You're quitting."

"What? Why?" Elle said, putting the cupcake wrapper down. "It's only a few hours a day, it isn't effecting anything, Kaylen."

"You done eating?" he asked. Elle's nose flared at his attitude. She sat back and crossed her arms.

"Yeah."

It was silent between them for a few minutes before Kaylen sighed heavily.

"I'm just trying to take care of you," he said. "Why can't you see that? Why are you making this difficult for me?"

"And I'm bored!" Elle yelled. "Why can't you see that?"

"Raising my kids is boring?" he asked.

"Don't even go there. Don't do that to me. I love Jayla, but why do I have to sit in the house all day? Huh? You're being selfish and unreasonable."

"This conversation is over," he said, as he began packing the picnic up.

"You brought it up!" she yelled. Kaylen gave her an eye that let her know she was getting too loud. "Baby, I just want to work a few hours a day. It's not that big of a deal."

"I don't want to talk about it anymore."

Elle huffed before struggling to get up. Before Kaylen could finish packing, she walked off back to the car without him. She wasn't quitting her job and she knew if they didn't compromise, this would evolve into a bigger issue for no reason whatsoever.

Seven

Love was something that Ava knew of, but wasn't used to. Up until she was eleven, she felt her father's love. She didn't care much for Kita and their personalities often clashed because they were so much alike. She spent most of her time with Rico, while Bri clung to their mother. It wasn't until after Rico's arrest that the love in their home was replaced with toleration.

In an attempt to fill that space with something more, Ava began to mimic Kita's actions. Sleeping around with different guys only provided Ava with soul ties and enemies. Meeting Elle, Kaylen, and Sunny gave Ava a chance to build meaningful relationships and rebuild the damaged ones between her twin and her mother.

The rape had destroyed her. She would never regret Angel, but somewhere deep inside she wondered how she had been able to love this child with everything in her being and forgive Romero for his participation in her living hell. After a while, the routine of life brought on a normalcy that felt stable and LaDanian was able to knock her back into her past insecurities.
It was something she couldn't fix. It was something Rico couldn't fix. Even Sunny couldn't fix it.

Why not turn to God?

And for the next couple of weeks, that's what she did. She hardly spent any time with anyone except Angel. She went to work and to church, trying to find what everyone there already had. The members at Charity's church welcomed her and a few tried hard at recruiting her for the choir. She still wasn't sure about that though.

She had been so engulfed in her new lifestyle that she hadn't seen how it was affecting everything else in her life, until one afternoon when Sunny showed up at the house after work.

"Hey, what's up? What you doing here?"

"What I'm doing here?" Sunny asked, frowning. "You are aware that it's been a week since I've seen you, right?"

"It hasn't been that long," Ava said, trying to add up the days in her head.

Sunny pulled Ava's body to his and hugged her close. His back had a slight hunch in it as he bent down to press his nose and mouth into Ava's neck.

"You mad at me or something?"

"There a reason I should be mad?" Ava asked, with her eyebrow raised. Sunny shook his head. "I just been busy, you know I joined church."

"Why didn't you ask me to go with you?"

His question startled Ava. She hadn't expected him to say that. Guilt and confusion set in because he was right, she assumed he wouldn't want to go and that was wrong.

"You can go with me this Sunday," she said. Sunny shook his head.

"I have to work, but I'm off next Sunday."

Ava nodded, hiding her smile. Sunny followed her up to her room and sat next to her on her bed.

"Where's my little momma?" he asked.

"Watching a movie with Bri," Ava said. "She's probably sleep by now."

Sunny nodded before kicking his boots off and taking his work shirt off as well.

"You want to talk about what's been going on?" he asked, tapping the Bible that sat next to her. Ava bit her lip before turning to him.

"Ever since Gelly's birthday, I haven't been feeling right. I went to church with Charity a few weeks ago and joining it just seemed like the right thing to do. I've just been reading the Bible and trying to figure all of this out, but I feel like it's the right thing to do," she repeated. Sunny studied her face for a moment before nodding. "It's a little confusing though."

"You should probably get a study Bible or something until you can understand more."

"A study Bible?" she asked.

"Yeah, they have all types that break it down in regular words and get deeper into the meaning to help you understand."

"How you know that?" Ava asked. Sunny laughed.

"I grew up in church baby, I know a little."

Ava gave him a small smile before nodding. "So you're with me on this?" she asked. Sunny bit his lip before running his index finger along Ava's jaw.

"I'm with you on everything baby," he said. "Remember that."

Ava sat at her desk, trying to listen to a customer's issue with their phone while her own blew up in her pocket. She was ten minutes away from being off for the weekend and Dre had called her six times. She hadn't had time to call him back since a sale had brought a lot of customers in.

She wished he'd chill until she had time to see what was so important.

"I'm just trying to get an early upgrade, girl," the customer said, laughing. Ava knew it was an attempt to play her so she gave the customer a weak smile.

"Well, you're still three months away from your upgrade, but you can go early with a fee," she said. The customer's face dropped as Ava pushed a few buttons on the computer to get the answer for the questions she knew was coming next.

"How much?"

"67.25, plus the upgrade price of whatever phone you're looking at."

The customer sucked her teeth before tossing her phone into her purse.

"Girl, I'll just wait it out," she said, before getting up and walking out of the store. Ava rolled her eyes before telling a coworker that she was done for the day. As she was walking back to clock out of work, she called Dre back.

"Is the studio on fire or something, my dude?" she asked.

"Man, you always ruining my good moods. I got some people who want to hire you."

"What do you mean hire me?" Ava asked, unlocking her door and sliding in the driver's seat. She put the key in the ignition, but didn't turn it.

"I sent the song you did for Solace and a few of your hooks to some industry folks I know and they all pretty much want you."

"You did what, Dre?" Ava asked, not sure how to take the news.

"You speak English, A, I'm not repeating myself."

Ava sucked her teeth before her brain began to process Dre's words.

"So when you mean hire me?" she said, drawing out the last word until Dre hopped in.

"They want you to ghost write for artists," he said. "Possibly well known ones and you can do however many you want. You'd have to fly to their offices though, they won't do contracts like that over the phone or nothing. It'd only be a month or so of traveling before everything calms down though. Just to get you started."

Ava smiled, the excitement of being in the music industry creeping up on her quickly.

"Dre, what does this mean?"

"It means money for you Ava, without the fame, just like you wanted."

"This is crazy. I don't even know what to say."

"Do you have a lawyer?"

Ava thought about the guy that handled the rape case after Bri pushed for a trial.

"Yeah," she mumbled.

"Okay, well get me his information so I can pass it along. We can all look at the contracts together."

Ava sighed. "Thank you, Dre."

"Yeah yeah, just don't let me put my name on the line for nothing."

Later that night, Ava slid down against the window seat across from her bed. The room was dark and quiet, something she felt she needed at the moment. A picture of Sunny and Angel danced across the screen of her computer and provided the only light. The carpet slightly irritated her exposed legs as she secured the towel around her body.

Her dark, wet curls fell heavy around her face as she lowered her head and closed her eyes. Taking a few breaths, she rolled her bottom lip against her teeth and put her head back against the wall.

"Why is this so hard?" she asked herself.

She hadn't known that Dre had been sending her songs to record executives until that afternoon when a letter came in to negotiate an independent ghost writing deal and he called her. She thought he was just sending her work to independent artists to sample.

The old Ava would have jumped at the chance to write music for the very artists who comforted her soul on a daily basis. The moment that record company executive offered her a position as a ghost writer, she would have been on a plane.

The new Ava, however, had a family to think about. Angel was four, getting into everything and learning new things every day. Sunny's job was stable and their relationship seemed to be on the same path. Rico and Charity were the most disgustingly cute newlyweds she'd ever see. She was finally getting comfortable with Romero and letting him spend more alone time Angel again.

If she took that job all that could possibly be gone.

Ava tapped her small foot against the carpet and picked at her finger nails. Shuffling on her bed made her look up to see Angel's piercing eyes questioning her position. Ava smiled before crawling over to the end of the bed and patting her back.

"Go on back to sleep," she coaxed the miniature version of herself. Angel fussed a little and mumbled something under her breath before her head dropped like a doll's, back onto the pillow.

She watched her sleep for a second before getting up to dress herself in comfortable clothing. Ava slid into the bed and cuddled with her baby, deciding to let sleep overrule her want to figure things out at that moment.

When Ava was contemplating anything, she always got real quiet. Everyone in the house noticed when it happened, all except for Angel, who was usually too busy talking herself. She had a lot of decisions to make. She didn't think taking the ghost writing position would be so hard except she had commitments at home. Her retail manager job wasn't too keen on missing a lot of days. Sunny usually had a fit if he hadn't seen her in a few days because of their work schedules and Angel had to have one of her parents present in order to go to sleep without a fight. Ava had just joined church and had plans on joining the choir soon. Traveling a lot would throw all of her plans off.

But, it was a dream job.

In middle school, around the time her and Bri became enemies, Ava kept a notebook with poetry or song lyrics in it and an mp3 player glued to her hip. Music was her only outlet for expression and although it had led to one of the worse experiences in her life, she could never turn her back on it. Things wouldn't be the same in her world if she couldn't do what she loved, but Ava had a feeling that if she turned down this deal, Dre wouldn't be too happy to work with her anymore. It had taken him awhile to get over the fact that Ava didn't want to pursue singing in that way anymore. He'd gone to bat for her and she didn't want to disappoint him.

All of these different reasons why she should jump on the opportunity and so many to pass it up, Ava had no idea what to do.

She sighed as she sat next to Angel at the kitchen table, feeding her breakfast before taking her to Elle's house for the day. Rico walked into the kitchen looking rough. He hadn't shaved and it was evident around his mouth and jaw line. His hair was dry and in need of a trip to the barbershop as well. His eyes were sleepy red. Ava thought he was off yesterday so she wondered why he looked so restless.

"Morning, Papi!" Angel yelled from the table, obvious annoyed that her grandpa hadn't acknowledged her all of the few minutes he'd been in the kitchen. He doubled back to the table and kissed her forehead. Ava groaned when he reached over and playfully pushed her shoulder.

"How's my favorite girl?" he asked. Angel cheesed and Ava rolled her eyes.

"Peachy!" she said, both Ava and Rico looked at her in mock surprise. Angel always said things that made her seem beyond her age.

"Charity left for work early," Ava said, eyeing her dad. He slowly nodded before side eyeing her past the refrigerator door. She hadn't forgotten about his suspicious behavior. She just liked making him sweat. It was a part of her past that she still let slip every now and then. One of the benefits of knowing someone was doing something that they didn't want anyone to know about was watching them figure out why you hadn't said anything yet. Ava knew a few years ago when Bri started school that Rico was up to something when he paid her first semester tuition. "What you do yesterday?"

"Huh?"

"You were off right?" Ava asked. "What you do, I didn't see you."

"Oh, I went to chill at Momma's." he said. "Hey, does Sunny still work for that construction place?"

"Yeah, why?" It was Ava's turn to side eye him. Rico's bottom lip pushed out a little before he shrugged his shoulders and shook his head.

"I heard they were laying some people off, that's all."

"He's good," Ava said, knowing Kaylen wouldn't let that happen. Angel jumped down from her chair, announcing that she was done. Ava looked into the bowl to see it empty before giving her permission to go play in the living room. Rico sat down across from her at the table.

"So what's this I hear about you not letting Romero see her again?"

"You heard wrong," Ava snapped. Rico eyed her for a second before she put her head down. "He can come see her over here, but like I told your nosey wife, he's not allowed to take her away from this house as long as his friend is in town."

Rico's nose flared. Ava knew the rape was a touchy subject for him as well. It happened when he was in jail and the fact that he couldn't do anything about it, ate him up inside. Everyone was upset that Ava hadn't shown up in court to testify, but at that point in her life she just wanted to move on.

"How long is he here for?" Rico asked. Ava wanted to smile. She knew he'd be on her side.

"I don't know," she said. "But I wish he'd leave."

Rico nodded before telling Ava that he was headed out for work. He scooped up Angel's cereal bowl and dropped it off in the sink. He then walked into the living room, while yelling for Angel to come say bye to him and give him his daily dose of love.

    Ava sat still at the kitchen table, staring at the dark wooden ridge designs on the smooth surface. She took a few deep breaths before closing her eyes. She hated feeling anxious.

    It was almost as if some unknown switch had turned on inside her. Ava's emotions took over in a split second and she had the urge to cry. It bothered her.

    She got up from the table and jogged upstairs to the bathroom. She frowned at her reflection after she locked the door. Her eyes had a red tint and her skin looked pale. Tears came full force and almost took her by surprise. She stumbled back a little, doubling over and sitting on the edge of the tub.

    Ava had no idea why she was crying. She hadn't cried like this in a while. She pressed her back against the cool tile of the shower door and realized her skin was burning up. Maybe she was sick.

    Her mind wandered back to the prayer that Sunny prayed one night after her nightmare woke them both up. She closed her eyes and tried to remember the words. She sighed once they came to mind, reciting the end.

    "God, we thank you for allowing us to move past this valley and grow," Ava whispered. "Get me out of this valley."

    She took a few minutes to compose her emotions before washing her face and getting ready for work.

    Elle's face was like stone as she walked into her job for the last time to turn in her badge. She promised to finish out the week at a few of her clients' homes. Kaylen stuck to his word about not wanting her to work. She was livid, but what could she do? After saying goodbye to the few friends she'd made, she walked back outside to the awaiting car. Kaylen watched her as she got in. She turned around to check on Jayla before pushing her back into the passenger seat and putting one hand under her belly.

"So you gon be mad about it?" Kaylen asked. Elle didn't respond. Kaylen laughed a little before driving off. "What you want to eat, baby?"

"You tell me," Elle snapped.

"What?" Kaylen asked.

"You make all the decisions, why don't you just pick what we eat."

Kaylen sighed heavily, but Elle didn't care if he was annoyed. She could only move furniture around so much. Being a wife and mother was fine, but why couldn't she do something else too?

Elle was almost six months pregnant. They'd found out recently that it was indeed a boy. Of course she knew she couldn't stress her body, but that part-time job was just something to do. Now she would just be with Jayla all day, occasionally adding Angel to the mix until Kaylen Junior was born.

"Jay baby, what you want to eat?" Kaylen asked, giving up on Elle's attitude for the moment. Once Jayla said Subway, Kaylen made his way to the closest one. Elle stayed in the car while Kaylen took Jayla inside so she could tell him what she wanted on her sandwich. Elle always got the same thing every time they came so he didn't need to try and get her to talk.

"What you want baby?" Kaylen asked, picking Jayla up so she could see.

"Ham and cheese!" she said, smiling. The woman taking the order smiled back at her.

"You're too cute," she said.

"I know," Jayla said. Kaylen frowned at her but the woman just laughed.

"Your daughter is too much," she said, eyeing Kaylen. He smirked.

"Yes she is, I need a two chicken breast foot longs, one on wheat and one on flat bread for my wife."

Her face dropped a little and it took everything in Kaylen not to laugh. A few minutes later, Kaylen and Jayla walked out of Subway with their food. Elle was on the phone when he opened the back door to put Jayla in her seat.

"I'll call you back," she said, before hanging up.

"Who was that?" Kaylen asked after getting back in the driver's seat.

"Kaylen, leave me alone please."

"What's the point of you being mad though? I should be mad that you snuck around and did all that after I asked you to let me take care of you," Kaylen snapped. Elle turned and positioned her back on the door, crossing her arms below her breast and above her belly. Kaylen groaned at the stone expression on her face. He pulled out of the parking lot and tried to hurry home.

"Excuse me, all mighty Kaylen, if I wanted to do something with my life other than sit around and birth your big head babies!"

"Hey!" Jayla said from the backseat.

"I love you, big head," Elle said, smiling for the first time that whole day. Jayla gave her a stern glare before unbuckling herself when Kaylen parked. "What did I tell you about doing that?"

Elle got out of the car and pulled Jayla from the backseat. She stalked up the stairs towards their apartment as Kaylen took his time following behind them with the food. When he got in the living room, Elle snatched the bag from him and took Jayla in the kitchen. Kaylen shook his head before following.

Besides Jayla talking a mile a minute, they ate in silence. Kaylen felt a little guilty but he just couldn't understand why Elle wanted to work so badly. Most women would love it if their husbands told them they didn't have to work and to just chill. Kaylen knew Elle wasn't most women; she hadn't been since he met her. He'd have to figure out a compromise to bring the peace back into his house.

Elle still wasn't talking to him after they ate, so he went up to Sunny's to play the game for a few hours. They were on their third game of Madden when Sunny paused the game.

"You gonna tell me what's up?" he asked.

"Un-pause the game, man."

"Kay, for real."

"Elle got a job, I found out about it and made her quit."

"You made her quit?" Sunny asked. Kaylen nodded. Sunny sat there for a second before un-pausing the game. Kaylen sighed because he knew Sunny had something to say.

"Say what you gotta say, yo," Kaylen said.

"I ain't got nothing to say, you did what you did."

"What the hell? She sitting up there pregnant and she supposed to be taking care of my kid. I'm the one working hard so she doesn't have to."

"That don't mean she wants to sit in the house all day, G."

"Shut up."

Sunny laughed before proceeding to throw a long pass to one of his players and score a touchdown. Kaylen cursed under his breath before tossing the controller on the couch. He was done playing.

"You just came at me with advice about me and mine, let me tell you something," Sunny said. Kaylen sighed before running both his hands down his face, stopping his hands over his nose. He exhaled against his hands before moving them. "She ain't working for money. She's hella bored, bro. You keeping her locked up in the house all the time. She's liable to go crazy. What happened to y'all trying to start a business together? She was all excited about that a few years ago."

"It never fell through," Kaylen answered.

"Well make it fall through."

They both looked towards the door as it swung open. Sunny smiled to see Ava in her work clothes. Angel popped up from around the door and ran towards Sunny. Ava shook her head before greeting both of them.

"What's up, bro?" Kaylen said. Ava rolled her eyes before punching him in his arm.

"I shouldn't even be talking to you," she said. "But I'll stay out of it."

Sunny smirked as Kaylen stood up.

"Yeah," he said, softly punching her in her shoulder. "Stay out of it." Ava groaned in playful disgust as Kaylen walked out of the front door and back down to his apartment. When he got back upstairs, it was empty. He looked at his phone to see Elle had sent him a message saying she and Jayla went to her mom's. He sighed before kicking off his shoes and sitting down on the couch. He ended up dosing off to sleep, being woken up by Elle calling his cell phone.

"Yeah?"

"I'm downstairs but Jay is sleep, can you come get her?"

He paused for a second, missing the sound of her voice. She hadn't spoken to him most of the day and then it wasn't as soft as it was now. He told her he would be down before hanging up, slipping his shoes back on and heading out the front door, leaving it open. Elle waited until Kaylen had the back door of the car open before getting out and going upstairs.

He put Jay to bed, taking his time and hoping that Elle would cool off a little. Once he finally entered their bedroom, she was laid out on the bed in his tee shirt that she wore to bed, rubbing her belly.

"You ready to talk?" he asked, kicking his shoes off.

"It's your world," she said, sarcastically. Kaylen rolled his eyes.

"You can cut all that out, I don't control you."

"Oh, well what do you call it then?" she asked, sitting up with her arms folded below her chest. "You made me quit my job."

"I'm your husband, I'm taking care of you!" Kaylen said, reaching his boiling point.

"Fine Kaylen," Elle said, turning towards the television even though it wasn't on. Kaylen shook his head and went to take a shower. By the time he got back, Elle was sleep.

Eight

Beep, beep, beep...

Sunny groaned while pushing his face into the mass of curls that lay next to him. The sun wasn't coming through the blinds of his bedroom window, but there was a light glow outside which meant it was time for him to get up for work. He only had to do the early shift two weeks out of the month but he hated it every time it came around. Sunny was usually a night owl; staying up and playing the game with Kaylen, but having to be at the construction site by six in the morning cut that out.

His usual routine changed a lot when he started working his legit job. Hustling wasn't exactly dream hours, but he always made his own unless something urgent called for more block time. At first his construction job bored him but now he welcomed the stability.

He opened his eyes to see nothing but black curls. Ava shifted a little but didn't move. Sunny pulled her into his side with one arm and she giggled into the pillow.

"Get up," she said. He shook his head. He felt her shift again before her arm stuck out and her hand fidgeted with his phone on the nightstand. After a few minutes it went silent. "You're going to be late for work."

Sunny ignored her comment and pulled her closer. His fingertips felt around the bed until they came in contact with soft skin. He loved when she spent the night. She didn't do it much because he only had one bedroom but whenever Angel was with Romero for the night, Ava would spend the night with Sunny. Since Romero's friend was gone, Ava was letting Romero take Angel again.

Ava slightly turned towards him while still lying on her stomach and lifted her left leg over his. She rubbed her hand over his fade before sighing and trying to go back to sleep. He kissed the tip of her chin before pulling on one of her curls.

Moments like these made Sunny wonder what exactly he was waiting on with the whole marriage thing.

"I wish you stayed with me," he mumbled.

"You just trying to get me to make you breakfast," she snapped back. Sunny smiled.

"It would be nice."

"I'm not getting out this bed for another three hours," Ava said. "At least."

Sunny sucked his teeth in slight irritation but couldn't say otherwise. It was rare that Ava would cook since Elle always did. He would luck up every now and then when she was up making breakfast for Angel.

He idly wondered if they got married would he be able to get home cooked meals when he wanted them. It probably wouldn't be every day like Kaylen.

"You ever think about us getting married?" he asked. Sunny almost hadn't realized he'd said it aloud until Ava's eyes flew open. She looked at him for a moment before closing them again.

"Not often, but I guess I do think about it," she mumbled. "Why? Do you?"

Sunny nodded but didn't say anything. After a few minutes, he kissed Ava on her forehead and got up to get ready for work.

"Mr. Diveno left your orders in the trailer," a coworker instructed Sunny as soon as he got on site. Sunny nodded before adjusting his coveralls and heading for the dingy, off white trailer that sat off to the right of the construction site. He wanted to laugh at his coworker calling Kaylen, Mr. Diveno. He still wasn't used to it but Kaylen had moved up to management so that respect came with the title. To everyone except Sunny, of course.

The door on the trailer was just about off the hinges as Sunny swung it open and walked over to the cluttered desk. Sunny nodded at the guy behind it as he handed Sunny the schedule. He glanced over it before inwardly groaning. Kaylen always gave him the hard jobs when he ran the schedule.

Once Sunny made it to his site post, the day seemed to swallow him whole. There were days when nine hours felt like a full twenty-four and other days where it went by fast. Today, there were too many problems and progress was stopped too much to get any real work done. By the time Sunny made it home, he didn't want to be bothered.

He was glad that Ava was gone so he could take a shower and walk around without clothes on. He checked his mail and realized he had a few past due bills that needed to be handled soon. This was another problem with working a legit job; you actually had to wait for a paycheck to come every two weeks to have money.

It hit Sunny that money was the reason he wasn't too pressed about proposing at the moment. Even though Elle didn't like it, Kaylen took care of his household and that was what Sunny wanted to be able to do. There was no way that Ava would quit working and be domesticated, but Sunny at least wanted to know that if she did want to quit her job it wouldn't be a problem for him to take care of his family. He wanted to be financially stable for kids. He loved Angel and had been around since she was born but he also wanted to see Ava pregnant with his seed. All he needed was a little boy to carry on his name and he'd be complete.

Sunny was hoping that Ava wouldn't read too much into the conversation they had that morning before he left for work. He wanted to marry Ava, that wasn't up for debate. Sunny just wasn't ready.

If it was one thing Ava hated doing, it was lying. She could count on her fingers how many times she'd actually lied in her lifetime and even that small number made her feel sick to her stomach. She never felt the need to hide any of her dirt from anyone who was bold enough to ask her about it. She had only remembered lying to Sunny about the rape because she didn't want to lose him. She didn't think anyone would believe her at the time anyway. It still sucked to have to lie.

This was why she felt so queasy on her way to Dre's house.

She was supposed to be at work for another three hours, but took a few vacation hours to handle some business. It wouldn't take that long, Dre said, but she wanted to be able to get her thoughts together before heading home.

It didn't make any sense, if she sat and thought about her decision logically. Not telling anyone that she'd taken the ghost writing deal wasn't making any sense;

however, in her mind right now, it was all going to work out. She was just testing the waters.

Ava pulled up to Dre's house and Dre's cousin, Omar, was sitting on the porch. She killed the ignition and rushed out the car and up the porch.

"Where's the fire?" he asked, with a smirk. Ava rolled her eyes.

"The door open?"

"Hi to you too, Ava," Omar said. Ava just pushed the door knob and walked in the house. A few years ago, Omar tried to talk to Ava before her and Sunny became official. At first, Ava was a little infatuated with Omar because he could sing. Now he was just annoying.

"Yo, Dre!" Ava yelled, knowing that Dre hated when she did that.

"I'm in the kitchen, Miss Ghetto."

Ava laughed before walking in and dropping her keys on the table next to a stack of papers.

"My lawyer hit you up already?" she asked. Dre didn't turn from the stove, but nodded. "Dang, he's fast."

"It's called doing his job, smartie," Dre said. Ava sucked her teeth before sitting down and glancing over the papers she'd already read twice.

"So what happens now?"

"You go to Atlanta."

"Come again?" Ava asked, sitting up with her elbows on her knees to lean forward. She turned her ear towards Dre.

"Next weekend we need to be in Atlanta for the record label to brief you."

"Dre, you do know I have a job and a child?" Ava asked, her tone showing that she wasn't amused or excited.

"You want to count responsibilities?" Dre asked, finally turning around with a skillet in his hand. "I have all of that, a couple girlfriends and car notes. Either you in or you out?" he said. Ava laughed before sitting back in the chair and shaking her head.

"I'll think of something."

"Think quick," he said, turning back around. "You eat?"

"If you offering food, make it to go," Ava said. Dre sucked his teeth.

"Naw, you doing too much now."

Ava laughed before picking up her keys and heading out. Omar looked up from a phone call.

"Dang, you leaving? I was just about to come chat with you," he said.

"Fortunately, I have better things to do," Ava said while she stepped quickly off the porch. She made her way back to her car and drove to Elle's to pick up Angel.

She didn't stay long, Kaylen and Elle were still acting weird so Ava used that as an excuse to head home. She sighed in relief when Rico's car was the only one in the driveway.

"Papi!" Angel said, while running through the front door.

"Stop running!" Ava said, closing and locking it behind her.

"My favorite girl is finally home," Rico said from the living room. Angel backtracked from the kitchen and ran straight into his arms on the couch. She burst into giggles once he began tickling her. Ava sighed as she sat down in the recliner.

"So, Dre got me a ghost writing deal," Ava said. Rico looked at her with raised eyebrows.

"It pay this time?" he asked. Ava nodded. "Good deal."

"It's with an actual record company. I have to go to Atlanta next weekend."

"Why you sound like you got a court date or something?" he asked. Ava rolled her eyes.

"Just don't know if this is the right decision," she said. "If I follow through with this I'll be traveling a lot."

"I see," Rico said, nodding while Angel snuggled up to his side and flipping through the television. "Well, you already committed right?"

Ava slowly nodded. "Looks that way."

"So you just gotta deal now," he said. "What Sunny say?"

"I'm not telling anyone but you right now," Ava responded quickly.

"You act just like yo momma," Rico said, laughing. Ava smiled at the mention of Kita. She missed her a lot. "That wasn't a compliment," he joked.

"Shut up!" Ava said. They both laughed. "Will you go with me to Atlanta?"

"You really aren't going to tell Sunny? How you just gon dip out of town?"

"I'll tell him it's for work and you're coming to visit some old friends," Ava said. Rico eyed her.

"Yeah, definitely got those lying skills from Kita Vine."

"Are you going or not?" Ava asked, slightly irritated.

"Yeah, but we gotta tell Charity. You ain't about to get me hurt. Plus, you'll need a baby sitter."

"Good idea, Pops," Ava said, getting up and walking out of the living room.

Ava was glad that Sunny had been working overtime that week. It gave her time to get her lies together. She hadn't wanted to, but telling Sunny the truth before she was even sure what was going to happen with this deal seemed like a lot of unnecessary drama. She knew Elle would have a fit that she didn't tell her, but with all going on in her house, Ava hoped she would be too distracted to care.

Ava had an early day at work and since Romero had Angel, she knew it was time to tell Sunny about her trip.

She used her key to get into his apartment, tossing her things onto the couch near the door. She could hear a buzzing sound in the back so she followed it to the bathroom. The door was open and she could see Sunny standing in front of the mirror, over the sink, lining his facial hair with his clippers.

At that moment, she remembered the day they first met. It was around the time she auditioned for the school musical to piss Bri off. He had gotten out of Kaylen's car to hug Elle. Ava remembered thinking he had the most gorgeous smile she'd ever seen on a guy.

"I was just about to come find you," Sunny said, snapping Ava out of her thoughts. She smiled.

"You were getting fresh for me?" Ava asked. Sunny smirked while dusting the hairs off his sink, and putting his clippers up. He lifted Ava onto the counter and kissed her. She frowned as a few loose hairs touched her skin.

"Where you been?" he asked, running his hands down her arms. Ava had to will her mind to concentrate.

"Chilling with pops," she said. "What you doing this weekend?"

"More overtime," he said, peering over the top of her head and into the mirror. He took his left hand and wiped the side of his face. "Why?"

"Gotta go to this work thing in Atlanta."

"Y'all got stores in Atlanta?"

"Yeah, it's a corporate meeting that my store is sending me to."

"You driving by yourself?" he asked, she shook her head.

"Pops got old friends down there so he said he'd drive. You know I don't like driving more than an hour," she said. Sunny looked down at her and laughed.

"You'll be sleep before y'all get out of Tennessee," he joked, patting her on the side of her thigh. He walked out of the bathroom, still laughing. Ava sat on the counter for a second to digest her lie.

"*That was too easy,*" she thought. Looking up at the ceiling for a moment, Ava assured herself that she would tell him everything once the time was right.

That following Friday, Rico and Ava were on their way to Atlanta. It was a three and a half hour drive so Ava drank an energy drink in order to stay up. Rico was driving, but she didn't want to fall asleep on him. Interstate 75 was a little crowded since it was the weekend. Rico coasted through the mountains and they made it to the Doubletree Hotel downtown Atlanta in good timing.

"This don't look like this from the outside," Rico said, complimenting the hotel as they walked towards the elevator. Ava laughed before hitting the *UP* button. The elevator was glass so they could see the floors of the hotel as they rode past them. The fifth floor had what looked like a little lounge with a few couches spread out and a few tables with chairs. The elevator finally stopped at the ninth floor before it dinged. The metal doors slowly slid open and Ava got off the elevator first.

"We should have got two rooms," Rico said.

"You don't want to share with me?" Ava asked, smirking as she slid the electronic key in the slot and waited for the light to turn green.

"No," Rico said. Ava sucked her teeth as Rico explained how bad she snored. Ava almost commented that Sunny had no problems with it. Knowing how sensitive Rico got about her even insinuating that she was sexually active, she kept that thought to herself. Instead, Ava smiled. She and Bri were half a year away from being twenty-two. Ava always said though, they'd been through more things than people twice their age. Sometimes Rico acted as if they were still the eleven-year-old girls who watched him being taken from their home in handcuffs.

"I don't have to meet with Dre until dinner," Ava said. "But I'm tired."

"You didn't do anything," Rico said, frowning at his daughter. Ava shrugged before falling back on the bed. Rico laughed. "I'll catch you later then."

Rico pulled the other room key from the small envelope that the hostess put it in, and tossed the empty envelope on the dresser near the television. Ava kicked off her shoes and curled up on the bed, already falling in love with the softness of the pillows. She watched Rico pull an outfit from his bag and lay it out on his bed. He grabbed a small, leather bag and headed to the bathroom. Ava was sleep by the time the shower turned on.

Ava woke up to a text from Dre with the address on where the dinner meeting was. Ava wondered why she couldn't just ride down to Atlanta with Dre, but knew he had to stay a little longer for business. It was a lot easier to pass off her story with Rico anyway. Ava went through her clothes and sighed once she looked at the outfit one of Dre's girlfriends had picked out for her. She wasn't used to these types of meetings so she had no idea what to wear. Dre sent his girlfriend to the mall with Ava the day before they left.

    She picked out a coffee colored sleeveless chiffon collared shirt with dark brown dots on it. The tan jeans she paired with it almost looked like slacks. She loved the simple, brown and cream wedges. Ava thought it looked more like a casual outfit, but Dre and his girlfriend approved so she went with it.

    She washed her hair in the shower and used the hotel dryer to give it a little volume. By the time she got dressed, she had a little over thirty minutes to get to the restaurant. She sent Rico a text to let him know she was headed out. She idly wondered where he'd gone, but knowing she had the car, he couldn't have gone too far. The strip their hotel was on was surrounded by bars, other hotels, and restaurants. Rico would be fine.

    Ava hated driving. It had taken her so long to even familiarize herself with Hamilton's streets and she lived there all her life. Bri often teased her about not knowing the names of streets. You'd have to tell Ava what something was by in order for her to know where it was.

    Rico and Ava had gotten a small rental car that had GPS. Luckily, the restaurant was only fifteen minutes from where she was. Ava pulled up to Pappaduex and licked her lips at the seafood sign. She knew she was supposed to be focusing on the meeting at hand, but the delicious smells that were seeping out of the restaurant almost made her want to run straight to the kitchen. That's when she realized she hadn't eaten all day.

"Yo!" Ava said, after calling Dre. "I'm outside."
"I gotta booth in the back. Nobody's here yet."
"Order me a drink," Ava joked, turning the car off. Dre just hung up on her instead of responding. She found Dre in a booth near the back, snacking on an appetizer.
"You always eating," Ava said, throwing her purse into the booth first and sitting on the side next to him. He elbowed her before he continued eating. Ava snuck one of his nachos before ordering a glass of water.
"You nervous?" Dre asked. Ava frowned before shaking her head.
"Why should I be?" Ava asked. "They want me."
"Man, you full of it," Dre said, laughing.
"I'm saying. Not to be all cocky, but they like my style so they need to be trying to convince me."
"This was a mistake," Dre said, shaking his head.
"Calm down," Ava said, laughing. "I know how to act."
"Could have fooled me."
Ava shook her head as her phone buzzed in her pocket. She looked at it and saw that Sunny was texting her. Immediately, she felt guilty, but she didn't have time to let it set in. Dre elbowed her again. She looked up to see two guys walking towards their booth.
One was your typical-looking record label rep. He was a stalky white guy with short, dark hair. He had on a full, three-piece suit and dark shades on his eyes. His face looked a little rough around his chin and jaw line. The other guy looked to be of mixed heritage. His jet black hair was slicked back into a ponytail that curled up on the ends. He was a little more built and clean cut.
Dre pushed Ava out of the booth and they both stood up to greet them.

"Dre? Ava?" the one with the shades asked, holding out his hand to shake Dre's.

"Yes."

"I'm Rich, this is Derrick," he said pointing to his partner. They both shook Ava's hand before everyone sat back down in the booth. "Nice to put a beautiful face to those words," he said. Ava smiled.

"Don't get carried away," Dre told him. All three of them laughed but Ava just looked at Dre, wondering how he felt so comfortable joking with him like that.

"It's nice to meet you, too," Ava finally said. The waitress brought her back the lobster bisque she ordered. She knew she'd still be hungry, but she hadn't known how long this meeting was going to last and she wanted to get dinner with Rico later.

"Is this your first time in Atlanta?" Derrick asked. Ava looked up at him and nodded.

"I haven't been too far from Tennessee," she admitted. "I'd love to travel though, but work and my kid keep me at home."

"You have a child?" Rich asked. Ava frowned.

"Yes, a little girl. She's four."

"I don't see that being a problem," Derrick said, more so to Rich than Dre and Ava.

"Why would it be?"

Dre slipped his hand on Ava's arm, quickly catching the attitude in her voice.

"Don't mind Rich," Derrick said. "He's all business. Seeing as this is a ghost writing deal, most of the time we don't need you present for you to work. However, we would need you to be available if a particular artist requests a vibe session before deciding to work with you. Would you be able to do that?"

Instead of opening her mouth to say something smart, Ava looked at Derrick and nodded. She silently apologized to Dre with her eyes. It wasn't everyday that she'd get this opportunity. Now that she was sitting down with them, it made it more real. She also didn't want to mess up Dre's reputation. She didn't know the extent to which he was known, but she knew that he'd gone to bat for her with these people. Dre had never shown Ava any reason not to be loyal to him. She'd hold up her end of the bargain.

"I have help," Ava blurted out. "With Angel. My daughter."

"Angel's a pretty name," Rich said, trying to smooth things over.

"She's far from an angel," Dre mumbled. Ava looked at him in shock and swatted his arm. Everyone laughed and the tension had been defused.

"Moving on to business," Rich said. Derrick rolled his eyes. "The four songs Dre sent us were too good for us to pass up getting you on paper."

"Thank you," Ava said, trying not to blush. Whenever someone complimented her on her passion for music, she felt unworthy.

"Do you know how ghost writing goes?" Derrick asked.

"My name doesn't go on anything, right?"

"Yes, but it's a little more complicated than that," Rich said. Ava looked between the two of them to see who would speak next. "Your employment will be on a contractual basis. Most of our developing artists don't get much of a choice on who they work with, so we decide who will write the song. Those cases will be more often than not that your services will be solicited. Other times, the times you want to happen, are when our big artists ask for you personally."

"How would that happen if they don't know who I am?"

"The artists knows you, no one else does."

Ava sat back in her chair and thought it over. She wasn't sure how she felt about not getting credit for her own words.

"We pay you for the rights. You'll make more than someone who wants acknowledgement on the back of an album that nobody reads anyway," Rich said.

The table grew a little silent as Rich put a manila folder on the table and slid it towards Dre and Ava. Dre slid it to her. He hadn't asked for anything in this deal, but Ava discussed him getting a percentage of her signing bonuses out of respect and gratitude. They argued about it, but Ava would have her way.

"This is what our lawyers discussed with yours, all that's needed is your signature."

"We have to run, but we need your decision before you head back home."

Once Rich and Derrick left, Ava still hadn't said anything. Dre cleared his throat and turned to her.

"You talked about not wanting to be famous but you love writing music, this is a way to do it," he said. "You know I wouldn't put you on something I didn't think you wanted. We been down for years and your talent is ridiculous. Yes, I'd rather you be singing your own songs and showing everybody what you made of."

"You know I can't do that," Ava mumbled.

"I know you can, but I also know what you been through so I won't press it."

"The money without the fame right?" Ava said, smirking at taking Dre's words. He laughed and nodded before eating one of his nachos.

"Well, enjoy the rest of the night. We should hit a club later," Dre said. "Y'all leaving tomorrow, right?" he asked. Ava nodded. "I may stay a couple days."

"I heard that," Ava said. "I think I miss Gelly already."

"Take a break, its only two days," Dre said, teasing Ava. She shrugged and smiled. This was the furthest she had been from her baby. Even when she went to Sunny's mom's funeral she wasn't that far. It was only an hour and half away from Hamilton.

"I should probably call and check on her and Charity when I get back to the room."

"Pops gonna go out with us though? I can't just roll with you like we together," Dre said. Ava frowned.

"Please, I'd make you look good," Ava said. Dre sucked his teeth. "He probably won't, but I got a friend down here who will roll." Dre gave Ava and questioning look. "Not that type of friend."

"Whatever."

"Just let me know when you ready, big head," Ava said, sliding out of the booth. "Thanks for lunch!"

Ava giggled as she heard Dre suck his teeth again while she walked away. When she got back to the hotel, Rico was on the phone with Charity.

"Mami said Gel is acting up," Rico said, when Ava walked in. Ava frowned.

"What is she doing?"

"Throwing a tantrum for you," Rico said. "I told you she's spoiled."

"No she's not. She just loves her mommy," Ava said, proudly. Rico eyed her before continuing his conversation with Charity. Ava kicked off her shoes and pulled her phone out of her purse to call Amaru. Amaru was Ava's first high school boyfriend. He was Ava's first everything. He was her first love, her first sexual partner, and the reason all the rumors that ruined her high school life started. Years after their demise, Amaru apologized and he and Ava became friends again. A couple of years ago, Amaru moved to Atlanta. A few of their other classmates moved down there as well.

"What's up, baby momma?"

"What if I told you I'm in Atlanta with my manager and I want to kick it tonight," Ava said.

"I'd say we in VIP!" he said. Ava laughed. "You for real? I thought you stopped singing."

"Writing deal, and yes sir I'm for real. What's the best club to hit on a Friday night?"

"I know a few places," Amaru said. "Your dude with you? I need a date?"

"No, just my manager."

"Cool, let me hit you back in a few hours."

Ava hung up and lay back on the bed. She flipped open the folder that Rich had given her at the restaurant and looked over the contract again.

"Hold on," she heard Rico say. He held his cell phone out to her.

"You have to buy me shoes for keeping your secret," Charity said. Ava laughed.

"It shouldn't be that hard for you to keep it."

"Romero called here earlier and asked and I didn't know if you told him or not so I just went with the story."

"Charity, you are such a horrible liar," Ava said. Charity sucked her teeth.

"I just forget things, that's all," she said. "That's why it's better to just tell the truth."

"Let me speak to my baby," Ava said.

"She just went to sleep and I refuse to wake her up before the Lord does."

Ava laughed at Charity's exhausted tone. "Stop acting like that."

"What are you two about to do," Charity asked.

"Probably get some dinner, I'm going out with Dre later."

"Out to a club?"

"Yes."

"Ava be careful," Charity warned. "You're still new to salvation."

"What does that mean?"

"You've been doing really good about not drinking and cussing and things like that. I'm just saying be careful not to fall back into that."

Ava sighed, a little confused. She didn't know all there was to know about living a saved life, but she'd knew a few people who went to church on a regular basis that still went out and had a drink every now and then. Ava didn't want to drink; she had no desire to, but she didn't think it was totally wrong. Ava guessed she had a lot to learn.

"I'll be careful," she said, not wanting to further the conversation. After a few more minutes of talking to Charity, she gave the phone back to Rico.

Later that evening, Ava got ready to go to Echelon 3000 with Amaru and Dre. Ava wore a pair of studded, blue jean shorts, a loose fitting red shirt that fell from her shoulders, and a pair of cheetah print wedges. She had plenty of time after she and Rico had dinner, so she flat ironed her hair.

Dre picked Ava up from her hotel. They would meet Amaru at the club. Ava asked Rico if he wanted to go, but he declined and stayed in the room. They drove for about thirty minutes before pulling off on an exit. When Dre turned towards a shopping center, Ava frowned.

"You going the right way?" Ava asked. Dre smiled, as if Ava told a joke. "What's funny?"

"It's right there," Dre said, nodding towards the middle of the center before turning to park. Ava looked for a second before laughing.

"They put a club in a shopping center? Next to a beauty supply!?" Ava laughed harder.

"It's nice inside, though," Dre said, turning the key in the ignition. The car immediately died down and Ava unbuckled her seat belt. "So who's this dude we meeting?"

"Dre chill, I told you he's a friend," Ava deadpanned Dre's curiosity. "You know I'm with Sunny."

Dre gave her a look as they stepped in the line for the club. Ava smoothed her shirt over her stomach as she observed the women in line. Their chests were exposed and some of them had shorts small enough to show all of their business. A lot of them had on way too much makeup. Ava smirked, knowing that a few years ago, that would have been her minus the makeup.

They stood in line for about ten minutes before Dre paid for them both to get in. There was a small window in the wall where a woman was sitting at a desk, checking

IDs. After they went through, they turned left at the corner and walked down a short hallway. Once it opened up, Ava had to admit that she was impressed.

She definitely wouldn't have guessed that the inside looked this nice. There were two big dance floors separated by bars, and in the back was a bar and grill. There was also another level that held VIP lounges with large glass windows that overlooked the rest of the club.

Dre saw the look on Ava's face and smirked. "Told you."

Ava rolled her eyes before walking towards the bar. Dre questioned her after she ordered a witch's brew.

"It's just juice."

Dre turned to order a drink just as someone came up behind Ava. She quickly turned around and smiled to see Amaru.

"Don't be in my city looking this good," he said. Ava giggled before hugging him. She leaned back and tugged on his short hair.

"When you do this?"

"Last year."

"Looks good. You look like a grown up!"

"I do what I can," Amaru said, licking his bottom lip and rubbing his chin. Ava smacked his arm. "You missed abusing me."

"I did," Ava admitted. "How you been?"

"Atlanta is treating me good," he said. Ava nodded.

"This is my manager Dre. Dre, this is Amaru," she said once Dre turned around with his drink. They greeted each other before Dre went to talk to a woman at the end of the bar.

"You looking good for real, baby," Amaru said. "How's my girlfriend?"

"My child doesn't even like you!" Ava laughed. "But she's good."

"That's cool. Dance with me."

Ava finished her juice before putting the empty glass back on the bar. She then followed Amaru to the dance floor.

Ava had never been to a club that played R&B and Rap. She was having a lot of fun catching up with Amaru. After so many songs, Dre came over and told them that they all had been invited up to VIP. The first person Ava recognized was Derrick. She introduced Amaru to him as they slid into the booth.

"You enjoying yourself?" he asked.

"Yes, thank you."

"I hope you're leaning towards a yes."

"Pretty close to it."

"You're from Tennessee, right?"

"Hamilton."

"I have an associate from there who owns a few studios in New York. You know Michael Taylor?"

"I don't think so," Ava said.

"Yes you do," Amaru chimed in. The look he gave Ava made her frown.

"I do?"

"Think about it."

Ava looked at him for a second while she thought about it. She wasn't a very friendly person and she didn't remember a lot of names. There was only one person she knew with the last name Taylor. That's when it hit her. Amaru could tell that Ava had figured it out. He cleared his throat to interrupt the awkward silence.

"We went to school with his son."

Derrick looked at Amaru and nodded. Ava closed her eyes. She felt like no matter what she did, she could never get away from LaDanian.

While Ava was waiting for Dre to finish his conversation with some woman, she and Amaru stepped outside. It was still pretty warm for after midnight. Ava imagined it was probably a little chilly in Hamilton right now.

The shopping center was closed except for the club. There were a few construction signs in the parking lot and there was no longer a line to get in. A few club goers were stumbling out as Amaru and Ava stood off to the side.

Ava was glad to see him. They were always good friends, ever since she'd met him. It was unfortunate that they became romantically involved and their friendship ended with the reveal of his true intentions at the time. Ava could admit that the hurt from being betrayed by him was something she thought she'd never get over. It wasn't until after the rape that she realized how silly it was to hold that grudge.

When Ava was pregnant with Angel during her senior year at Hamilton High, Amaru looked out for her. He'd bring her food in the morning and give her rides home before she and Sunny got back on good terms. Their friendship had grown and she appreciated it.

"So what's up?" Amaru asked.

"I got this ghost writing deal, but it may cause me to travel a lot and I'm not really trying to be away from my family like that."

"You only been here for a day and half right?" he asked. "Did they say you'd be gone for more than that?"

"They didn't say much of anything," Ava mumbled. Amaru shook his head and laughed. "What?" Ava snapped, frowning.

"What you trippin' off of?"

"I'm not tripping off anything, I'm just trying to make sure I make the right decision. I have Angel to think about."

"You sure this is about Angel?"

"Amaru, quit while you're ahead," Ava warned him, but Amaru just shook his head.

"You always running from something you want, Ave."

Ava smiled at the nickname, but shook it off at his statement. "I do not run!" Ava said. "I've never ran, you know that."

"You don't run from bad things that happen to you, but you run from good things," he said. Amaru took Ava's silence as an okay to continue. "You sang in front of everybody in school to prove a point, but when it came down to making it a career, you ran from it for a while."

"Yeah and when I stopped running, look where it got me!"

"It got you Angel," Amaru said quickly. Ava huffed but didn't say anything. He gave her an apologetic glance. "Ava, your heart is in music, it may have started off rocky but think about it. If you didn't have a passion for it, you would have been done. You stopped singing but eventually your heart led you back to being involved with it."

"I don't know," Ava said, upset that her voice cracked as her throat got dry. Sometimes she hated her emotional side.

"Ave, I know you're scared," Amaru said. "I know you been through some things. Hell, even I had a hand in your pain, but you grew from that. You grew so beautiful baby you can't let fear hold you back."

Ava looked at Amaru before he pulled her in for a hug. She sighed before telling him thank you.

"No problem," he said. "Just make sure you make the check out to Amaru Jackson."

Amaru laughed as Ava swatted his arm. He laughed harder when she punched him in the chest.

"You're stupid!" she said.

The next morning, Rico and Ava decided to go to Lenox and shop a little before heading home. Ava hadn't gotten much sleep the night before. They stayed at the club a little longer last night but Ava's mood was disheartening. She hadn't even thought about LaDanian's connections in the music industry. He was in New York, she didn't think to worry about it all the way in Atlanta.

Obviously they were more extensive than Ava thought. It only made her blood boil more as her hatred for him grew. She couldn't explain it. She knew why she'd gotten over Romero's involvement in the situation. Ava could admit that she didn't even hate Davion; Bri's ex boyfriend, as much as she hated LaDanian.

Ava had never met LaDanian's dad. She'd always heard he was this big shot producer that had LaDanian and his mom sitting in a nice house on the richer side of Hamilton. His mom was always snotty, Kita never liked her, but Kita hardly liked anyone when she was alive. Ava could look back and realize that her mom never really had any friends. The men that she dated after Rico went to jail seemed to be her only company.

Ava never remembered actually seeing his dad. Not even a picture of him all those times she was in LaDanian's basement studio before the rape happened.

"How was the club?" Rico asked, as they walked past the first floor of the food court.

"It was nice," Ava said. "Amaru came."

"He stay here?"

"Him and Bri's old friend, Jaiva," Ava said. Rico nodded. "Speaking of Bri, she said she wants shoes too."

"Well, you better get to looking," Rico said. "I learned never to pick Charity's shoes out a while ago."

Ava laughed before they looked around for a shoe store. She loved spending time with Rico. It was a little weird, because she hadn't really became a daddy's girl until a few years after he went to jail. When she got old enough, she was the only person who even visited him. Besides Charity and his mom, Ava was the only one who wrote him letters. She was grateful through it all that he was only a little over an hour away from their home the whole time he was incarcerated. They'd been through some emotional times together, despite the distance. Their biggest argument came when Ava told him that she was pregnant and he immediately accused her of being like Kita. However, as soon as he got out, they were inseparable. It took Bri some time to come around, but eventually she did.

While Ava looked around at the shoes, her heart became heavy at the thought of Rico going back to his illegal ways. She would be lying to herself if she said she wasn't suspicious of the way he had been acting and how extra money just seemed to show up. Ava was adamant on not saying anything to him until she had proof. She had no idea how she would get that proof, though.

Her cell phone rang to a tone that made her roll her eyes at her forgetfulness.

"Hey love," she said, answering Sunny's call as quickly as she could. "Sorry I didn't call yesterday. Things got a little busy."

"Whatever man," he said, his attitude very apparent.

"I love you," she said, sweetly. She could hear him suck his teeth and she held back from laughing.

"What time you coming home? We need to talk."

"We should be hitting the highway in a few hours," Ava said. "Charity and Bri wanted shoes. What's wrong?"

"Come here when you get back."

"I have to get Gelly," Ava said, now worried about what was wrong with her boyfriend.

"Come here after you get her, Ava."

"Okay."

Ava looked at her phone for a second after Sunny disconnected the call. She sighed, not looking forward to Sunny being upset with her. It only happened rarely, but Sunny was the type to keep silent and ignore his issue. Ava was vocal about when she wasn't happy.

She picked out shoes for Charity, Bri and Angel before going to find Rico. While she walked around the mall, she called Elle.

"How's Atlanta?" she asked. Ava felt a little guilty for not telling Elle the real reason either.

"It's pretty nice, weather is about the same. How you feeling?"

"I've been having pains all morning," Elle groaned. "This little boy is kicking my butt!"

"They bad?"

"Not really," Elle said. "Just real uncomfortable. I want some tea but I don't feel like getting up to get it."

"Tell Kaylen to get it, Elle."

"I'm not talking to him. He got Jay for the day so I'm chilling."

Ava sucked her teeth. She knew that Elle was still upset that Kaylen made her quit her job, but Ava felt like Elle went about getting what she wanted in the wrong way. She tried not to comment on it. Ava wasn't married, so she didn't want to give a married woman advice, even if it was her best friend.

"Y'all are silly," Ava said. Elle sucked her teeth.

"Naw, he's silly!" she said. Ava laughed at her tone.

"Shut up. I'll see you when you get home."

"Okay."

Ava found Rico in a jewelry store, looking at watches. He was having a conversation with the salesman about two different styles, so Ava just sat down in a chair near the door. Someone tried to come over and talk to her, but she just smiled and said she was with Rico while pointing to him.

"Come tell me which one of these you like," Rico said, calling her over. Ava switched the shoe bag from her left to her right hand before walking over. Both of the watches were by Movado. One was stainless steel with a rectangular face, small diamond baguettes around the pearl white face. The other one was gold with a circular face but everything else was the same as the other watch.

"I like that one," Ava said, pointing at the stainless steel piece. Both Rico and the salesman smiled, as if letting Ava in on a secret.

"Me too," Rico said, nodding at the salesman. He took that as his cue to put the other one up before cutting the tag off the one Rico wanted. He asked him if he would be wearing it out of the store. Rico told him to box it up.

"How much was it?" Ava asked.

"You counting my money now," Rico looked at her, smiling. Ava looked at him for a second before slowing shaking her head. "It's on sale."

"You got anything else you want to do?" Ava asked, suddenly anxious. "I'm ready to hit the highway." Rico reached for the bag and his receipt before they walked out of the jewelry store.

"Nah, we just need to go to a gas station first."

"Well, let's go."

"You alright, kid?" Rico asked.

"I'm good," Ava lied. "Just ready to go home."

The sun was gone when Rico pulled into the driveway of their home. He shook Ava awake after turning the car off. Although the drive was only a few hours, he was tired.

"Finally," Ava said, stretching. Rico frowned.

"You slept the whole way!"

"Sorry," she said, sending Sunny a message that she was home. It was almost nine. "I gotta go. Sunny says he wants to talk."

"Go ahead and go. Angel's probably sleep by now anyway," Rico said.

"Thanks," Ava said. She was glad she wouldn't have to go in and pack Angel up. She was a fussy child when she was woken up out of her sleep. "I'll drive the rental and drop it off in the morning."

Rico tossed her the keys before going in the house. Ava followed behind him, dropping her things off in her room. She walked past Angel's room to see her television still on. Ava walked in, kissed her forehead, turned the television off, and left.

When she got to Sunny's apartment, he was standing outside, leaned against the rail. Ava frowned, wondering what was on his mind. She knew that Charity and Bri wouldn't have told him the truth so he couldn't have known the real reason she went to Atlanta. He watched her walk up the steps, but didn't say anything. Ava frowned when she realized he was smoking. He knew his job could do random tests so she hated for him to risk it. Sensing that he wasn't in the best of moods, Ava decided not to nag about it.

"Hey," she said, standing close. Sunny looked at her out of the side of his eye for a second before pulling her to him by her waist. She relaxed a little; at least he wasn't mad enough not to show her love. She laid her head against his shoulder and sighed. "I missed you."

"Didn't act like it," he mumbled.

"I said I was sorry about not calling," Ava said. "I just got busy, but that doesn't mean I didn't think about you."

"Don't try to sweet talk me right now," he said. Ava couldn't help but laugh.

"You missed me?"

Sunny turned around and walked into the open door of his apartment. Ava followed behind him, closing and locking the door once she was inside. Sunny turned around and looked at her as she sat on the couch and kicked her shoes off.

"I thought you had to get Gel."

"Daddy said she could stay there tonight," Ava said.

"What's been going on?" Sunny asked. Ava hated the way he was looking at her at the moment. Since she'd gotten out the car, all she wanted to do was kiss him, but it looked as if that wouldn't be happening at the moment.

"What you mean?"

"All this, 'I been busy,' stuff you been pulling, not telling me what's going on in your life with church and stuff. You trying to leave?"

Ava sat back against the couch and frowned. Him asking her that felt like someone was trying to knock the wind out of her.

"Why would you ask me that?" Ava snapped, now upset. Sunny shook his head before running his hands down his face.

"You been tripping..."

"I been busy with work why are you tripping?" Ava said. "I don't do that when you take overtime."

"You know what I'm doing and when I'm doing it," Sunny said. "Don't play with me."

"Sunny, I'm sorry," Ava whined, not wanting to argue. Sunny laughed a little. "What's funny?"

"Everything don't work the way you want it to Ava. Mess around and let me find out something crazy," he said, not even finishing his sentence.

"I'm real mad you sitting here accusing me of cheating on you!" Ava said, jumping up off the couch.

"Well what you doing? Because when I come at you on real stuff, you come with a excuse that could have easily been said before it became a problem!"

Ava bit her lip. She wasn't one to cry, but Sunny's tone with her right now wasn't soothing. She scratched her head, pulling at one of her curls before digging her toes into his carpet. She heard him sigh and move towards her. Ava let out a breath that she didn't know she was holding as Sunny wrapped her up in his arms.

"I told you I was with you on anything, baby," Sunny said, as his lips pressed against her forehead. "You know I need you around me. You can't be dipping into my time without a good enough excuse."

Ava knew he meant that as a joke, but the fact that she'd lied about why she went to Atlanta and the extent of her work with Dre was eating at her. Sure, Sunny said he was with her on anything, but would he be with her on something that would definitely interrupt their time if she had to travel a lot?

"I'm sorry," Ava said. She felt him nod. "Now kiss me."

"You think you got it like that?" he asked, looking down at her with a smirk. Ava stood up straight and nodded. Sunny laughed before gripping her hips and kissing her like she wanted him to.

The next few weeks went by as normal, but unfortunately in the Diveno household, arguing seemed to be the new normal for them.

Elle had become distant from Kaylen. It seemed as if she had just been going through the motions. Elle started to question everything their relationship was built on. When her mom, Janet, put her out for even dealing with Kaylen, he had become her sole provider. Elle wouldn't lie and say he hadn't taken care of her just as he promised, but now she wondered about their dynamic. Kaylen always got his way. Throughout their dating and even the last few years that they had been married, if something didn't go as Kaylen planned, he was upset about it.

When they first moved to Hamilton, Kaylen had a problem with Elle wanting to finish school and get her diploma. He kept saying all he wanted to do was take care of her but Elle wanted to finish school for her own reasons. She eventually won that argument, and even got Kaylen to agree that she'd take some college courses once she graduated. That plan got put on hold when Jayla was born. Elle was so caught up in being a mother and rekindling the relationship she had with her own mother that she forgot about her dreams. Just when she was building up the courage to tell Kaylen that she wanted a job, here comes their baby boy.

Elle was very excited to have a son. She knew that Kaylen was hiding the extent of his excitement, just because he was Kaylen. In the beginning of their relationship, Elle remembered lying up with him and giggling as he talked about the future Junior she would have and how he would dress and things like that. They were young and it was cute. Elle wasn't young anymore and she wanted more out of life.

"I don't know why he doesn't get that!" Elle said to herself, in frustration. Jayla, who was sitting against her side with her head next to Elle's belly, looked up at her mom and frowned. "Sorry baby."

"I can't hear Phineas and Ferb," Jayla said, with a lot of attitude. Elle laughed before telling Jayla that she was sorry. It amazed Elle how well Jayla and Angel talked for their age. Even though Angel was eight months older than Jayla, she kept up pretty well with Angel's progression because they spent so much time together.

Elle sat back as a sharp pressure weighed down on her hips. She groaned as the baby inside of her moved quickly. Elle looked down at her belly and could see her son's head pressing against the skin. Jayla saw it too and quickly put her small hand over it.

"My brother coming soon?" she asked.

"We still have a few months to go, darling," Elle said. Jayla sucked her teeth, rolled her eyes and went back to watching the Disney channel. Elle laughed at her attitude before scooting off the couch. "I'll be right back, Momma."

Elle's feet seemed to drag across the tan carpet sluggishly as she walked towards the kitchen. Drinking tea had been calming her nerves for the last few days, but she hadn't drank any on that particular day because she didn't feel like making any. She wished Kaylen wasn't at work so he could do everything, even though she barely said more than she had to around him at the moment.

While Elle tried to make her tea, the pain shot around to the top of her butt bone. She used the counter in front of the microwave to support her, and tried to breathe normally. The microwave beeped four times, letting her know that her water was done. When she opened the door, she stumbled back a little.

"Oh!" she yelled in pain, abandoning the cup and the open microwave door to get back into the living room as quickly as possible. She flopped down on the couch next to Jayla and reached for her cell phone.

"Baby, go put your shoes on," Elle said, gently pushing Jayla off the couch to get her attention off of the television. Jayla didn't respond, or take her eyes off the television until she got to the wall that separated the hallway from the living room. She then skipped off towards her bedroom. Elle scrolled through her contacts until she got to Sunny's name.

"Yo!" Sunny answered.

"I need to go to the hospital," Elle said as calmly as she could.

"Why?" Sunny asked,.

"Something's not right," was all Elle could think to say.

"I'll be right down," Sunny said, before hanging up. Elle slid on her house slippers and sat back on the couch.

"Hey," Elle said in a soft tone, before pressing both of her palms to each side of her belly. "Why are you acting up kid? Is it because I don't like Daddy right now?"

Jayla came running back into the living room with some sparkling boots on. Elle giggled, not even having the strength to tell her to change.

"Where we going?"

"To check on your brother," Elle said as Sunny came through the open front door, pulling his hoodie over his head.

Once they got to the hospital, Elle was taken to an outpatient section of the emergency room. They checked her vitals before her doctor came in and discussed what was going on with her.

While the nurses ran in and out, Elle thought about her first pregnancy. When she carried Jayla, all she could remember was being happy. It was around the time Ava had come clean about being pregnant when Elle found out she was expecting as well. She and Kaylen were both equally excited. She remembered celebrating every little thing about her pregnancy; when she first started showing, when Jayla first kicked or when they first heard her heartbeat.

Elle felt bad because she hadn't been as happy while carrying her son. Her home was filled with tension, she was lying just to have something to do other than sit on the couch and now she was in the hospital having pains.

Elle wasn't sure what all this meant, but she wasn't happy about it at all.

Elle winced as the nurse put an IV in her wrist. They could never find her veins and she hated it. Once the nurse finally figured out what she was doing, Elle exhaled and turned her head away from the IV.

"Do you have someone waiting for you?" the nurse asked. Elle nodded.

"My brother-in-law and my daughter are in the waiting room," Elle said.

By the time Sunny was allowed back in the room, Jayla was sleep in his arms. Sunny lay her on the bed next to Elle before sitting in the chair.

"I need to call Kaylen," Elle said. "Call Ava too."

"Okay," Sunny said, pulling his phone out. "What am I telling her?"

Kaylen's office phone rang but he picked up on the first ring. Elle ignored Sunny's question once Kaylen said hello.

"You need to get to the hospital," Elle said, rubbing Jayla's head with her other hand and looking up at Sunny. "I went into premature labor."

Nine

Elle pushed her head into the stark, white hospital pillow and tried to wish everyone away. She had been moved into the maternity ward and the chill of the room helped her relax. Everyone who came in complained about it being cold, but Elle's fever had yet to break. Elle couldn't wrap her head around everything that happened. She hadn't been afraid one time during this pregnancy. She figured it would go smoothly like Jayla's did. She was wrong.

Yesterday, November 20, 2010, she had Kaylen Jr., six and half weeks early. She had been in the hospital for two days. Her doctor was trying to stop her contractions with some type of medicine and bed rest. They held off for 26 hours but after that, everything happened so fast. One minute she was sitting watching the only cartoon channel the hospital had with Jayla, and the next the nurses were saying the baby's heartbeat was weakening. They monitored her close for an hour before the doctor decided it was best to deliver.

Elle was tired, frustrated and mad at the world. Her blood pressure was up and she'd had a fever ever since she left delivery. The list of things that were wrong with her and her son ran through her mind like subtitles in a nightmare.

She was thankful that Ava had come and taken Jayla with her. She'd been hysterical ever since Elle was admitted into the hospital. Elle knew that being around Angel would help Jayla calm down. It was good that Kaylen was a manager now instead of working on sites. It didn't take him three hours to get to the hospital like before. Elle would have been happier about that in other circumstances. She was thankful that her son was alive, but she was mad.

Elle was mad that her mom had been grilling her ever since the doctor told them what caused the premature labor. She was mad that her son had apnea which was caused by Bradycardia and RDS. She was mad that she wasn't sure what all that meant. Most of all, Elle was mad that it was all Kaylen's fault.

"Are you going to tell me what the doctor said about my grandson?" Janet asked. Elle huffed.

"When are they bringing him in?"

"You heard what I said to you, Trish!" Janet said. Elle rolled her eyes.

"His heart rate is too low and he can't breathe on his own," Kaylen said, from his spot in the corner.

Elle looked up at the ceiling and frowned. "And it's all his daddy's fault."

"Trishelle, you losing your mind, for real," Kaylen said. "But I'ma help you find it quick."

"Oh what, you going to hit me? I wish you would! Kaylen you'd be in jail so quick your head would spin!"

"Ain't nobody say nothing about hitting you, you need to get your mind right! You don't see how all this dramatic ass mess just affected my son!?"

"Your son, Kaylen!?"

"You two need to quit!" Janet yelled, causing both of them to be quiet. "I can't believe y'all. My grandson is laying up in a bubble, only three pounds, and we want to play the blame game. It doesn't matter!"

"Mommy, calm down," Elle whispered, not used to being yelled at by her.

"No, the both of you need to start acting like grownups with kids!" she said, pointing between the both of them. "I'm going to see if I can find the doctor myself."

The room grew quiet as Janet left Kaylen and Elle alone. Elle roughly wiped the tear that fell down her face. Kaylen sucked his teeth.

"What you crying for, babe?"

"Leave me alone," Elle said.

"I been doing that and now they saying high stress caused you to have our son early, Trishelle. Do you think that's still the solution?" Kaylen said. "It's been months. Why you still mad? I'm not mad that you lied to me."

"Yes! I'm mad that you want me to sit up in your house, barefoot and pregnant, while you make all the money and all the rules."

"You act like I treat you bad," Kaylen said, finally walking towards the bed. "I treat you wrong? Don't I give you want you need?"

"Why is it bothering you so much that I want to work, Kaylen?" Elle asked. He bit his lip and shook his head. Elle's eyes got watery again, but Kaylen walked out of the room before she started crying.

Kaylen pushed his hands through his dreads as he stalked down the hallway of the maternity ward. He stopped near the glass that separated the nursery and looked for his son. His heart broke to see him in the back, away from the healthy babies, in an incubator. He was so skinny, but at eighteen inches, the nurses said he was a normal length. Kaylen felt like punching a wall; his son couldn't breathe on his own and there was nothing that Kaylen could do about it.

Kaylen felt someone next to him. He looked up to see Janet standing there and he tried not to suck his teeth.

"I'm not going to say nothing to you," Janet said. Kaylen rolled his eyes, knowing that was a lie. "You can go in a see him." Kaylen didn't move. "What's really the problem? We all know you can take care of your family."

"I been doing that ever since you put her out," Kaylen snapped. Janet frowned. "And you just said you weren't going to say anything."

"Don't be disrespectful," she said. "We're over that. She only forgave me after you pushed it, so I know you're just talking out of your neck right now."

"Man," Kaylen said, pushing his palm to the glass in front of him. "I'm her husband. That's my family. I'm supposed to take care of my family."

"Ain't nothing wrong with that, Kaylen," Janet assured him, putting her hand on his back. "My baby is bored."

"It don't matter now," Kaylen mumbled, set in his decision.

"Y'all need Jesus," Janet said, shaking her head.

"You didn't work!" Kaylen pointed out. Janet put her hand on her hip and rolled her neck a little.

"And how well did that work out for me?" Janet asked. Kaylen didn't respond. "Everybody knows how broken up I was when Trish's dad passed. I went through it. Took it out on my baby and didn't even try to see where she was coming from with her love for you. I couldn't take care of myself. You're half my age and you took care of my child better than I could."

"Miss Janet, what's the point," Kaylen said, tired of the conversation.

"You know more than anybody that I am the one person that she doesn't want to be like."

Kaylen looked up at his mother-in-law for a second before she gave him a knowing look.

"I'm not hustling no more," he said.

"It doesn't matter," Janet said. "She has to know she can take care of herself."

Kaylen ran his hands up his face before tugging on his dreads a little. A nurse stepped out asking if they wanted to come in to see KJ. Janet nodded but looked at Kaylen.

"Go ahead. I'm going to call and check on Jay."

"What's up?" Sunny said, after he answered the phone. "How's little man?"

"Same," Kaylen said. "What's my baby doing?"

"Her and Gel tearing my living room up," Sunny said. Kaylen smirked, knowing that Sunny was going through it.

"She eat? You need some money?"

"Come on man," Sunny said, slightly insulted. "We good."

"Alright," Kaylen said, not really even sure what he could do at this point. "I'll probably come get her soon. Miss Janet taking her tonight."

"Cool it," Sunny said. "When Bri gets off to get Gel, me and Ava will bring her up there."

"Thanks bro."

"It's nothing."

Kaylen hung up his phone and turned back to the glass. He watched Janet smile as the nurse instructed her on how to reach through the small gloves that let them into KJ's incubator and touch him. Kaylen smiled, seeing that his color was getting a little darker. The doctor said he hadn't shown any signs of improvement but hadn't gotten worse. Kaylen looked at him closely, trying to find any sign that would assure him that his son would be okay. When he couldn't find anything, he stalked over to the nearest bench and sat down, leaned over and put his head in his hands. He sighed and said a prayer.

Ava laughed as Angel sang along with a Kirk Franklin song on the radio.

"Sing baby!" Ava said, before joining in with her.

"Mommy you have a pretty voice," Angel said. Ava blushed.

"Thank you, Momma," Ava said. "You excited to go shopping with Daddy today?"

"Yeah!" Angel yelled, throwing her hands up. Ava looked at her a little before laughing. Ava pulled up behind Charity's car and turned hers off. She had just come from picking Angel up from daycare. Even though she had the day off, Ava still took Angel to daycare so that she could sit at the hospital with Elle. Everything had been crazy since KJ came early. Elle was being released tomorrow, but KJ wasn't as lucky. He had gained a half a pound, but he wasn't gaining or eating enough to go home yet. He was also still having some trouble breathing. Good news was that his heartbeat regulated.

After getting Angel out the car, Ava went through the garage since it was open and into the house through the kitchen. It was empty but she could hear the television on in the living room. Angel took off running as Ava locked the door and called Romero on her way upstairs.

"What time are you coming to get her?"

"Let me call you back in like ten minutes and I'll let you know," Romero said, quickly. Ava huffed and hung up. Ever since LaDanian left, Romero had an attitude with Ava.

He felt like Ava was wrong for monitoring his interactions with Angel while LaDanian was in town, but Ava didn't care. Ava felt that she was justified.

Ava rolled her eyes, already having had enough of Romero for the day. She went into Angel's room and looked for an outfit. Angel always came back from daycare with stains, so Ava never sent her in her good clothes. Even though Romero was acting out, she still wanted Angel to be ready if she needed to be. After she laid her clothes out, she and Angel went into the bathroom.

"Hey, I thought she was going with Romero?" Bri asked, walking past the bathroom with her textbooks in hand.

"You know I don't send her anywhere looking crazy," Ava said, pulling at Angel's shirt.

"I can do it!" Angel whined. Ava put her hands up in the air. Bri laughed and walked away.

"Well, do it then!" Ava said, turning the water in the tub to warm.

About an hour later, Angel began to get antsy. She hadn't said anything, but Ava knew that she was wondering where Romero was. Ava could hear Angel banging toys around in her room. She asked Angel to clean up after her bath. Ava walked past her open door, just in time to see Angel throw a doll into her little, red toy box and flop down on her toddler bed.

Ava tried to keep her temper down as she pulled her cell phone out of her back pocket and called Romero.

"Your daughter is waiting on you," she said, not even giving him time to say hello. Ava heard Romero curse under his breath.

"I didn't know this would take that long," he said. "Pass her the phone."

Ava sucked her teeth as she walked further into Angel's room. She held the phone out and Angel put it up to her ear, her eyes never leaving the television. She talked to Romero for a few minutes before handing the phone back. Ava hung up without saying anything.

She put her hands on her hips, watching Angel for some type of reaction. Angel was a sneaky child. She'd wait until anyone least expected it to act up. She was that way in day care as well. If another kid did something that she didn't like, she'd wait and plot her revenge. She was like Ava in that way, so she couldn't really blame her, but Ava did try to keep it under control.

She remembered Kita used to complain about being paid back for the things she did to her mother through her own journey with motherhood. Wondering just how true that legend was, Ava prayed every night that God had mercy on her.

Suddenly, Angel looked over at Ava with a frown on her face.

"What?" Ava asked.

"Can you take me instead?" Angel asked. Ava sighed before nodding. Even though she hadn't wanted to go to the mall, especially the toy store, which was what Romero had promised Angel, it was only right. When he didn't deliver, Ava went out of her way to make sure Angel got what she wanted. The smile that spread across Angel's face as she jumped off her bed would be worth spending her last bit of money on whatever toy Angel wanted.

"Go see if Ti-Ti B wants to go while I change," Ava said, patting Angel's butt as she scooted out of the room. Ava laughed as she followed behind her.

Hamilton Square Mall wasn't much to brag about. They had the usual department stores like Macy's and JC Penny, but the rest of the stores usually didn't last long. There was a small arcade and only a couple of restaurants in the food court. The only reason Ava still went there instead of a mall in a near county was the toy store.

Angel definitely had more than enough toys, but it seemed like her collection kept growing. Ava looked forward to the day when Angel outgrew toys, but then again, she wasn't looking forward to Angel growing up.

"This mall stinks," Bri said, kicking at the carpet as they walked down the first hall. "Who puts carpet in a mall?"

"I've seen it in other malls," Ava said, laughing. Angel walked ahead of them, determination on her face.

"What you buying her today," Bri asked, shaking her head. "She's so freaking spoiled."

"Don't act like you don't have a hand in her rottenness," Ava said. Bri smiled, but didn't say anything. "Right, anyway. Ro was supposed to bring her, but he bailed."

"Figures."

Ava decided not to say anything. It seemed like Bri was still holding on to what happened. Ava always thought it was funny how she could forgive him but Bri couldn't. She didn't even want to think about what would happen if Bri saw Davion again.

They turned in the toy store and Ava groaned at all the noises coming from the live demonstrations of toys that were turned on. Bri giggled before she ran after Angel and pretended to be as excited as her. Ava followed close behind, shaking her head.

It took Angel about twenty minutes to settle on a toy. They'd argued about a water gun and some other army toy that was made for boys. Bri told Angel that boy toys were ugly and Angel almost had a fit. Ava sat back and watched her twin argue with her daughter and wanted to smack them both. Angel finally agreed on a Disney princess megaphone that came with a CD.

"Really?" Bri asked, as Ava paid for it and smiled.

"If my baby wants to sing, she can."

"Oh please," Bri said. "You aren't fooling me. I hope she can sing better than you!"

Ava laughed hard as she handed Angel the bag and they walked out of the store. Ava was putting her debit card away when she felt Bri nudge her arm. "What, girl?"

"What did Romero say he had to do?"

"I don't know," Ava asked, looking at Bri. "Why?"

Before she could respond, Angel screamed and took off running.

"Daddy!" she said. Ava panicked a little but it was replaced with anger when she saw Romero a few stores ahead of them with a woman. He turned around, confused, but smiled once Angel got to him.

"What's up, beautiful?" he asked, picking her up and kissing her cheek.

"Aw, she's cute," the woman said. Ava and Bri stopped in front of them and frowned.

"What ya'll doing here?" Romero asked. Bri laughed as the frown on Ava's face deepened after looking at Romero's guilty expression.

"Mommy bought me a toy since you couldn't," she said. Ava wanted to smile at how Romero's face broke once Angel spoke up, but it wasn't the time.

"This why you busy?" Ava asked, looking towards the woman. She stepped back and looked at Romero before looking back at Ava.

"I'm Melody," she said. "Romero's girlfriend." Ava and Bri didn't say anything. Melody turned to Romero and Angel. "Hi pretty girl."

Ava was about to snatch Angel back but before she could Angel held her arms out and turned away from them. Ava took Angel from Romero and sat her down on her own feet. Angel slid behind Ava and Bri, hugging Ava's leg. Ava could feel her blood boiling inside. She closed her eyes for a second before she heard Bri tell Angel to come with her to the candy machine near the exit.

"Ava, I…" Romero said. Ava shook her head.

"It was nice meeting you, Melody," Ava gritted out, before turning and walking off, not even acknowledging Romero. She walked faster to catch up with Bri and Angel.

"Did you know he had a girlfriend?" Bri asked, once they got in the car.

"This the stuff I be talking about," Ava mumbled, not wanting Angel to hear. "He thinks he can pull slick stuff like this and expect me to trust him with my kid."

Seeing that Ava was very upset, Bri didn't respond. Ava started the car and pulled out of the parking lot. The whole ride home, Romero kept calling Ava's phone. She didn't even bother to ignore it, but she let it ring without even thinking of picking it up.

Ava had no problem with Romero having a woman, that wasn't even the point. He'd broken a promise to Angel to spend time with his girlfriend. Ava wondered if he had planned it. Why even promise Angel a trip to the toy store? Why even tell Ava that he would have Angel that day? Ava then wondered if it was something sporadic, at that moment

Melody just decided she wanted to go to the mall and wanted Romero to take her, and that then and there Romero abandoned any thoughts of spending time with his daughter to please his girlfriend. Ava's anger grew by the second.

"Ava calm down," Bri whispered, lightly thumping her twin's thigh. "He's not worth it. Angel's fine, she got her toy."

Ava glanced in the rearview mirror and smiled. Angel had taken the megaphone out of its wrapper and was singing along to whatever was on the radio. Ava sighed.

"You're right," she said. Bri beamed like she did any other time she was right. Ava laughed.

"Shut up, you don't say that often."

"Not my fault you have no common sense," Ava joked.

"Alright, that's cool," Bri said, nodding her head. "I'll take your little jokey jokes right now, but remember that later. Gel's going to help me beat you up!"

"Hecks no!" Angel said. Bri and Ava both laughed.

"Don't say that anymore, Angel Na'mya Daniels!" Ava said sternly, trying not to laugh. Angel slouched in her seat from mild embarrassment. Bri turned around in her seat and puckered her lips at Angel, blowing a kiss. Angel smiled at her aunt and all was right in their world.

"He's so ignorant," Bri said, Ava laughed as she crossed her legs under her body and leaned back against the couch. Angel was curled up in Charity's lap in the recliner while Ava and Bri were on the long couch. They had gotten home and once Charity saw how upset Ava was, she demanded to know what happened. Rico was on the love seat, but he was so into Sports Center, he wasn't really listening to what his girls were saying.

"So you didn't even know he had a girlfriend?" Charity asked.

"He said he was going to bring her to the party, so I planned on meeting her there, but then all that stuff happened and she didn't show up," Ava said, shaking her head. "I wonder if she's been around my kid."

"He's not that silly to not introduce you but have her around," Bri said. Ava sucked her teeth.

"How come he ain't?" she asked. "He's silly enough to cancel plans with Gel for something stupid." Ava looked to see Angel sleep and was glad that she wasn't listening to the conversation. Angel was smart but Ava knew that she hadn't known the extent of the situation. Angel had been sad that Romero cancelled their plans, but once Ava brought her a toy, she was good to go.

Bri laughed and everyone looked at her.

"Remember the first time she spent the night with him?" Bri asked, still laughing as Ava smiled. "You were so paranoid. You kept calling every five minutes until Momma threatened to punch you if you called again."

"Man, I was flipping out!" Ava said, finally laughing. Charity looked on with a smile. It was rare that the twins were vocal about fond memories of their mother. Ava shook her head. "I just need to know who is around her," she said. "I cannot for the life of me understand why he doesn't see that."

"He's a guy," Charity said. Rico side eyed her. "They don't understand a lot."

Ava watched as Charity rolled her eyes at Rico, who had already turned back to the television. She didn't know what was up with Charity, but she'd been acting weird the last few days. Ava wondered if Charity was having the same suspicions that she was about him being back in the game.

Someone knocked on the door, causing everyone to turn and look at it. Ava stretched out her legs and got up, knowing that it was probably Romero. She laughed a little as her assumption was right.

"What?" Ava said. Romero sighed.

"Can you just hear me out?"

"Why? You keep lying about what's going on with you, yet you expect me to let you get Angel whenever. No, let me correct that. You want my child when it's convenient for you!" Ava said, her temper showing its ugly head.

"I didn't think it would take that long, she had to pick something up for her mom," Romero said. Ava sucked her teeth.

"The fact that you think I care why is irrelevant, but funny," Ava said, crossing her arms under her chest. Romero shifted on the front of the porch.

"Can I come in and talk about it?" he asked, looking to see if anyone happened to be outside. He hated arguing with Ava, because she usually got loud.

"Nah, you good."

Romero sighed in irritation before looking square in Ava's eyes.

"I'm sorry that I didn't introduce you to Melody before, but she hadn't met Angel."

"I don't believe you."

"I don't really care at this point!" Romero said.

"You should!" Ava snapped. "First LaDanian and now this? You're pushing it."

"I don't trip about Sunny," Romero said. Ava looked at him for a second before laughing.

"That's a lie but it doesn't matter, Sunny was around before you were even allowed to see Angel so go there if you want."

"That's not my fault."

"We aren't getting anywhere," Ava said, turning to go back in the house. Romero stepped up and grabbed her arm. She quickly glared at him and he let her go.

"Just hold on," Romero said. "Like I said, my bad about not introducing you to Melody before, but I didn't want her around Angel just yet. We only been together for a little minute."

Ava sighed, realizing that Angel and Melody weren't supposed to meet yet, according to what he was saying. She could respect that.

"Well, you definitely have to apologize to your daughter," Ava said, looking down at the porch as she leaned against the door. Romero smiled and nodded. "But she's sleep right now."

"I'll come get her tomorrow?" he asked. Ava nodded before going back into the house.

"Was that him?" Bri asked. Ava nodded. "What he say?"

"That he was sorry for bailing but they weren't supposed to meet yet because he hasn't been with her long," Ava said, flopping back down on the couch.

"That's understandable," Charity said. Bri rolled her eyes.

"He's still a clown," she said, leaning over and putting her head in Ava's lap. "And a lame."

"Y'all talk too much," Rico mumbled.

"Well turn on something other than sports and we'll be quiet," Charity said. He sucked his teeth, but began to go through the TV guide.

Rico rode around the diner in Jasper, frustrated that Tyler hadn't arrived yet. They were supposed to meet twenty minutes ago, but he wasn't answering his phone. Rico had just gotten off a long shift at work and all he wanted to do was lay up under his wife and go to sleep. Tyler called him on his lunch break, asking him to pick up a package once Rico got off work.

He pulled into a recently vacant parking spot that was in clear view of the entrance to the lot. Rico rolled his neck backwards, reaching up with his right hand to massage it, hoping to relieve some of the tension. The pain in his shoulders made him want to wake Charity up when he got home. It was nearing midnight, so he knew that plan would get him anything but a massage.

"Finally!" Rico said, seeing Tyler's car pull in. He honked his horn to get Tyler's attention, before watching him park policemen style next to his car.

"You do know I just got off a shift right?" Rico asked.

"Man, calm down, working man," Tyler said. "I had some things to handle," he said, before smiling. Rico could tell that he was high. He sucked his teeth.

"Man, I told you about smoking on the job," Rico said. Tyler laughed.

"Don't worry, the boss won't get me," Tyler joked. Rico shook his head, trying not to laugh at how goofy his cousin was acting at the moment.

"What you got for me?" Rico asked, rubbing the stubble on his chin. He was tired and didn't have time to joke around with Tyler. There was only about a five year age difference, but Tyler was very immature. Rico knew he got it from his father, who was his mother's brother. They weren't very close, but that didn't stop Tyler's mom from coming around Ran and Rico when they were younger.

"How's Auntie Ran?" Tyler asked. Rico frowned. "Tyler!"

"Alright, alright," Tyler said, throwing his one of his hands. "I don't have the package yet, that's why I'm late. They claim it wasn't ready so we're giving them two days."

"What, man?" Rico asked, shaking his head. "That don't even sound right."

"I know, that's why we're checking on it."

"You could have called and told me that," Rico said. "Saved me some gas."

"You ain't hurting," Tyler said, smirking. "I'll hit you up in a day or so."

"Whatever man," Rico said, starting his car. The fact that Tyler had just wasted his time; time that could have been used to get home and sleep, made Rico very upset. Once he finally got home it was nearing one in the morning. The house was still and Rico was grateful for it. He traveled upstairs, frowning as the smell of his work day caught up to his nose. He double checked the front door lock, turned the alarm on, and headed upstairs to him and Charity's room. The television was on, but the receiver had turned off leaving a cable network logo to bounce around the screen. Charity was lying on her side, with her back to the door and one foot peeking out from under the cover.

Rico slid his shirt over his head as he softly kicked his shoes off. They landed with a light thud before he scooted them near the wall. He grabbed his red dry towel and headed back out of the room and into the bathroom.

Rico sighed, looking at the mess most likely left by his granddaughter. He constantly got on Ava about cleaning the bathroom up. He would make them start using the one downstairs if they couldn't keep this one clean.

The hot, steaming water from the shower almost felt as good as a massage would have. Rico was glad that he was off the next day, hoping that he wouldn't even make it out of bed until well into the afternoon. The bathroom steamed up quickly and the euphoric feeling that settled over him let Rico know that as soon as he hit his bed, it was over for him.

A few droplets from the faucet dripped as he stepped onto the mat and wrapped his towel around his waist. He wrinkled his nose as he pulled some tissue from the holder on the counter. He took his right hand and wiped it across the mirror, clearing the steam, only for it to come right back. Rico threw the tissue near the waste basket, but missed it. He groaned before bending down to pick it up.

"The hell?" he asked, seeing something sticking out of the waste basket. He blinked his eyes, running his hand over them before widening them to see if he was focusing on what he thought he was looking at. It was a small, white stick with a pink top covering a small, brush-like top. Rico shook his head, not thinking much of it. That was until the small, bright blue plus sign became visible.

His first reaction was to wake everyone in the house up and demand to know who'd taken the pregnancy test. He prayed that it wasn't Ava; two kids at twenty-one would not be a good thing for her. Yes, she was doing pretty well with Angel and handling her business, but the reality was that she was still in his house. Even if she wasn't there, she'd probably be living with her boyfriend and Rico wasn't feeling that scenario either. The thought made him want to punch Sunny in his face, but he knew that wouldn't go over well.

    Rico silently cursed. He didn't want to deal with it right now. The exhaustion was outweighing his anger at the moment. He cursed again before wrapping the test up in tissue, sliding it in the drawer of the counter, and going to bed.

    Ava woke up the next day, wanting to go visit Elle before her afternoon shift. Bri's class was cancelled for the day, so she offered to watch Angel. Ava had to admit that she was grateful that she never had to worry about day care or things like that. Even though Angel went on occasion, it wasn't something she had to depend on. Her family always had her back when it came to Angel. It made her remember how when she was first born, Kita would make sure her schedule worked around Ava's so that Angel wouldn't be in a day care. Kita was dead set on spending as much time with Angel as possible. Ava knew that was because Kita knew her time was limited.

    On her way to Elle's, she'd been listening to an album that Charity gave her. It was filled with gospel songs from various artists. The current song was by Tye Tribbett and it was called *Chasing After You*. Ava thought it was one of the most beautiful melodies she'd heard. She wasn't used to listening to gospel music, but most of the songs that the choir sang were old hymns that usually threatened to put her to sleep. This song was different.

    She didn't usually like very slow songs, but this one seemed to draw her in. It spoke of never being satisfied with your relationship with God, in a way that you always wanted more of Him. How her mind usually worked when she thought up lyrics for a song, she would get inspired by hearing something or seeing something. She'd never been inspired to write by listening to gospel music, but this song was capturing her. It was a weird feeling, but Ava hoped the lyrics in her head would stay there until she got somewhere to write. Right now, she had to focus on her best friend.

She knew that Elle would be freaking out about KJ still being at the hospital now that she was home. She was right.

"Where's Jay?" Ava asked, seeing Elle sluggishly move over to the couch after letting her in.

"With my mom," Elle said. "Where's Gel?"

"With Bri."

"So what's going on?" Elle asked, sighing and running her hand over her forehead. Ava frowned.

"You okay?"

"I have a fever," she said. "I'm just all messed up, best friend," Elle said. Ava nodded. "I want him home like now, but it seems like since I ain't together yet, it's good that he's there."

"He getting better?"

"He's breathing on his own but he's not really gaining weight like he should," Elle said, her voice cracking a little. "Makes me feel so helpless and useless, you know?"

Ava nodded, she was blessed that Angel was born healthy, especially with all the stress that was going on in her life at the time. She couldn't imagine how she'd feel in Elle's shoes.

"You eat anything?"

"Kaylen brought me some whack soup, but I ended up throwing it up."

"Are you two talking yet?" Ava asked. Elle looked at her for a moment before sighing.

"I'm really trying to get over the fact that he doesn't want me to work, but no matter how hard I try, I still feel like me going into premature labor was his fault," Elle said. Ava could tell that she was getting emotionally. "All I wanted to do was work a few hours a day! It wasn't even that big of a deal."

"You still handled it the wrong way," Ava said.

"I know that," Elle admitted. "But it doesn't make him any less wrong and you know that!" Ava threw her hands up in surrender, sensing that the topic was still a sore one.

"Well, I have three hours before I have to clock in so we might as well eat some ice cream and watch our favorite movie," Ava said. That got a small smile from Elle. Satisfied at her small victory, Ava got up to fix them two bowls of mint chocolate chip ice cream. After bringing them into the living room and handing one to Elle, Ava turned to see the beginning credits of *Clueless*. She looked back at Elle, curiously. Elle smiled.

"I watched it last night," she admitted. They both laughed as Ava sat down on the couch and got comfortable. About halfway through the movie, Ava could tell that Elle was in better spirits and it warmed her heart. Elle had been Ava's rock through the whole rape situation. Even when Elle didn't approve of Ava trying to lie about it, she was still there. Ava couldn't have asked for a better friend in Elle. Ever since they met, Elle had Ava's back and loved her enough to tell her the truth. She even credited her for hooking her and Sunny up, since it was all a part of her plan in the beginning. Even back before Ava and Bri became close again, Elle was like the missing sister Ava could confide in.

"Hey, thanks for cheering me up," Elle said, elbowing Ava. Ava playfully pouted and wiped fake tears from her eyes. Elle laughed. "You're goofy."

"You know I got you."

Someone knocked on the door and Ava got up to answer it. Her stomach twisted a little, in a good way, to see Sunny at the door.

"You saw my car?" she asked. Sunny kissed her forehead quickly but shook his head.

"Kaylen told me to come check on Elle."

"You only came because he asked you too?" Elle asked. Sunny sucked his teeth as he walked into the living room. Ava closed and locked the door.

"Stop playing," he said, walking over and sitting down next to her. "You good?"

"I want to go see KJ," she said.

"Ain't you sick?"

"It's just a little fever," Elle said. Sunny shook his head. "For real, I won't even go in the nursery but before we pick Jay up we can just ride past there so I can see him. Please Sunny!?"

Ava watched in amusement as Sunny tried not to look at Elle, who was giving him her big, puppy dog eyes. Watching them was like watching siblings bicker. Sunny groaned before telling her okay.

"You better not try to go in the nursery," he demanded. Elle smiled.

"I'll just have his Uncle Sunny kiss him for me," Elle said, leaning in to kiss Sunny's cheek. She and Ava both laughed as he blocked her with his hand.

"I cannot afford to be missing work."

Ava frowned at his tone when he said it. Something was off.

"You okay, babe?" she asked. Sunny looked over at her for a second before nodding. Ava walked over and sat on his leg and he wrapped one arm around her.

"Ugh, here y'all go," Elle said. Ava told her to shut up. Elle pushed herself off the couch.

"Y'all better be done with all this lovey stuff when I get out the shower," she said.

"Don't be mad because you and yours ain't in love right now," Ava said. She giggled when Elle threw up her middle finger but kept walking towards the bathroom.

Ava looked at Sunny for a few minutes before narrowing in on his eyes. They were shifting from the television to her, as if he were uncomfortable.

"What's up with you?" She asked.

"What you mean?"

"You acting weird."

"Man, you think everybody act weird, you ever think it's you?"

"Huh?" Ava asked. It wasn't the fact that she hadn't heard him, but his tone and what was said made her confused. She wondered if he was still upset about them not spending that much time together lately. Ava understood where he was coming from, but he was all talk. In the last couple of weeks since their argument after she came back from Atlanta, Ava made more of an effort to be there for him. Problem was, every time she tried, he was either working overtime or tired.

At first, Ava thought he was lying about getting more hours at his job. She even went as far as to ask Elle to ask Kaylen if it were true, without bringing up that Ava was the one who wanted to know. Sunny was telling the truth.

"Let me ask you something," Ava said. "Why is it okay for you to work all the time and not me?"

Sunny sucked his teeth and looked at her sideways. "What?"

"I'm supposed to be okay with you having all this overtime all the sudden?" She asked.

"Yeah."

"Why?" Ava frowned when Sunny hesitated. "Why!"

"Because I have things to take care of."

"And I don't?!" Ava asked, sliding off of his lap, barely wanting to look at him. "I guess you and Kaylen really are brothers."

"Ay, don't do that. This is something totally different."

"Yeah, whatever," Ava said, turning back to the movie that was almost over. She was done with this conversation. Apparently, Sunny was too.

Elle came from her room, looking refreshed but still under the weather. She had on a pair of red sweats with Hamilton High in white block letters down the right leg, and a long sleeve white thermal. Her hair was up in a bun and she had on red and white Nikes.

"I'm ready to go see my son," she said. Ava looked at her phone.

"I'm headed to work," she said. "Send me a picture, I don't have one yet."

"Okay."

Ava headed towards the door, not even acknowledging Sunny anymore. She heard Elle ask him what was going on just as she was closing the front door behind her.

When Ava got to work, she was still trying to push Sunny's attitude to the back of her mind. Days when her mind was elsewhere was when she got the worst customers. It seemed like every time the door swung open, Ava had problems. She didn't do any new lines that day and by the sixth customer that had come in with a repair issue, Ava was ready to go. The phone she was working on now obviously had water damage. She couldn't wait until her head manager hired someone else to work the floor, until then it was her duty as assistant manager to fill in.

"Well sir, you aren't eligible for upgrade until next March," she said. We have some used phones if you don't want to pay full price for a new one."

"Great, how much?"

"Our used phones are 50% off retail price."

"Well, that one was a penny," the customer said, laughing. "What's half of a penny?"

Ava signed, hating to have this price conversation for the thousandth time. Nobody ever paid attention to contract terms.

"You got this one for a penny because you renewed your contract, but the retail price is 200. So if you want this exact phone used it will be a hundred dollars." Ava tried her hardest not to laugh as the man's face contorted from humor to confusion and frustration.

"I'm not paying for a phone I got for free!" he yelled.

"Well, what do you suggest then?" Ava asked, frustrated.

"I want a free phone," he said, looking at her as if the answer was obvious.

"You not getting one," Ava said, totally out of work mode. "Any other ideas?" Ava could hear one of her co-workers snicker behind her.

"Excuse you?" he asked. "The customer is always right!"

"Not in this case."

Before either of them could reply, Ava's manager looked out of his office. He told one of the other employees to take over for Ava.

"You got a call," he said, pointing at Ava. She frowned, but happily walked away from the customer.

"Who is calling me at work?"

Ava walked into the office and waited until her manager left out to pick up the phone.

"Hello?"

"Ava," Bri cried into the phone.

"What's wrong?"

"Charity and I are on the way to the hospital."

"Where's Angel?" Ava asked, placing the palm of her right hand on her manager's desk, feeling her heart drop at the thought of something being wrong with her daughter.

"She's with Ro."

"Bri, you know you're supposed to call me first before…"

"Ava, shut up!" Bri yelled. "Daddy got shot!"

Ten

July 15, 2007

Ava frowned once she saw Angel in her playpen crying. She was about to get her when the phone rang.

"You get the phone and I'll get Angel," Sunny said walking over to the playpen. Ava nodded as she dropped her bag at the door and reached for the phone.

"Hello?"

"May I speak with Kita Vine? This is her boss, she was due at the office over two hours ago."

"Well, I just got in so let me see where she is and I will have her call you right back." Ava said before hanging up. "That's weird."

"What?" Sunny asked as he got Angel to calm down.

"Ma missed work today," Ava said.

"Maybe she's still asleep."

"Let me go wake her up," Ava said as she jogged upstairs to Kita's room. She yelled for her to wake up as she swung her bedroom door open.

"Ma, get up, your boss just called," Ava said, flopping down on Kita's bed. Kita didn't respond. Ava smacked her lips.

She pushed on Kita's shoulder, but Kita moved right back into place without hesitation. Ava slowly looked over Kita's back to see that her chest wasn't moving. Kita wasn't breathing.

Ava frowned as she moved Kita's hair from her face, trying to see if she really wasn't breathing.

"Ma!" Ava yelled as she began to panic. She began to violently shake Kita as she yelled for Sunny to come help her.

"Kita, please don't do this!" Ava said as she laid Kita on her back. Ava tried to remember how to check a pulse when Sunny came walking into the room.

"What's wrong?" Sunny asked with Angel in hand.

"She's not breathing! Please call somebody," Ava screamed as tears ran down her face. She shook her again, this time by both arms. Sunny ran out of the room just as Ava screamed.

The next hour wasn't clear. Ava wasn't sure how she'd been able to even explain to her manager why she needed to leave work early. It was almost as if she was floating outside of reality as she drove to the hospital.

All she kept thinking about was the day she found Kita. Angel crying in her playpen. Kita lying lifeless in her bed. Ava screaming.

She gripped the steering wheel tight, praying that she didn't have to do this again. She squinted as her vision became blurry and without her consent, tears spilled down her cheeks. She parked haphazardly near the entrance and threw the car in park. Once she got through ER, Bri was the first person she saw. Bri's face was just as bad.

"Oh my God, Ava! We just got a call from someone saying they saw him get shot!" Bri cried as she latched on to her twin's shoulders. "We didn't know what to do. Charity freaked out, she's been throwing up and crying none stop. Granny is complaining about everything and they won't tell us what's going on!"

Ava couldn't form words. Bri pulled her down the hall and the further they walked, the more Ava felt like she was going to faint. The hospital seemed to have an eerie calmness, despite her family's trauma. There were only a few nurses in blue scrubs walking in and out of a few different rooms. The waiting area was only occupied by a few people waiting and although they looked ill, nothing was as serious as this.

When they turned the corner, Ava saw Charity hunched over on a small, grey couch. Her shoulders were moving slightly, so Ava knew she was crying. Granny Ran was seated a few chairs down on her cell phone.

"Charity, sit up," Bri said, gently pushing her shoulder. Charity looked around and slowly sat up. Her eyes were red and puffy. She pulled Ava down next to her and Bri sat on the opposite side.

"I feel like I'm going to throw up again," Charity said, covering her mouth. She ran off towards the bathroom, causing everyone's eyes to follow.

"Where is Tyler?" Ava heard Granny Ran say. Ava quickly looked in her direction. "Are they arresting him for that? Well, find out what's going on with your son so I can do the same!" she yelled before hanging up.

"Was that Uncle Ryan?" Bri asked, referring to Granny Ran's brother. She nodded. "Tyler was with Daddy?"

Bri was confused, but when Granny Ran nodded, Ava became furious. She knew what Tyler did for a living. That was who Rico had been leaving in the middle of the night to meet up with. He was dealing again.

"I should have said something," she mumbled. Granny Ran and Bri both looked at her.

"What child?" Granny Ran asked. Ava didn't respond but looked at her. Granny Ran was well into her 60's but didn't look much older than Rico. Ava often joked about them aging well, but their relationship still wasn't 100 percent. Granny Ran hadn't gotten over Kita's behavior after Rico went to jail, but Ava didn't feel like it was her place.

"He'd been leaving really late and I'd see him but I wouldn't say anything," Ava said. "He had all this extra money to help Bri with school…"

"What are you saying?" Bri asked. Granny Ran just shook her head. Ava looked at Bri for a second before she frowned. "No," she said, shaking her head. "He promised."

"He promised what?"

Everyone looked up to see Charity standing with her hands fixing her ponytail. She'd washed her face and although it was flushed, it wasn't as puffy.

"How did you not know what your husband was doing at night?" Granny Ran said. Charity frowned.

"Excuse me?"

"Granny!" Bri said. Granny Ran shook her head.

"As a wife you are supposed to make sure your husband comes home at night."

"He does!" Charity said. "What are you even talking about? How dare you question my marriage like that."

"How dare I?" Granny Ran said. "My son was shot twice, I can say what I want."

"He's my husband!"

"Well, how come you didn't know he was dealing again?" Granny Ran said, immediately looking around to see if anyone had heard her. Ava could have sworn Charity's face turned green.

"No, he's not," she said, unsure.

"He got shot running with Tyler," Bri said. Charity violently shook her head.

"No," Charity said, "No, he promised me!"

"He promised all of us!" Ava shouted, her anger boiling over. Tears fell from her eyes again as she felt like her lungs were closing. "I can't do it again. I can't. I can't see another parent lifeless!"

Bri roughly pulled Ava to her side and cried with her. Charity kept repeating that he promised and eventually she and Granny Ran began arguing again.

"Shut up!" Bri yelled. "This isn't our fault! It's his fault. He promised us!"

"Child, don't talk like that," Granny Ran said, finally sitting down. "He'll be fine."

Silence fell over the waiting room.

"He has to be," Charity said. "I'm pregnant."

It had been an hour since Charity revealed that she was pregnant, and no one had said anything. Ava finally calmed down and sent a text to Sunny, letting him know the situation. He told her that he would be there as soon as he got off of work. A nurse had come to speak to them, letting them know that Rico was still in surgery. He was stabilized, however any little thing could send him into cardiac arrest. He had been shot in the chest and his side. One bullet hit his side and broke a rib, but then went straight through. His chest wasn't so lucky.

  Bri was sleep with her head on Ava's lap. Ava played in her twin's curls, seeing that she would need to dye her dark roots soon if she wanted to keep her hair honey brown. Granny Ran had made some type of bed out of a couch and was trying her best to sleep. Ava and Charity were wide awake.

  Charity was sitting across from Ava with both hands wrapped around her stomach. She would blink ever so often, but her face was emotionless. There was such a mix of emotions in that waiting room. They were hurt, scared, upset and confused. Why would Rico risk his life again?

  This was definitely worse than jail to Ava. At least when he was locked up, Ava knew he was there and healthy.

  "Please Lord," she thought. *"I need my daddy."*

  "Will you get in trouble for leaving work," Charity mumbled. It took Ava a moment to realize she was talking to her. Ava shook her head.

  "When did you find out?"

  "I took a test about a week ago," Charity said. "Went to the doctor yesterday."

  "Does Daddy know?" Ava asked. Charity shook her head. "Y'all too old to be having kids," Ava joked. Charity cracked a smile.

  "That's what we have you and Bri for," Charity said. "And I am not old."

WHEN ALL ELSE FAILS

She wasn't but Ava felt they needed a little humor at the moment. Although Rico was forty-five, Charity was thirty-six. It wasn't uncommon for women her age to get pregnant. It happened all the time.

Ava smiled, knowing that Rico would flip if he finally got the boy he used to beg Kita for. She could remember their constant bickering about another baby, Kita always giving Rico a hard time about him not being able to make anything but girls. It would always end up in some type of sexual joke that would gross Ava and Bri out and make them laugh.

"Did you know he was back in the streets?" Charity asked.

"I assumed it," Ava responded, truthfully. Charity bit her lip and shook her head.

"I feel stupid," Charity said. "Not knowing what my husband was up to. I guess I kind of knew something was going on, but I just kept praying and praying…and praying," Charity stopped because her voice was cracking. She took a moment, closing her eyes and exhaling. "I can't take this."

Ava wanted to assure her that Rico had learned his lesson. That if and when he pulled through this, he would be totally done. The truth was, Ava wasn't so sure. She'd been here when Rico first got out of jail, right before Angel was born. He'd promised her and Bri that he wasn't going to jeopardize his family again. One thing Ava hated was for someone to go back on their word. She wanted to be mad at the world. She wanted to be mad at Tyler for offering Rico the opportunity, she wanted to be mad at Rico for taking it, and she wanted to be mad at whoever pulled the trigger that sent him to the emergency room.

She wanted more than anything for it all to just go away.

After another three hours past, Ava had to go deal with Romero. He was working midnights, so Angel had to come home. Since Romero's house was closer to the hospital, Ava called him to let him know that she would pick her up.

She wasn't in the mood. Nurses had no idea why the surgery was taking as long as it did, or even if they were still operating. Ava hated hospitals. Besides the fact that Rico was fighting for his life, they always reminded Ava of her suicide attempt.

She sighed as she drummed the steering wheel. Why was everything all of the sudden reminding her of the darkest years of her life thus far?

Romero's front door opened and Angel's little body was the first thing she saw. Ava couldn't help but jump out of the car to hug her. Still, that little girl was the only pure light in her life.

"I missed you," Ava said, hugging her tight. Angel struggled against her.

"I just saw you this morning," she said, in a matter-of-fact tone. Ava laughed to keep from crying. She stood up and grabbed Angel's hand, looking at Romero as he handed her Angel's backpack.

"How's your dad?" he asked.

"Fine," Ava lied. Romero nodded before looking around.

"We should probably talk?" he asked. Ava shook her head.

"I have no energy to deal with you right now," she said. Romero sucked his teeth.

"Why everything always gotta be on your time?" he asked. Ava frowned before throwing Angel's bag over her shoulder. She turned and walked to the car, putting Angel in her seat in the back and closing the door.

"If you wouldn't keep lying we wouldn't have to keep doing things on my time," Ava shouted back, just as Romero reached his porch. He turned to look at her as she got in the car and drove off.

Ava groaned. She didn't want to bother Elle to watch Angel and everyone one else was at the hospital. She had no choice but to take Angel with her.

"Why we here!" Angel yelled. "I don't want no shots."

"Papi is a little sick," she said. Angel's face broke down.

"He gotta get shots?"

Ava's heart dropped and her mouth felt dry. She struggled to swallow as she rounded the corner.

"Something like that baby," she managed. "We won't be here long."

Angel took her mother's word for what it was worth, and began to skip down the hallway next to her. The waiting room came into view and Angel took off towards Bri.

"Hey Ti-ti's baby!" she said, once Angel was in her lap. "What you doing here?" Bri asked, while looking up at Ava.

"Mommy said Papa has to get shots," Angel said. Everyone looked from her to Ava. "He might need me to hold his hand."

"Aw baby," Charity said, before clearing her throat. "He already got his shots. He's just resting now."

Ava got up and sat next to Charity and whispered so that Angel couldn't hear.

"He's out of surgery?" she asked. Charity nodded.

"He's stable but they still have him in ICU until he wakes up," she whispered. "So you can go home. She doesn't need to be here."

Ava nodded, feeling a little relieved that at least Rico was out of surgery.

"When did Granny leave?" Ava asked.

"About ten minutes ago," Charity said, sighing in frustration. "That woman is going to be the death of me!"

Ava wanted to laugh, because in that moment Charity sounded like Kita.

"Learn to live with it," Ava said. "You know how she is and we can't do nothing about it."

"Don't I know it," she said, shaking her head. Ava noticed that Charity kept one hand on her belly.

"You excited?" she asked. Charity looked at her for a moment before nodding and smiling.

"I really am," she said. "You know I love y'all but watching Angel just always made me want a baby."

"It's okay to be excited," Ava said. "I was excited even considering everything that was going on at the time."

"Really?" Charity asked. Ava nodded, while looking over at Angel.

"I just knew she'd be everything," Ava said. Charity smiled before patting Ava's knee.

"Well, I hope Papi is as excited as we are."

Ava sighed, still not happy with Rico's decisions. She wanted to just be happy that he had survived, but if something didn't change in his mind soon, she wasn't sure how long he would in the long run.

"Bad news baby," Ava said. Angel turned around and frowned.

"What?"

"Papi's shots made him sleepy."

"What?" Angel said, exaggerated. Bri, Charity and Ava laughed a little. "I don't like those shots."

"I'm sure he'll be up soon," Bri said. "But you have to go to sleep, too."

"No," Angel said. Ava rolled her eyes, knowing tonight would be a hassle getting that little girl in bed.

"Come on Gel," Ava said, standing up and pulling Angel off of Bri's lap. Angel planted both her feet onto the ground and bent her knees. Bri shook her head as Angel yelled for her to help her.

"Stop acting up, girl," Bri said. Ava tapped Angel's bottom to straighten her up. Angel stood straight up and began to cry. A few of the nurses walking by began to ask her what was wrong. Ava just brushed them off while she bent down to wrap Angel up in her arms.

"You are way too spoiled," Ava said, sternly. "Quit all that crying."

"Bye Ti-ti!" Angel said, waving sadly at Bri was they walked down the hall. Bri couldn't help but laughed.

"I'll be home soon, niece!"

"Shut up, Bri," Ava said. Bri laughed harder.

"Did Papi get shots in his arm?" Angel asked as she sat on the bubble mat in the middle of the tub. Her curls were covered in tear-free shampoo and her skin was shiny from the soapy water.

Ava sat on the edge of the tub. She sighed as she dipped the hand towel into the warm water and ran it over Angel's back.

"No, they aren't in his arm baby," was all Ava said. She was trying to not lie to Angel, but that didn't change the fact that Angel didn't need to know all the details.

"His arm gonna hurt," Angel said, ignoring Ava's response. She tilted her head back to the side and dunked her pink princess face towel in the water.

Ava couldn't believe how advanced Angel was. Her little four-year-old mind turned like someone twice her age or more. Sometimes Angel was too smart for her own good. She had a smart mouth.

"Can I call Daddy?"

"After your bath."

"Wanna tell him good night."

"I said after your bath."

"I heard you, ugh," Angel said, rolling her eyes. Ava sucked her teeth.

"Catch a whopping little girl," Ava said. Angel slumped her shoulders and shrunk down into the tub. Ava laughed as she hid most of her body under the bubbles and shifted her eyes from left to right.

"I don't want to catch it," she said, lifting her lips above water level.

"Well, don't make me throw it."

Angel nodded in obedience and Ava smiled.

"I need to call Sunny, too."

"And your daddy? Girl, you need a cell phone," Ava joked. Angel giggled. "Well, you know what you have to do to get out of this tub."

"Yes ma'am."

"Colors, numbers, or letters?"

"Colors."

Ava began to point to random objects throughout the bathroom with Angel proudly stating the color of each. She only slipped up twice and Ava knew she was just acting silly.

After they finished getting ready for bed, Ava grabbed her phone and hopped in Angel's bed next to her. Bri had sent a text message saying that Rico had finally regained consciousness and he was being moved into recover. Ava sighed in relief.

"You want to call Sunny or Daddy first?" Ava asked, going to her recent calls and looking at both names.

"Daddy talks longer, so Sunny," she said. Ava giggled before hitting the heart next to Sunny's name on her touch screen. It rang a few times before he picked up.

"What's up, love?" he answered. Ava smiled.

"Gel wants to talk to you before she goes to sleep," Ava said.

"When she goes to sleep, can I come put you to sleep," he asked. Ava laughed from Sunny's outburst.

"You know you too loud," she joked. "Plus, Charity and Bri will be home soon."

"When they get there, come over here," Sunny pressed.

"We'll see," she said. "Here's Gelly."

"Sunny where you been?" she asked in her exaggerated tone. Ava laughed before getting out of the bed and putting the stray toys on Angel's floor away.

"I been working baby girl," he said. "I miss you though."

"You better," she said.

"Don't get tough with me," Sunny said. "Keep it up and I won't give you what I bought you the other day."

"No! I'm sorry," Angel said. "I love you!"

Ava giggled at their interaction. Sunny and Angel's relationship was too funny.

"I'll see you in the morning, Gel. Go to sleep."

"I gotta call Daddy first," she said.

"Well, go to sleep right after. I miss Mommy," he said. Angel giggled.

"Okay, love you. Bye!"

Before Ava could even get back to the bed, Angel had hung up and dialed Romero's number. Ava continued to clean up Angel's room while she held a conversation with Romero. Ava had to admit that their conversation was almost cuter than Angel's and Sunny's. Ava had to take a moment and thank God for Sunny and Romero, even if she wasn't completely happy with their situation. The fact that Angel had so many father figures in her life, including Kaylen and Rico, Angel would never have to go through what Ava and Bri went through when Rico was in jail.

"Mommy, Daddy wants to talk to you," Angel slurred, letting Ava know she was a few minutes away from sleep. Ava took the phone from her and kissed her forehead.

"What's up?"

"Ava, I'm sorry about Melody."

"I'm not trippin' about that."

"Yes, you are," he retorted. Ava sighed.

"I'm not anymore."

"She's a good chick," he said, slowly. "I really like her."

"And that's fine. I have no problem with that."

"If you want I can bring her over so you both can meet her together," he said. "She'll be around for a while."

Ava couldn't help but smile at the way Romero was acting as if she was his mother and he was bringing a girlfriend home.

"It's whatever, homie," she said. Romero chuckled.

"Alright, I'll call my mini me tomorrow."

Ava just hung up. Romero knew Ava was sore about Angel looking more like him and he meant that to be funny. She walked back into Angel's room to see her sleeping. Ava went back into her own bedroom and called Sunny back.

"Why you acting like a teenage boy right now?" she asked, laughing. Sunny sucked his teeth.

"Can I be honest right now?"

"Don't play with me."

"Me and Kaylen just left the strip club."

"It's not even ten on a Thursday, Sunny," Ava said, sucking her teeth this time.

"Man, we wasn't even there long. Chill out, baby."

"I got something you can throw some money at."

"All I gave them were ones," Sunny said. "And baby, please believe you worth more than that."

Ava smiled. She wouldn't lie and say she was happy about him at a strip club, especially since Kaylen needed to be home trying to make up with his wife. What he said was a good cover though.

"Just for that, I'm not coming."

"Stop playing. They home yet?"

"No."

"Man, I'm on my way."

"No you aren't," Ava laughed. "I'm thinking about becoming celibate anyway," Ava said to see what Sunny thought of it. She looked around her room as he got quiet.

"You serious?" he asked after a moment.

"Yeah."

"...Until when."

"Until someone changes my name," Ava said, holding back her laugh. Sunny sighed deeply.

"First of all, what you mean someone?"

"Are we married?" Ava asked.

"Are you messing with someone else?"

"Don't get hurt," Ava said.

"I'm saying, you came at me like that. All you had to say was you were waiting on me to change your name. Now it's someone like you trying to be funny."

"It doesn't matter until it happens," Ava said.

"Okay...okay," Sunny said. Ava laughed.

"Baby quit playing," Ava cooed, trying to smooth the situation over. "You'll wait for me?"

"I'm saying baby you keep asking me to do all these things for you, what you doing for me?"

"Excuse you?" Ava asked, laughing.

"You heard what I said," Sunny replied back. "We can talk about this celibacy thing tomorrow if you serious, but I really need my woman to come take care of me right now." His voice was low, just above a whisper. Sunny knew what he was doing. Ava bit her lip.

"I'll let you know once everyone gets home."

"I love you," he said. Ava couldn't help but smile. Knowing that was the God honest truth made her blush every time he said it.

"I love you, too."

Realizing that she still had on her work clothes, Ava jumped in the shower. By the time she was out and dressed, Charity and Bri were back home.

"I'm going to bed," Charity said, beyond exhausted. Ava and Bri stood in the hall and watched her walk into her and Rico's room and shut the door behind her. They looked at each other.

"Can you believe she's pregnant?" Bri said. "It better not be a girl!" Ava laughed but nodded in agreement. "What if she has twins? Are they on Daddy's side?"

"Girl, I don't know," Ava answered. "You in the house for the night?"

"Yea, you going to Sunny's?" Bri asked, with a knowing smirk.

"If you keep an eye on Angel."

"That girl sleeps harder than me," Bri said, waving Ava off as she walked towards her room. Ava laughed.

"I'll be back in the morning."

Ava traced the tattoo of Sunny's mother as he traced her lips. The silence in his room usually bothered her, but seeing as they went nonstop for the last hour and a half, Ava welcomed it. The darkness of the room would soon pull her into a deep sleep, but Sunny seemed to be wide awake.

"You know what today is?" Sunny asked.

"The 12th," she replied after thinking about it for a moment. Sunny smirked and made a little 'umph' sound in his throat.

"Five years ago on December 12, I rolled up to Hamilton High with my bro to get my in-law." The smile on Ava's face spread quickly as she realized what he was talking about. "You ain't worth nothing for not remembering," Sunny said. Ava laughed and moved closer to him.

"Baby I remembered I met you in December, but the date didn't dawn on me," she said, kissing his chin. He playfully pushed her off and she laughed harder. "Aw, baby. I can't believe it's been five years already."

Ava and Sunny both began to reminisce about the last five years of their lives. From the very beginning it seemed as if Elle was plotting on them being together, but it was nice to know her work wasn't in vain. They had been through a lot. With both of them losing their mothers, dealing with Ava's rape and attempted suicide, their brief break up before Angel was born- it was definitely a bumpy ride.

Ava wouldn't trade it for anything.

When Sunday rolled around, Rico was up but still in this hospital. Although the situation wasn't perfect, Charity and Ava walked into church with smiles on their faces. Ava noticed that Rico was in the bulletin under the prayer list and Pastor Davidson had been to visit him the morning before. Charity was in high spirits although she still hadn't told Rico he was going to be a father again. Ava told her she should do it as soon as possible, but Charity wanted to wait until Rico was released and at home.

Ava was a little relieved that she didn't have to deal with Angel during the service. She was with Romero and his family that day, attending their church. The day before, Romero brought Melody over to meet Ava and Angel. Angel was hesitant to open up, which was natural. Ava, on the other hand, was not in the mood to make any new friends. If Romero said she was cool, then Ava would give her the benefit of the doubt for now.

To make his cancelled trip to the mall up to Angel, Romero kept her last night and promised Angel a trip to the zoo the following weekend. Ava tried to get Bri to come to church with her and Charity, but she slept in as usual.

"It's packed in here today," Ava said. Charity looked around and nodded as they walked to their usual seat on the right side of the church, three pews from the front. Ava noticed there were a lot more people in the choir stand than usual. She got excited. The church's choir was pretty good, probably one of the best in the city.

"Oh, Zemira is back."

"Who?"

"The pastor's niece," Charity said, pointing to a chocolate skin girl who looked around Ava's age. "She's been away at school."

"She's from here?" Ava asked, not remembering her face. Charity nodded.

"Her mom stays in Jasper."

Ava nodded, idly wondering how Erik had been. She hadn't seen or talked to him in years. She prayed he was okay just as the deacons called for devotion.

Throughout the service, Ava could tell that Pastor Davidson was excited about having his niece being back. He kept thanking God for her return, and proclaiming her accolades. Zemira looked embarrassed but Ava thought it was sweet how humbled she seemed. After offering, Pastor Davidson stood up with a smile on his face. His wife playfully nudged Zemira in her side but she shook her head and tried not to smile.

"Before I give the word today. I need Zemira to bless us with a selection," he said. A lot of people in the congregation laughed and cheered, yelling for Zemira to sing. Ava looked on, seeing as how everyone was excited for her to sing.

"She sounds really nice," Charity said. "You two should do a song together." Ava laughed, she wasn't even in the choir.

Zemira finally stood up and walked shyly over to the organist. She whispered something in her ear and they both nodded before Zemira went over to the microphone.

"Always trying to put me on the spot," she said, smiling at her uncle. He blew her a kiss and she laughed. "It feels good to be home. I've been praying and asking God what was next for me. Most of you know my situation with my mother and the last place I wanted to be was home," Zemira paused to clear her throat and ward off the tears. "But God spoke to me and he placed a spirit of forgiveness in me and it brought me back home."

"Amen! Hallelujah!"

"So this song has been in my spirit for a while and I know it's my uncle's favorite," she said. Pastor Davidson clapped hard and she laughed. "But I did put my own little twist to it."

Zemira began to sing *Angus Dei*. Her range was crazy. Ava was amazed at how smooth her low tenor was and how powerful her soprano came out. She sang at the original tempo but switched it up in the middle, having the whole congregation clap along while she sped it up. Before she could even finish singing, the Spirit overcame several members in the congregation.

Ava kept her eyes on Zemira and watched her emotions. Tears slid down her face as Pastor Davidson went over and wrapped his arm around her. She cried harder as he gently rocked her and patted her back. Her right arm went straight up in the air with her palm facing the ceiling.

Ava's heart went out to her. She didn't know her situation or her circumstance, but one thing she could tell was pain. Zemira's pain was laced throughout her beautiful voice and that was something that Ava could relate to.

After church, Ava was waiting for Charity to leave when Pastor Davidson walked up to her with Zemira at his side.

"Ava! I'm glad I caught you. I want you to meet my niece, Zemira. Mira this is Charity's step-daughter, Ava.

"Girl, my uncle keeps telling me about you," Zemira said. Ava looked on, shocked.

"Nothing bad," he said. "You two just have a lot in common as far as musical talents," he said. Both of them nodded.

"So I'll be seeing you at choir rehearsal this Saturday?" Zemira asked with a smile. Ava looked at Pastor Davidson, who looked around and avoided her stare.

"I see he got to you, too," Ava said. Zemira laughed.

"I'm trying to get this choir hip girl," Zemira said. "I could really use your help."

"She'll be there," Charity said, entering the conversation. Ava looked at her and sucked her teeth.

"Please?" Zemira asked. She clasped her hands together in front of her and gave Ava a puppy dog look.

"Okay," Ava said. All three of them smiled. "I'll be there."

That following Wednesday, Rico was released from the hospital. Charity and Granny Ran had to work and Bri was at school. Ava and Angel were left with the task of picking him up. She was debating on whether or not she would bring up the fact that his cover had been blown. She wasn't very happy with him at all.

Angel skipped through the plain hallway, her sneakers tapping against the tile and squeaking just a little. Ava watched her, amused by her fascination of the lines that separated each tile.

"Papa been here too long for shots," Angel said. Ava sighed, wondering why her four-year-old chose to remember everything she told her.

"His shots made him a little sick. He wanted to stay here so he wouldn't get us sick at home," Ava explained.

"I love Papa," Angel said, nodding her head to prove her point. Ava smiled at her before telling her to stop skipping. They were now in front of Rico's door. It was open, so he saw them from his position. He was sitting on the edge of the bed, sliding his feet into a pair of black Polo loafers that he usually only wore around the house. He was already dressed in the outfit Charity had brought over to him before her shift.

"Hey," he said once he saw them. "There's my favorite girl."

"Papa, your shots made you sick!" she said, letting him know as if he didn't. Rico looked up at Ava.

"You got shots in your arm like she got for school," Ava said. Rico nodded in recognition.

"They did make me sick baby, but I'm good now." he said. Rico groaned a little from picking Angel up. She hugged him and Ava could tell he was in pain, but he didn't have to pick her up so she didn't feel bad for him.

"You ready?" she asked. Rico nodded before telling her to grab his bag.

Ava was quiet as they left the hospital, letting Angel talk Rico's head off. She popped her knuckles to calm her nerves. All she wanted to do was confront him.

"Tyler is in jail if you're interested," Ava said, without looking from the road. She glanced in her rearview to see if Angel was paying attention, but she was playing with her toys contently.

"Oh yeah?" Rico asked. Ava nodded. "I'll have to call Unc to see what went down."

"You're really going to do this?"

"Do what, Ava?"

"Lie to my face?" Ava asked. "You aren't really about to play me like this are you?"

"Watch your mouth and talk to me like you got some sense," Rico said sternly. Ava shook her head, fighting back tears.

"I watched you," she said. "I watched you leave at night, come up with mysteriously large amounts of money before payday. I gave you the benefit of the doubt that you wouldn't be that stupid," Ava said. "How could you?"

"Ava, look," Rico started. "You really don't understand everything. We need to talk about this later," he said, glancing back at Angel to see if she was paying attention. Often times she'd act like she wasn't, but her ears would be wide open.

"I don't even want to," Ava said, shaking her head. "It's whatever. Dig your own grave."

"Ava!" Rico said, "Stop it."

Ava folded both of her lips in and shook her head, fighting the tears back.

"There's nothing to talk about it," Ava said. "If you don't care about your family, what's the point?"

"Ava!" Rico said. "That's enough."

Ava pulled into the driveway and quickly turned the car off. By now, Angel could tell that something was wrong with her mom and her grandpa. When Ava got her out of her car seat, she immediately started crying.

"Don't start," Ava yelled. Angel closed her mouth, but tears ran down her eyes.

"Give her here," Rico said, seeing that Ava was becoming emotional. Ava ignored him and held Angel's hand until they got in the house.

Rico watched as two of his girls went upstairs and he shook his head. He would have gone after them, but he was still pretty sore. All he wanted to do was take a shower and lay down. He decided on using the downstairs bathroom, knowing it would take him too long to get to the one upstairs. Rico noticed the quiet of his home, but welcomed it over the beeping of the machines he was hooked to at the hospital. He shook his head as he walked past the kitchen and down the main hallway with the bathroom in view. He tried to remember what happened the morning he got shot. At first, he couldn't really remember anything that happened last week, all he knew was Tyler was running off at the mouth as usual and the situation went from bad to worse in a matter of minutes.

Rico had gotten off another night shift and drove to his mom's house where he knew Tyler was waiting. He parked his car in his mom's driveway, only to see Tyler's car parked on the street, but it was empty. Tyler was next door at some girl's house. Rico only knew that because it wasn't the first time Tyler got caught sneaking out of that married woman's home when her husband was on midnights. Rico saw it was almost five in the morning. Tyler was cutting it close.

"Yo," *Rico said into his phone.* "I'm out front."

"Here I come," *Tyler said. Rico could hear the woman complaining in the background.* "Guh, calm all that down. I'm not your man."

Rico shook his head and laughed, hanging up on his cousin. Within minutes, Tyler was jogging out the front door as he slammed it behind him. He looked back at the house and smirked.

"What?" *Tyler asked.*

"You need to quit before she tells her man on you," *Rico said. Tyler looked at his older cousin and laughed.*

"And get us both killed? She ain't crazy," *Tyler said.* "Come on." *He patted Rico on his chest before pointing to his car. Rico walked over to Tyler's passenger side while Tyler jogged to the driver's side.*

"We going to the diner?" *Rico asked. Tyler turned up his radio and nodded. Rico laughed. All Tyler listened to was old 2Pac and Jay-Z albums. For him to be so young and goofy, he was adamant that modern rap wasn't good and only listened to old school. Rico could respect it.* "And you're sure they there?"

"Rico, cuz, quit tripping," Tyler said, *finally glancing at his older cousin while he drove.* "Everything is under control."

"Yeah, that's what you said last time."

"This ain't last time."

Rico looked out the window and tried to relax. His body was telling him it was time to lie down, but he wanted to get this done and over with. Anything that was keeping him from lying up under his wife at the moment was the enemy.

He thought about Charity and asking her to speak with the girls about the pregnancy test he'd found. He still hadn't said anything, because he knew his mind wasn't in the right place. She'd be able to talk to them a little nicer than he would.

"Granny tell you Pops is sick?" Tyler asked. *Rico shook his head.*

"Nah," he replied. "He cool though?"

"Yeah, he just need to chill out and quit acting so young," Tyler replied. *Rico was sure he could say the same about Tyler, but he left that issue alone. Tyler and Ryan hadn't always had the best father/son relationship. They were just now able to be around each other without Tyler snapping out about Ryan missing most of his childhood years. Tyler always said he was nothing like Ryan, but they were alike in more ways than one.*

"How's Tina?" Rico asked. Tyler smirked as a small smile of pride showed on his face.

"Getting big man," Tyler said. Rico nodded. "She got about a month left before my baby boy drops."

They talked a little about how Tyler was nervous about his first born, but his on-and-off girlfriend Tina was keeping him grounded. It would be her second child so she had more experience than Tyler. They were often at odds about their relationship status. Tyler always wanted to act like he wasn't bothered if Tina spoke to other guys, but Rico knew it was a matter of time before Tyler got it together, especially since he was about to be a father.

When the cousins pulled up to the diner, the usual crowd was there. Rico looked around, idly expecting to see Sunny or Kaylen, but neither was present. He nodded a little before walking towards an empty booth and taking a seat. Tyler slid into the booth seat across from him, the maroon plastic seats yielding to their weight. A few moments later, a giddy college girl bounced over and asked if they wanted anything. Tyler asked for a drink while Rico shook his head.

"No thank you,"

"Man, why you bugging?" Tyler asked once the waitress walked off. "Chill out."

"This isn't a chill situation."

"Stop acting like you don't know the game," Tyler said. Rico sucked his teeth.

"I know what got me locked up," he said. Tyler smirked before shaking his head.

"Yet here you are."

Rico didn't respond. He knew he would come off wrong if he took it there with his cousin, but the fact that Tyler was right didn't pass by Rico's mind. In fact, all of his current thoughts began to decipher the situation. What was Rico doing?

The bell ringing caused Rico to look up towards the door. A short, dark skin man with a low cut fade ran his hand over his face before looking around. The guy with him was a little stockier, but not too much taller. His brown skin was scarred under his eye and a few other places on his face, but that was the most visible.

Tyler followed Rico's gaze behind them and nodded towards the pair, waving them over to the table. Tyler slid closer to the window and allowed room. Rico didn't move. The one with the scars pulled a chair from a nearby table and sat on the end. The dark skin one sat on the edge of the booth with Tyler.

"This my cousin Rico," *Tyler said.* "This Match and Kyle." *Rico watched Tyler point to the one with the scars and then the darker one. Rico nodded in greeting.*

"What's good?" *Kyle said.*

"I'd rather just get down to business," *Rico announced. Match snickered a little and exchanged a glance with Kyle.* "It seems to be some miscommunication going on with how business should be handled."

"Your fault," *Kyle said. Rico adjusted his position and leaned on the table.*

"Excuse me?"

"What he's trying to say is, the miscommunication falls on your end, not ours," Match said. "Business enough for you?"

Rico narrowed his eyes. "Man, Tyler what type of mess you got me on?"

"What?" Match said, standing up. Kyle smirked before running his thumb and index over the corners of his mouth.

"We all need to calm down," Tyler said.

"Point is, after this deal, I'm out," Rico said, throwing his hands up. "I got too much to lose and y'all can't get stuff straight. Find another cat. Tyler let's go!"

Tyler sighed as Kyle got up to let him out. Rico took off towards the door before Tyler could catch him. Tyler pulled out his keys to hit the lock and they both got in the car.

"Man, cousin..."

"I don't want to hear it Tyler," Rico said. "Get me back to my car."

Tyler sighed before putting the key in the ignition. They hadn't even gotten a good block away from the diner before they heard tires screech and guns go off.

Rico smiled in appreciation at his wife's thoughtfulness. His soap, razor, lotion, pajama pants, and a tee shirt were neatly on the granite marble top. He wasn't even concerned about how she knew he'd end up in the downstairs bathroom. Charity knew so much about him and that was the reason he felt guilty about keeping his side business from her. He'd done it out of protection, but in the end he left them clueless.

Rico slowly sat on the edge of the tub and turned the silver knobs inward. A short hiss came from the pipes before the water came out. The water spat against the bottom of the tub before filling out past the stopper. Rico tilted his head side to side to stretch his neck before carefully peeling off his shirt. He looked down at his chest, realizing he wouldn't be able to take a bath. Rico groaned as he leaned down to pull the stopper up to allow the water to go down the drain. He then pulled the small round handle to switch the water to the shower head.

After his shower, he was a little more relaxed. He smiled when he heard his wife's voice in the living room.

"Papi!" she said, throwing her arms around him. "Is it okay if I hug you?"

"Yeah," he lied, already feeling sore but not up for denying his wife that opportunity. They both needed it. Rico held in a groan as Charity pressed her body to his. She sighed and pulled back, wiping tears from her eyes. "I'm good baby."

"Are you really?" Charity said, her concern laced with sarcasm. "I thought your job was paying you good?"

"What you talking about?"

"Why were you with Tyler, Rico?"

Rico sighed before sitting down on the couch. "You been talking to Ava?" he asked. Charity shook her head.

"No, your uncle told your mom. Are you selling drugs again? I'm not doing this with you, Rico!"

"You not doing what?" he asked. The tone of his voice caused Charity to step back a little. "You leaving? Nah, you aren't, so chill out."

"Why are you talking to me like you've lost your mind?" Charity yelled back. "Do you know how it feels to sit up in a waiting room thinking any minute a doctor is going to tell you that your husband is dead because he's too stupid to learn from his mistakes?"

"Charity," Rico said in warning. "Sit down and lower your voice."

"No! You don't get to tell me to calm down." Charity said, kicking off her white and red sneakers that matched her scrubs. "I find out that I'm pregnant and not even two days later my husband is laid up in the hospital from getting shot!"

Silence fell over them as Charity studied Rico's face. She cried harder as he watched her, realizing she could really be raising her child alone. She covered her mouth with her right hand to quiet the sobs.

"That was your pregnancy test in the bathroom?" he whispered. Charity nodded, but only cried harder. When she groaned, Rico sighed. "Hey," he said, lifting both his hands from his thighs and motioning towards her. "Come here."

"No."

"Baby, come here," Rico pleaded. Charity dropped her hand and walked towards the couch. When she was close enough, Rico pulled her down next to him. "I'm sorry. I'm done okay?"

"I don't believe you."

"I know you don't," he said, laughing a little. "None of my girls do, and I don't blame you."

"Rico, the girls were freaking out. Your mom was blaming me and I had no idea what to do," Charity vented. Rico grabbed her neck and kissed her forehead. He really needed to talk with his mom about how she treated his wife. He never understood her issues with the women in his life.

"We'll be okay," he said, sliding his hand across her belly. Charity giggled. "Lord, this better be a boy."

Eleven

Trishelle bounced up and down, tapping her feet against the tile of the nursery. Kaylen smirked at her actions, but didn't say anything to her. They still weren't on speaking terms, but today was a joyous occasion.

Kaylen Jr. was finally coming home.

It was five days before Christmas and Kaylen Jr was exactly one month old. He was nine pounds and gaining and Elle couldn't have been more excited. They weren't expecting him for another week, but everyone was happy to hear he'd be home for Christmas, especially Jayla.

"Mom, you want to dress him?" the nurse on duty asked. Elle nodded eagerly before pulling the Polo outfit they'd purchased on the way there out of the bag.

Elle exhaled as she walked over to the basinet and KJ's brown eyes shifted to her. His color had changed so much; he was almost the same dark caramel color that Jayla was. His black hair was still sticking to his head with small ringlets coming up on the top. His top lip was small, but his bottom one stuck out just a little. Elle was in love with her mini Kaylen as she called him. He almost made her not mad at the original version.

"I bet you two are tired of coming up here," the nurse said.

"It wasn't too bad," Elle said. The nurse smiled.

"Dad came up every day," she said. Elle frowned and quickly looked at Kaylen, who made it clear he wasn't going to look at her. "The mid day staff knew him by name."

"Had to check on my little man," he said. Elle carefully slid the white onesies over his head before pulling it down his body.

"Hey handsome," she said, smiling down at him as he waved his arms. The nurse announced she'd be right back with some paperwork. "You came every day?" she asked, not looking up at Kaylen while she dressed her son.

"Lunch breaks."

Elle's heart softened just a bit, but she tried hard not to show it. She slid the long sleeve body suit on and made sure she didn't pinch his neck with the zipper. She smiled while holding the small hat in her hands.

"I can't wait to get you home, munchkin."

"You sure you don't want to run off to work," Kaylen said behind her. Elle glared at the wall above KJ's basinet, but didn't respond. "Your Nana and your big sister are waiting for you, too."

The nurse came back in and Kaylen signed the release papers while Elle put KJ in his car seat.

"*Thank you, Jesus*," she thought, as she covered his car seat and walked out of the hospital with Kaylen in front of them. He opened the back door of his car and Elle slid in with the baby. After buckling him in, she pulled the cover back and smiled. When he grabbed at her finger, Elle's heart dropped. She hadn't seen him since the day before and a sudden feeling of guilt came over her. How did she even go a day without seeing him? Of course she was sick and had to take care of Jayla, but Kaylen had made time every day to see their son. What was she doing?

"We home, little man," Kaylen said, turning the car off. When he was met with silence, Kaylen turned around to see Elle looking down in the car seat and crying. "What's wrong? Is he okay?"

"He's fine," Elle said, crying harder. "He's perfect."

Kaylen hurried out of the driver's seat and pulled open the door to the side that Elle was sitting on. He reached past her and un-clicked her seat belt.

"Come on, Elle."

"I'm a horrible mother! And wife!" she sobbed.

Kaylen looked at her and frowned.

"Quit playing, it's cold," he said, trying to get her out of the car.

"What's going on?"

Kaylen stood up and looked towards their apartment to see Janet peaking out of the door. She had volunteered to stay with Jayla while they picked KJ up. Kaylen jogged around to the other side and got KJ out of the car, meeting Janet on the steps. "What's wrong with her?"

"Give me a minute," Kaylen said, handing her the car seat "She's just emotional."

"Be nice, Kaylen," Janet warned while turning around and heading back upstairs. Kaylen went back to Elle's open door. She hadn't moved and hadn't stopped crying.

"What was I doing that I couldn't see my son every day?" Elle cried.

"Baby, is this what you crying about? My job ain't far from the hospital," he said, kneeling down between the car and the open door and pulling Elle to the edge of the seat. She shook her head.

"I'm a horrible momma."

"Trishelle, look at me," Kaylen demanded. She turned towards him, but didn't look up in his eyes. "You heard what I said!"

"Kaylen," she whined.

"Nah, I'm not about to let you sit up and do this," he said, grabbing her chin. "You breaking my heart." Elle cried more.

"I'm sorry!"

"You ain't never gave me a reason to doubt you. We got two kids who won't have to ask for nothing. Don't sit up here and say this mess about you being a horrible wife and mother no more," he said. "You been my wife since you was sixteen." Elle cracked a smile.

"You sound like a perv," she said. Kaylen licked his lips before smiling.

"Now you cracking jokes?" he asked, leaning up to kiss her. Elle closed her eyes and shook her head before gripping the shoulders of his coat.

"Thank you," she whispered. Kaylen kissed her again.

"Can we get out the cold now?" Kaylen asked. Elle nodded before Kaylen helped her out of the car. "You big baby," he said, laughing. Elle swung her arm and hit him in the chest.

"Shut up," she said, before jogging up the first flight of stairs and going into the apartment.

"Aw, look at my babies!" Elle said, seeing Jayla sitting on the couch. Janet was sitting next to her and she had KJ halfway in Jayla's lap, helping her hold him. Elle hurried and pulled her phone out.

"Jayla you say hi to your baby brother?" Elle asked. Kaylen came into the apartment and shut the door. Jayla looked down at him and nodded. She placed her hand on his head, but she was a little rough.

"You have to be careful baby," Janet said. "He's not ready to play with you yet."

"Well, he needs to hurry up," Jayla said. Everyone laughed.

"Don't rush him," Elle said. Kaylen stood behind her and kissed her neck, before patting her thigh. Elle blushed.

"Ohhhh," Janet said, smiling while taking KJ out of Jayla's lap. "Looks like the love is back."

"It will be in about two weeks," Kaylen yelled from the kitchen. Elle gasped with a shocked look on her face. Janet laughed.

Ava sighed as she walked into the local pizza place holding Angel's hand.

"I don't want pizza," Angel whined.

"I don't care," Ava said, mocking her. Angel stood up straight and frowned. "Get beat up in here."

"I want Daddy."

"He right there," Ava said, pointing to a booth in the back. Angel looked up with wide eyes and ran towards him. Ava rolled her eyes as she got her thoughts together, walking slower. She watched as Romero slid out of the booth just as Angel made it over and wrapped her up in her arms. He kissed all over her face and Angel giggled. Ava looked at Melody, who was sitting on the same side of the booth that Romero was sitting. She was smiling up at Angel and Romero's interaction.

She took the time to commit Melody's profile to memory. She was a little shorter than Romero, a few inches taller than Ava. Her skin was a smooth milk chocolate color and her eyes were hazel. When Ava had seen her at the mall and when Romero brought her over her hair was in a short bob, now it was in a short, spiked cut with a dark red tint.

"What's up, Av?" Romero asked when Ava finally reached the table. She nodded before sliding in the empty side. Angel was sitting on Romero's lap. "Sit next to Mommy so we can order food. You want cheese pizza?"

"Yes, I love pizza!" Angel said. Ava looked at her and rolled her eyes.

"You are such a trader," Ava said. Romero and Melody frowned but Angel just giggled.

"Angel, you remember Melody," Romero said. "She's daddy's girlfriend."

"Hi Angel," Melody said in an overly enthusiastic voice. "You remember me?"

Ava wanted to laugh when Angel shook her head.

"Don't be rude, say hi," Ava said. Angel sighed heavily before speaking to Melody.

"Um, let's order," Romero said. Ava could tell he was uncomfortable. She felt a little bad so while he ordered, she decided to be nice.

"Melody, you from around here?" Ava asked.

"No, I'm from Georgia, but I go to Jasper," she said. Ava nodded.

"How did you meet?"

"You know I play at the gym out there some times," Romero said. Ava really didn't know, but she nodded anyway. "We met about six months ago. She plays volleyball."

"Gelly likes volleyball too," Ava said, looking at Angel. "Don't you baby?" Angel nodded while sipping her juice. "Can you tell Melody what color your volleyball is?"

"It's yellow and red!" Angel said. They had been working on their colors, so Ava knew she'd be excited to say that.

"Aw, I bet that's pretty," Melody said. Angel finally smiled at her and began talking. Romero looked at Ava.

"Thank you," he mouthed. Ava waved him off before pulling Angel closer to her. "What are we doing about C-H-R-I-S-T-M-A-S?" he asked. Ava sighed.

"She didn't give you her list?" Ava asked. Romero frowned. "She had a list that she separated between all of us."

"Who is us?" Romero asked.

"Me, you, Bri, Sunny, Rico and Charity got one, and your mom," Ava said. Romero's eyes widened.

"Dang," Romero said. "That's smart though."

"Don't encourage it."

"You got her spoiled, too."

Ava shook her head before unzipping Angel's backpack. Sure enough, Romero's list was folded in the pocket. She'd helped her write it a week ago, even though Christmas was next week. She handed it to Romero and he looked over it. Melody leaned over and looked too.

"I work at Target for the holidays so you can use my discount," Melody told him. Ava held her palm out towards Melody and smiled at Romero.

"There you go."

"This ain't bad," he said, reading the list.

"She's not that spoiled," Ava said, defensively. Romero smirked. Ava could tell he was about to get on her nerves. She didn't need to go to work agitated. "Are you going to be good for Daddy while I'm at work?" Ava asked Angel.

"She's always good for Daddy," Romero said with a smirk. Ava rolled her eyes.

"That's because Daddy doesn't know how to say no," Ava said. Angel smiled. Ava shook her head before kissing Angel's forehead.

"I'll drop her off in the morning," Romero said. Ava nodded before sliding out of the booth.

"Have fun at work, Mommy!" Angel said before focusing on her pizza. Ava snickered before telling her she loved her and saying bye to Romero and Melody.

Rico parked in front of his mom's home, realizing he hadn't been there since the night of the shooting. He looked around to see no one outside. There was only one house on the street that had Christmas decorations up. He looked towards the door to see his mom opening it and waving at him to come in. He turned the car off and got out.

"What were you doing?" she asked. Rico shook his head before jogging up the steps. "Well get in here, letting my good heat out."

"How you doing, Ma?" Rico asked, hugging his mother.

"I should be asking you that," she said. Rico closed the door and put his coat in the hall closet. "I just made some soup. You want a bowl?"

"Why wouldn't I?" he said. She smiled.

"Don't get smart."

Rico followed Ran into the kitchen and inhaled the aroma that filled the room. He sat down at the table while Ran made him a bowl of homemade chicken noodle soup.

"You done shopping?"

"Me and Charity just finished about an hour ago."

"Hope you got your mother something nice."

"You know I got you."

Ran sat the bowl down in front of him and sat in the chair across from him.

"Tyler got out on bond," she said. "If you want to know." Rico just nodded, not really having an opinion. "Does that girl even cook?"

"What girl?" Rico asked, frowning. "You can't be referring to Charity."

"Why can't I?"

"That's my wife, not that girl."

"You are aware that I'm your mother right?" Ran asked, inching her way towards where Rico sat.

"Ma, what's your problem with my family?"

"I don't have a problem. I just gave her a few pointers, that's all."

"What you call pointers ain't always helpful, Ma."

"Rico, nobody knows how to take care of you like I can," she said. Rico looked at her and sighed.

"I'm grown, Ma," he said. "Let me run my family."

"But..."

"But," he said, cutting her off. "Let me run my family."

"Fine!" she said, throwing her hands up. "But you better make sure you're running it into the right direction."

"What, Ma?" Rico asked, confused.

"Don't keep repeating history, son. You talked a lot of smack about Kita and how she lived, but you weren't that different."

"Ma, that's not..."

"No," she said, cutting him off this time. "You will hear this. She thought she could do whatever she wanted and it caught up with her. You just got lucky that God keeps giving you chances. Stop taking those chances for granted."

"Merry Christmas, Mommy!"

Ava smiled as she pushed her cover from around her neck. She opened her eyes to see Angel standing at the side of her bed with a small box in hand. Ava took in her daughter's appearance and laughed. Angel's hair was all over the place. She hadn't even washed her face which was evident by the dried slobber on the left corner of her mouth. She had on pink and purple Cinderella pajamas with the buttons to the top done the wrong way. Ava leaned over and kissed her nose.

"Sing the song, Ma!"

Ava giggled before clearing her throat.

"Today is so special, not because of gifts, not because of toys or any of this." Ava began to sing. Angel smiled and bent her knees, swaying side to side. It was a song they learned when Ava took Angel to children's church for the first time a couple of weeks ago. Angel began to sing along. "Today is about Jesus. He's the greatest gift!"

"Good job, baby," Ava said. Angel smiled before holding her hands out. "You got me a gift, Gelly?"

"Sunny helped me!" she said. Ava looked towards the door to see Sunny leaning against it. Her insides warmed as she smiled. He'd gotten a clean cut. He wasn't dressed up; just a simple Nike sweat suit with his Cool Gray's.

"Merry Christmas, baby," she said, pulling Angel into the bed with her. She turned and patted the empty spot next to her. Sunny pushed himself off the door frame and walked along the side of the bed. Angel snuggled into Ava's side before pushing the gift on her belly.

"I guess I better open this, huh?" she asked. Angel nodded. "I thought you were supposed to open your gifts first?"

"Mommy!"

She laughed as the whoosh from Sunny landing on the other side pushed a burst of air her way. She smiled at him and he leaned over, kissing her forehead.

"Baby girl wanted to wait until you opened yours to open hers," he said. Ava nodded before tearing at the paper. The white box had a "P" on it and she smiled, knowing it was from Pandora.

"Babe, you finally started my charm bracelet?" she asked. She gasped when she opened it to see there were already five charms on it. "Aw!"

"This one is me!" Angel said, pushing her finger into a small charm with a sapphire in the middle.

"It sure is! What color is that Gel?"

"Blue!" she said. "Sap-fire."

"That's good baby," she said, laughing a little. "And this one is for Sunny and what color is it?"

"Purple. I can't say that other word."

"Amethyst," Sunny said, getting closer to them. His was a small heart with his birthstone in it. The one for Ava was actually two charms with two girls holding hands for her and Bri. There was a dangling music note and an "S" silver charm for Sunny's name. Ava knew the charms were expensive, but the thought into it meant a lot. She had been meaning to start a bracelet ever since Angel turned two.

"Thank you, loves," Ava said, kissing all over Angel's face. She giggled before standing up in the bed.

"Now my turn!"

"Go ahead and wake Ti-ti B up and let Mommy brush her teeth," Ava said. Angel nodded before jumping off the bed and running out of the room. Ava took the moment to move closer to Sunny.

"I love it," she whispered.

"I'm glad."

"You're gift is in the closet."

"I can wait until after Gel opens her stuff," he said. Ava nodded. "What time you and Bri going to the graveyard?"

"After breakfast," she sighed. "To get it over with."

Sunny nodded before pulling Ava into his body. She

smiled and enjoyed a quiet moment before getting up to get her Christmas started.

The house was incredibly still upstairs. She could hear her family moving around downstairs and wondered if they decided not to wait on her. Ava hurried, brushing her teeth and washing her face quickly so she wouldn't miss Angel opening her gifts. Ava was pretty sure Angel had gotten everything she wanted from everyone. She would have to wait until Romero came and got her after breakfast to get everything from his side.

Sunny waited until Ava was ready before they headed downstairs. She jiggled her bracelet in Bri's face and smiled.

"Who you think helped pick the charms out?" Bri said. Ava looked at Sunny and gasped. Everyone laughed as she hit him in his chest.

"I didn't tell you I picked them out," he said, laughing.

"Yeah, yeah," Ava said, sitting down on the carpet next to Angel, who was already trying to see which gifts were hers.

"Well, I already got my gift," Rico said, rubbing Charity's belly as she sat on his leg. She put her hand over his and blushed.

"Aw," Bri said.

"Stop it," Ava replied. Rico rolled his eyes and Charity sucked her teeth.

"Don't hate, your little brother loves you," Charity said.

"You better hope it's not another girl," she joked. Rico frowned.

"Don't even play like that."

"Which one is mine?" Angel said, interrupting their teasing. Bri sat one in front of her. Angel got up and kissed Bri on the nose before rushing back to open her gift. Ava shook her head.

"That little girl is something," Sunny said, as he sat down next to her.

"You hear me?" she said, agreeing. Angel was too caught up in her gifts to hear them discussing her. That was how most of their morning went. Angel even began to open gifts that weren't hers. She began pretending that she could read, and coincidently, every gift under the tree said Angel.

"Oh, I forgot! Zemira called the house for you this morning," Charity said, looking at Ava. "She said she didn't have your cell and wanted to tell you Merry Christmas."

"Aw, that was sweet."

"Who is Zemira?" Sunny asked.

"My pastor's niece," Ava said. "They been trying to hook us up." Ava laughed at Sunny's face. "Not like that, Santana. She sings and they trying to get me to join the choir.

"You should," he said. "You haven't done anything with singing besides writing hooks and stuff every now and then."

Ava nodded quickly before turning back around. She caught Bri looking at her with a knowing smirk. She hadn't really thought about the weight of her lies until that moment because it was never brought up or questioned.

"So what's up with breakfast?" Bri asked. Ava looked at her with a silent thank you. She hadn't even known how to move on from the conversation.

"I'm not," Charity said, stretching out on the couch. "I'm thinking of taking a nap."

"Oh please!" Ava said. "You ain't that pregnant."

"Bri and Ava it is," Rico said. "Sunny, help me put this doll house together."

"Yes, help!" Angel said, pulling at Sunny's hand. Sunny quickly nodded and Ava wanted to laugh at how Angel had them all wrapped around her finger.

"Why doesn't he know again?" Bri asked, as they walked into the kitchen. Ava quickly looked back to make sure Sunny hadn't heard Bri.

"Any louder? Please!" Ava said. Bri rolled her eyes.

"What's your problem? You remember the last time you lied to him right?" Bri asked, referring to when Sunny found out that she was raped and not just jumped by some girl and her friends over a guy.

"This isn't like that," Ava said, brushing her twin off as she walked over to the refrigerator to get the ingredients from their Christmas breakfast. Bri shook her head before walking over to the pantry. "It isn't, Briann."

"I heard you the first time, Ava," Bri said, mocking the way Ava said her name. "I'm out of it."

"Thank you," Ava said. Bri sucked her teeth, but did not respond. "What's up with the guy you've been talking to anyway?"

"What guy?"

"For real. I knew about Donte, what makes you think I don't know about this dude?" Ava said with a knowing smirk. "Keith, right?"

"You are a nosy, heffa."

"That's what twins are for!"

They laughed as they began to make breakfast. Bri made the waffles while Ava cooked the scrambled eggs with cheese and the sausage and bacon. After everyone ate, Ava gave Sunny his two gifts; one from her and one from Angel. Sunny helped Ava load the car with the things she had gotten for Jayla and KJ. She put the gift she helped Angel pick out for Romero in the car as well. Rico and Charity were heading over to Granny Ran's house. Ava was going to drop Angel off at Romero's before she and Bri went to visit Kita's grave. Later she was going to meet back up with Sunny at Miss Janet's where Elle and Kaylen were while Bri headed to Granny Ran's. Ava hadn't made her mind up on whether she would go there later or not.

"Is his girlfriend there?" Bri asked. Ava frowned as she turned on Romero's street.

"Probably, it is Christmas."

"I don't like her."

"You have no reason not to," Ava said. Bri shrugged before looking out the window.

"I just get a bad feeling from her. You know like when you rub those vinyl covered notebooks and get that nasty shiver over your skin?" she asked. Ava looked at her for a moment and then laughed, glancing back at the road. "You know what I'm talking about?"

"No, psycho, I don't."

"Whatever."

Ava sighed when she pulled up in front of Romero's house. She turned to see that Angel was sleep and Ava was glad she didn't hear Bri talking about Melody. Angel liked to run her mouth to Romero and he would love to know that Bri and Ava were discussing his new girlfriend. Ava looked at her sleeping child for a second before pulling her cell phone out.

"Where you at, yo?" Romero asked. Ava sucked her teeth.

"I'm outside, yo," she mimicked him. "Come get the kid, she's sleep."

"What she sleep for? She needs to open her presents!"

Ava didn't even respond, she just hung up the phone as she saw Romero's front door open. He looked up at her and shook his head as he jogged to the car.

"You hella rude, yo," Romero said. Ava looked at him and smiled. "How long she been sleep?"

"Car ride," she replied.

"Hi Bri," Romero said, opening the back door and securing Angel in his arms.

"Hi," Bri said back, dryly without even looking at him.

"I'll be back to get her later."

Romero nodded before using his foot to close the back door and turning to walk back towards the house.

Knowing where she and Bri were headed brought an inevitable gloom on Ava's day. The change from watching Angel open gifts and marveling at the innocence of Christmas to driving through the cemetery was heart breaking.

"I don't remember where it is," Bri admitted, biting her lip in embarrassment.

"Over by the tree near the gate," Ava replied. "In the back."

Ava drove slowly on the narrow path and parked near the tree. Bri was the first to get out, beating Ava to Kita's grave. She pushed the old flowers away with her foot while Ava bent down to remove some of the weeds. It was a little hard, seeing as it was December and the ground was cold. Bri laughed out of nowhere. Ava looked up at her and frowned.

"What?"

"I bet she's thinking, 'why are these fools sitting at this grave in December?'" Bri said, imitating Kita's voice. Ava slowly smiled and nodded, standing up straight and dusting her knees off.

"Sounds like her."

"It doesn't feel like it's been that long."

Ava thought back to the day she found Kita, lifeless and cold. She shivered and wrinkled her nose, fighting off the tingling feeling that was usually the introduction to her tears.

"It's crazy how three years went by so quickly," Ava said, finally responding. They leaned against the tombstone just as they always did.

"Why do we come here?" Bri asked. Ava sucked her teeth.

"You ready to go or something?"

"I was just asking, hot head," Bri said, rolling her eyes at Ava's attitude. Ava looked around and shrugged.

"As weird as it sounds, it's peaceful here," Ava thought aloud. "Like, I know it's just her body and not her, but I feel closest to her here."

"I think I have baby fever."

"Briann, why are you so random?" Ava asked, laughing. Bri shrugged, just as Ava had done moments ago, and smiled.

"You're one to talk."

"We don't run the same race, but we run it the same," Ava quoted something they'd read about twins awhile ago, before Kita died.

"Slightly," Bri answered. "How you think Sunny is going to take your career move?"

"I don't know honestly," Ava said. "I've prayed about it though. Hopefully he'll understand."

"I saw you reading the Bible," Bri said. Ava looked at her. "While I was walking past your room last night."

"You got one?"

"Never thought about it, I guess," Bri said, shrugging. Ava knew that meant Bri wasn't really interested.

"I'm going to buy you one," Ava tested, carefully watching Bri's body language.

"Don't waste your money," Bri said. "I don't really read."

"This is different," Ava thought, but decided not to push her. Ava didn't really know why she suddenly took an interest in Bri reading the Bible anyway.

"Let's go," Ava said. "I'm getting cold."

Ava dropped Bri off at Granny Ran's, went back to get Angel from Romero's, and then headed to Miss Janet's house.

"About time you got here!" Elle said, pulling Ava into the house while Angel ran over to where Jayla was playing.

"Merry Christmas!" Ava said, handing her KJ's gift. Elle smiled before handing it to Kaylen. "Jayla, me and Gelly got you a gift!"

When Ava looked over, Jayla had already handed Angel the gift Kaylen and Elle bought. Ava laughed as Angel tore through the wrapping. She sat down next to them and helped Jayla open her gift.

"Lord, these kids are spoiled," Miss Janet said, coming in with a tray of cookies.

"Look who's talking," Elle mumbled. Kaylen patted her on her thigh. She gave him a knowing look before picking KJ's gift up. "Look son!" she said, holding the gift out. KJ was seated on his father' lap, busying himself with trying to grip his pacifier.

"I see someone made up," Ava said smiling, "Where's my man?"

"Bathroom."

"I think I want to take him out of town for his birthday," Ava said. Elle smiled.

"That would be dope, he never does anything," Elle said, never tearing her eyes from the box. Ava smiled when she opened it. It was a black and red Polo outfit with the shoes to match.

"This fly, bro," Kaylen said. Ava rolled her eyes, but didn't comment on the despised nickname. She turned to the left to see Sunny strolling down the hallway and she smiled.

"Hey," she said, reaching for him. He leaned over and kissed her head before ruffling Angel's curls. Angel giggled before swatting his hand away.

"You good?" he asked. Ava nodded. She heard Elle giggled before she turned to see Kaylen getting up and walking in the back.

"I swear he's trying to get me pregnant again," Elle said. Ava frowned.

"Ugh."

"Shut up, we're married!" Kaylen yelled while coming back in the room. Ava looked at him for a second.

"Once again…ugh!" Everyone laughed.

"Don't you have to wait like six months?" Sunny asked.

"We can tell you don't have any kids," Janet said.

"Yes, I do," he said quickly, glancing at Angel. Ava bit her lip to keep from smiling so hard.

"It's six weeks, love," she said. Sunny nodded.

"Yo bro! I saw Dre the other day," Kaylen said. Ava's heart dropped a little, but she willed herself to keep her facial expression intact.

"I ain't seen dude in a minute," Sunny said. Ava sunk down a little, hunching her shoulders as she tried to keep her focus on Jayla and Angel. Elle watched her quietly.

"Yeah, he said bro is in high demand now," Kaylen said. "Some people trying to get hooks from her quick!" Ava knew the tone in Kaylen's voice was a proud one, but she wanted him to shut up.

"That's what's up, bae," Sunny said, gently nudging Ava's arm as he sat down on the ground next to her. She smiled faintly. "Why you ain't tell me?"

"Yeah, why you ain't say anything?" Elle said. Ava glared at her.

"Just been busy with work, I guess." Everyone looked at her for more of an explanation. She wanted to shout, "Thank you, Jesus!" when her phone rang, but groaned to see that it was Romero.

"Yes, baby daddy," she answered, getting up and walking in the kitchen.

"Ay chill with that, what's my baby doing?"

"Playing with Jayla, about to eat."

"You bringing her back?"

"I just picked her up."

"More family just rolled through."

"The price of tea in China is high."

"Stop playing, you get on my nerves!"

"We had a deal, you get her tomorrow remember?"

"But I got way more family than you," he said. "What? Nah, she's tripping." He was now talking to someone in the background.

"Who are you talking to?" Ava asked. "And about me."

"Man, Mel was just asking…"

"Oh, I didn't know you and her had a kid."

"You always so dramatic," Romero said.

"I'm just saying, if Gel has a brother or sister we should probably introduce them. They should know each other."

Romero got quiet, but sucked his teeth. "Bye dude."

Ava laughed when Romero hung up the phone. Somewhat satisfied with annoying him, Ava put her phone in her pocket and walked back into the living room.

"So, I have an announcement," Kaylen said.

"What you do?" Ava asked. Elle laughed as she cradled KJ on her shoulder and burped him.

"Shut up," he said, reaching in his pocket. "I have to give my wife her gift."

"Yes! Give it here!"

"Hold on woman," he said. "I got something to say first."

"Oh Lord," Sunny said. Kaylen ignored him.

"We been rocking for a long time. Even when the world was against me, you stayed down. You believed in me and I made sure I kept every promise I made to you. We got married in a court house with only Sunny and Moms there for support."

"It was so sad," Sunny joked. Ava laughed, but hit him in the arm.

"Shut up!" Elle said, almost in tears as Janet took KJ from her.

"Now that you and your mom cool again and I can afford to give you better, I'm going to do that."

"Aw!" Ava and Janet said as Kaylen got down on one knee in front of Elle, who couldn't stop smiling.

"Will you marry me again, big head?" he asked, opening the ring box to reveal a pink sapphire and diamond princess cut, white gold ring.

"I sure will!" Elle said, pushing her left hand in his face. Kaylen laughed a little, licking his lips as he slid the ring up her finger until it clicked against her wedding band. "It's so fly, baby. You did good!"

"I finally get to plan a wedding," Janet said. "We need to set a date."

"Chill out lady," Elle said, still admiring her ring. "We're going to do this all the way right this time."

"I'm going to be fly in a suit," Sunny said, stroking his chin.

"You're so conceited!" Elle said, side eyeing him. She then smiled before jumping on Kaylen. He hugged her while she kissed all over his face.

"I got a ring, too!" Jayla said, pushing her small palms into the couch and leaning towards her parents. Elle smiled before looking at Jayla and touching the small ring that dangled from a thin, white gold chain around her neck.

"That's beautiful, boo," Elle said.

"Daddy got it!" Jayla said. Elle nodded before leaning over and kissing her nose.

Ava watched them and smiled. Elle and Kaylen were always like a dream to her. Even through their obstacles, Ava knew what her best friend had was raw, unconditional love. She thought back over her relationship with Sunny and although he stayed down, she knew there were times he wanted to leave and had done so in the past. She wondered would she ever be as confident in them as Kaylen was in him and Elle.

She could say that in most times of panic, he stayed or eventually came back around. Ava knew her life was a mess and she needed Sunny to be someone whose first thought wasn't to step back, but to step up and help her clean it.

Ava groaned as Angel fought her, totally against the orange and yellow dress that Ava picked out that Sunday morning. It was the beginning of the New Year and Ava was not optimistic about it at all. She was leaving for New York soon, but planned on telling Sunny about her ghost writing deal and didn't know how he was going to take it. She had slacked on their church attendance at the end of the year, so she wanted to start off right. Angel was making that very difficult.

"I wanna pick!" Angel shouted.

"Angel Na'mya, we don't have time for you to pick your clothes today," Ava said, pulling Angel to her. "Stop before you get hurt."

Angel tested the waters and she kept struggling. Ava quickly popped her twice on her thigh. Angel's nose scrunched up and her movement halted, allowing Ava to get the dress over her head. Angel began crying, but Ava sucked her teeth at her daughter's dramatics.

"Ava, Sunny's here!" Bri yelled. Ava smiled before pushing Angel's white baby doll shoes into her hand.

"Go ask Sunny to put your shoes on." Angel gladly accepted her escape and ran off. Ava sighed before going to her room to finish getting ready. She frowned to see Bri in her bed.

"Get out!"

"Your bed was closer than mine," Bri mumbled into Ava's pillow.

"You need to get up and go with us."

"Ugh!" Bri said in irritation. A minute later she slid out of Ava's bed and stalked out of the room. Ava smiled before putting her shoes on.

"We're going to be late," Sunny said. "What you do to my baby?" he asked. Ava rolled her eyes.

"Don't start."

"I'm not trying to argue with you baby, especially since you leave tonight." Ava just nodded. She was catching a red eye to New York and coming back Tuesday. Of course, Sunny thought it was for work again. "I hope they promote you soon, since they keep sending you off."

He was standing a little close now, so she could smell that faithful CK-One before she actually took a look at his church attire. He was semi-casual, but his jeans went well with his dress shoes and button down.

"You're looking pretty handsome, Santana."

"I'm sure."

Sunny laughed as Ava rolled her eyes and walked past him out of the room. Ava picked her phone up and her heart dropped when she saw the date. It was exactly a week away from the anniversary of the rape.

"What's wrong?" Sunny asked from behind her.

"Huh?"

"You stopped moving," he said. Ava turned her neck to look at him and then down at Angel, who was also looking at her.

"I'm good, let's go."

Ava tried to stay engaged in her conversation with Angel about children's church on the ride. Angel had been so excited about it since the first time she went. Sunny's eyes shifted from Ava to the road and Ava prayed that he wouldn't ask her what was wrong again.

Ava was more upset than anything. No matter how much she thought it was easier to deal with, there were always these little triggers that threw her off. First it was the nightmares, then LaDanian coming back in town and now the anniversary.

"*I can't win for losing,*" she thought.

As soon as she walked into church, Ava ran into Zemira.

"Hey Ava!" she said, smiling. "Good morning, little momma."

"Hi Z!" Angel said. Ava smiled, her spirits somewhat lifted already.

"Zemira, this is Sunny. Sunny, Zemira."

"Nice to finally meet you," Zemira said. Sunny returned her greeting. "I have to run something downstairs, do you want me to take Angel to Lissa's room?"

"You want Zemira to take you downstairs?" Ava asked, bending down to Angel's level. When she nodded, Ava kissed her forehead. "I'll come get you in a little bit."

Ava and Sunny waited until Angel skipped down the stairs with her hand in Zemira's.

"You cool with that?" Sunny asked. Ava looked at him to think about what he was asking. It was obvious that Ava was very protective of Angel. She had been since she found out that she was pregnant. At the time, Angel was the only reason that Ava even regretted her suicide attempt… Angel and Sunny.

"I trust her," Ava admitted. Sunny's eyes got large and Ava laughed as she led him into the sanctuary.

"Shut up, I'm not that bad."

"Baby, don't lie in church."

Ava shook her head and smiled, trying not to say anything else. They found Charity and Rico and took a seat next to them as the service began. Ava sighed as her thoughts swarmed around like bees. She wasn't prepared to deal with the anniversary, not prepared at all. Something that happened so quickly had this everlasting affect on her life and she hated it. Ministers and therapists alike always told her to focus on the positive in the rape, which was Angel. She was Ava's focus, yet it killed her to admit that some days she felt it wasn't enough. Angel would always be a constant reminder that Ava's past allowed men to believe they could degrade her and treat her like an animal. Angel would always be a connection between Ava and Romero from that night. No matter how much light Angel provided Ava's life with, there would always be darkness surrounding it.

Throughout the service, Sunny seemed too comfortable. This was the second time he'd been to church with her due to his schedule, but Ava couldn't help but note the difference between when she first started going and when Sunny started. Ava remembered Sunny saying he was brought up in church, but she didn't really know what that meant.

Ava closed her eyes for a moment when the choir began to sing their second selection, realizing that she hadn't been focusing on the service. She hated going to church and not feeling as if she had learned anything. It was such a different experience than she was used to. Ava hated learning in school or sitting for long periods of time, but this was different. She never cared about school. Ava always felt it was pointless for life. Church, however, made her feel like she was becoming a better woman and mother for Angel; slowly but surely.

Sunny laced their fingers together during closing prayer and Ava felt a tug at her heart. It wasn't like the good ones Ava usually got when he showed affection. This tug actually hurt. Ava knew it had to be guilt.

"You can head to the car," Ava said. "It'll only take me a second to get Gel."

Sunny nodded before heading out the door with Rico and Charity. Ava made her way to the room where children's church was and smiled to see Angel waiting at the door with a picture in her hand.

"You're getting better with your coloring, love," Ava said, grabbing a hold of her hand.

"I practiced!"

"I can tell. What you learn?"

"You have to tell the truth!"

Ava's heart dropped at Angel's quick response.

"Huh?" she asked, while opening the front door of the church.

"You said when I lie about breaking stuff it hurts your feelings. When we lie, God's feelings hurt."

Ava's throat felt dry as she searched the parking lot for Sunny's car.

"Did you know that Momma?"

"No I didn't baby, so you taught me something, too."

That made Angel smile and drop the subject. Ava was relieved. Once they got near the car, Sunny got out and helped Angel in the back. Ava got in the passenger seat and waited for Sunny to pull out of his spot.

"Sunny, don't lie!" Angel said.

"What?"

"She learned why she suppose to always tell the truth," Ava said. Sunny nodded in recognition.

"I don't lie, baby," Sunny said. "That's why Mommy loves me so much."

"Ew!" Angel said. Sunny laughed, but Ava didn't.

Early that next morning, Ava was beside herself as she and Dre exited the JFK airport towards the lot that held their rental car. It was cold, but Ava didn't care. She had never been to New York and she hoped to see all she could in the next 48 hours.

"I hope you drive better here than at home," Ava joked. Dre sucked his teeth before getting into the car. Ava kept quiet, expecting a witty comeback but it never came. "What's wrong?"

"Tired," he mumbled, but his tone was loud enough for Ava to get the point. She buckled her seat belt and turned to look out the window. She wanted to see all the buildings, but ended up falling asleep on the way to the hotel. Dre woke her up when they arrived and she called

Sunny and Angel to let him know she was safe. She had to be more careful since she planned on telling him the truth soon. He rushed her off the phone anyway, because he and Angel were playing the Wii, but not before telling Ava to buy him a New York Knicks hat.

"We don't have much time," Dre said as they walked down the hall to their rooms. "We have to meet them at noon so be ready in thirty."

"You need a hug or something?" Ava asked, frowning at Dre. He shook his head.

"Not from you."

Ava sucked her teeth while sliding the key card into the door. She unzipped her bag and found the warmest thing she packed. She knew Dre would have a fit about the black and white Timberland boots she was going to wear, but her number one priority was to keep warm. The coldest it had gotten in Hamilton in a while was mid 50's and the hotel television was reporting high 30's. She pulled out a pair of dark denim jeans and a white, thin turtle neck sweater. After making sure she had everything laid out, she took a quick shower and got dressed. She met up with Dre in the lobby and they headed to the studio.

"So tell me about the artist," Ava said, now in work mode.

"You have similar styles, he wants a club hit but he's better at ballads."

"Is there any others sitting in?"

"Nah, he's really particular, says he wants to co-write with you and no one else. So only him, the producer and you."

"And you?" she asked.

"Not the whole time," he said. Ava sighed. "You got it."

"You know I don't like being around unknowns," she said. Dre smirked.

New York traffic showed them no mercy. They barely made it to their session on time. Ava looked at the small building with mild disappointment. It looked to be in a neighborhood instead of a business community and it was only two stories. It didn't have a parking lot, so Dre parked across the street. Ava zipped up her coat and followed behind him into the front entrance.

"What's the guy's name?" Ava whispered, realizing she didn't know it. She wasn't sure if Dre heard her ask him or not, but he didn't respond.

"Dre and Ava for Studio C," he said to the receptionist. Ava rolled her eyes, annoyed with Dre's attitude. The receptionist looked at something on her computer screen before handing them two electronic passes. Ava slid the black lanyard around her neck, while Dre used his to let them in.

The inside definitely looked better than the outside. It was clean, professional, and expensive looking. Ava tried to peak in the door to Studio A, but the small window was too high up. She sucked her teeth, following up behind Dre and into Studio C. The quietness of the hallway was completely washed away when Dre opened the door.

After her eyes adjusted to the dim light, Ava took everything in. It looked like a studio on television. She never learned much about the mechanics of a soundboard, but she had learned to tweak things in order to make something sound better. There were two guys at the board with their backs to Ava and Dre. They seemed to be mixing the beat they were listening to because it kept looping. Ava glanced at the back profile of the guy sitting nearest the booth. Something about him was oddly familiar, but since she didn't know anyone in New York, she brushed it off. That was until Dre pushed him in the shoulder.

"What's good, cousin?"

Ava frowned as both men turned around in surprise. She stood frozen as Omar smiled at her, but greeted his cousin.

"Can't believe y'all on time," he said. "How you doing, miss lady?" Omar stepped towards Ava and she quickly stepped back. He laughed.

"This a joke?"

"Ava," Dre said, sternly. She cut her eyes at him, definitely not in the mood to hear his voice. The other guy cleared his throat and smiled.

"How you doing, Ava? I'm Lean."

"Nice to meet you," she said, shaking his hand. "Please tell me you have another artist coming in." Dre and Lean laughed.

"Naw baby, just me. I'm a big deal around here and I got you hired on this project, so play nice."

Ava's nostrils flared as Lean and Dre moved over to the soundboard.

"Why Omar?"

"Because we got great chemistry," he said. Ava sucked her teeth. "Don't play, you know we flow tight in the booth."

"We do sound good together," she admitted. "But I don't sing anymore."

Omar smiled. "I know."

Ava sighed, hating the way that Omar kept smiling at her. She instantly remembered when she'd seen him the day she and Sunny got back together after Sunny's mom passed. Dre had a barbecue and Omar had been overly flirty. It was the first time she'd seen Sunny get jealous.

Ava heard Omar had left a few months after because he'd gotten a development deal with a label, but didn't think it was true since she'd seem him at Dre's not too long ago. She loved his voice, always had, but his cocky attitude repealed her. She didn't take lightly to anyone disrespecting her relationship.

"This is ridiculous," she said, sitting on the couch near the wall, realizing she had been set up. Omar laughed, sitting next to her.

"Chill out and let's make this money."

"Fine," Ava said. "Why not?"

"Don't be stubborn."

"I said fine."

"I can't believe Dre didn't tell you. I mean, I told him not to, but I figured he would."

"Right," Ava mumbled. She'd already made up in her mind that she would have a talk with Dre later. She made him promise to take her to Times Square, so she'd wait until then. Now it was time to be professional.

Ava had to admit that despite Omar's obvious attempts to flirt, their session was great. Their chemistry was undeniable and as soon as Ava heard the music and Omar sang what he had, Ava could practically feel the song. It was a love lost type of song that Ava was used to him singing, but this time it was more emotion in it.

Ava watched him in the booth for a minute before tapping Lean on his shoulder.

"What's up?"

"Stop him real quick, I have an idea." Lean and Dre frowned. "Trust me!"

"What's up?" Dre said once the music stopped. Ava leaned over the board.

"Can you try the bridge in that falsetto you do?" she asked. Omar looked at her for a second and smiled.

"I knew you missed me," he said. Lean laughed and Ava sucked her teeth.

"Shut up and do it!"

Omar smiled, but did as told. Lean smiled.

"That, my friend, is a hit!"

"So how did all this happen?" Ava asked Omar as they sat in the lunch room at the studio. It was pushing into the late afternoon, but neither of them were tired. They'd finally got the song how they wanted, but planned for Omar to clean up a few parts after their break.

"I had to get out of Tennessee," he said. "My dream was too big for it."

"You don't get home sick?"

"Nah, didn't have much family besides Dre."

"How'd you end up in New York?"

"I was in love."

"Oh Lord!" Ava said and Omar laughed.

"With the city," he added. Ava nodded. "Something about it was calling. You seem different."

"How?" Ava asked. Omar shrugged.

"Just do."

Ava left the conversation alone and continued to eat her food. About ten minutes later, the door opened and a man walked in. He had a muscular build, but he didn't seem that tall. He had African-American features, but held a foreign look as well. Everyone in the room took heed to him, letting Ava know that he was very important.

"Who is that?" Ava whispered.

"The boss."

"Omar, how's the session going?" the man asked as he reached the table.

"It's going well, Mr. Taylor," Omar answered, standing up. "Especially since I have my little hit-maker here."

Mr. Taylor had a curious smile when he looked at Ava.

"Welcome to T Suites," he said.

"I'm Ava Daniels," she stood reaching to shake his hand. Ava and Omar both frowned when he pulled his hand back.

"Is that a joke?"

"Why would it be?"

"Because there is no way in hell that the little whore that tried to ruin my son's name is standing in my studio."

Ava immediately stepped back as if someone pushed her and she began to recognize the features in Mr. Taylor's face that she couldn't shake. With his smugness on full display, Ava was surely squaring up with LaDanian Taylor's father.

Twelve

"So he just put you out?"

"Barely let me get my stuff, Bri."

"That's too ignorant," Bri replied. "I knew dude was boogie."

Ava sighed and shook her head. She was sitting outside of a bar and grill with a perfect view of Times Square. The heater next to her table blocked the winter air as the busyness of the street actually calmed her. After being thrown out of the studio, all Ava wanted to do was get home to Angel and Sunny. She couldn't remember being so embarrassed. Not even in high school when everyone teased her about the guys she slept with.

She almost resorted to her old ways. Mr. Taylor started talking about the trial and how Ava tried to run his son's life and take his money. That wasn't what she wanted. Ava didn't even want the trial, it had all been Bri's idea. All she wanted was Angel and when Mr. Taylor questioned that all she wanted to do was bash his face in.

"That's messed up, twin," Bri said. "What Dre say?"

"I'm not even trying to hear it," Ava said. "Dude knew whose studio it was."

"That's all bad."

"Cheer me up."

"Let me tell you how wild your kids is, bro!" Bri said. Ava was already laughing. She knew that Angel liked to test people.

"What she do?"

"We were talking about Dr. McStuffins right?"

"Really Bri?"

"Shut up, the show is awesome," she said. "Anyway, Charity comes in, all pregnant, trying to join the conversation." Ava laughed at how animated Bri was. "This kid says, 'this is a A-B convo so C your way out."

"Man, did you whoop her?"

"I couldn't!"

"Why not?"

"Because she was right! A for Angel, B for Bri and C for Charity."

Ava laughed, definitely feeling more homesick by the second. "She's too smart for her own good."

"Your fault."

Ava glanced out of the corner of her eye and saw Dre walking towards her. She sighed.

"I'll see y'all tomorrow night."

"Yep!" Bri said before hanging up.

"I got you clam chowder," Dre said. Ava nodded and took the cup of soup from him. "You want to talk about it?"

"Not really."

"Can I at least explain?"

"You can do what you want," Ava said, sipping the soup carefully. Dre sighed before turning towards her.

"I'm sorry I put you in that position. It was messed up, but I didn't want you to miss out on this opportunity."

"That wasn't your decision to make, Dre."

"You're too calm right now," Dre said, nervously. Ava just stared at him. "I messed up. I would never intentionally hurt or embarrass you. I care about you too much to do that."

Ava's heart softened a little at the sincerity in his voice, but the tone scared her. She was still upset, but now confused.

"Dre, don't…"

"Ava, I'm a man," he cut her off. "I respect you and dude and I know my cousin has a little thing for you, but somewhere down the line I fell for your crazy self."

Ava leaned back in her seat and looked out towards the traffic in the street. She thought back over the years that she had known Dre. She tried to remember a time where Dre's behavior or attitude would have given off his true feelings. Only thing she could recall was them bickering and playing around like brother and sister. Ava wanted to laugh. It wasn't fair that she had to keep dealing with things like this. She looked at Dre, who was watching her to gauge her reaction. Right now, she didn't have one.

"We should go," Ava said. Dre sighed. "We have an early flight."

Dre opened his mouth to speak, but Ava glared at him before he hunched his shoulders in defeat and nodded.

Ava was glad to be home. It had been a long eighteen hours. Ever since Dre confessed his feelings, she hadn't spoken one word to him. She was beyond mad. Ava couldn't understand why he would ruin what they had like this. Everyone in Hamilton knew how Ava was about Sunny and no one could change that. Why did Dre think he could?

Ava was tired by the time she got home, but Rico and Angel running around made her curious as to what was going on.

"What's up?" Ava asked, confused.

"Momma!" Angel said. "Papi finally not alone!"

Her excitement and Ava's confusion made Rico laugh. "We're having a boy!"

"Thank God," Ava said, while hugging Angel. Rico laughed harder.

"How was it?" Rico asked. Ava's eyebrows raised and she dipped her chin to look up at him. "That bad?"

"And beyond."

"Wanna talk?" he asked. Ava just shook her head.

"Just want to hug Gelly and sleep."

Rico looked at her for a second, as if examining her, before nodding his head and walking out. Ava wasn't sure of herself at the moment and that was one thing she desperately hated. Too much confusion made her numb. For the next couple of days, Ava was on autopilot. She'd only written a few songs and with the deadline to turn them in approaching, she became anxious. She hadn't seen Dre since the New York trip and had no idea what to expect.

She tried to push it out of her mind as she headed to Elle and Kaylen's with Angel to plan Sunny's birthday trip in a couple weeks.

Ava swerved when Angel's headband flew past her face and landed on the dashboard.

"Little girl!" Ava yelled, but focused on the road.

"Sorry," Angel whimpered as Ava reached back and thumped her leg, giving her the headband. "Don't take it off again!" Ava demanded.

"It's too tight!"

"You been stretching it out!" Ava said. Angel began to whine as Ava pulled into her usual parking space in the lot. After turning the car off, Ava eyed Angel through the rearview before getting out and opening the back door to get her out. Angel slyly slid out of the seat belt and her booster seat and down on the pavement in front of Ava. She looked up at her with those big, brown eyes but at the moment, Ava wasn't falling for it.

"Get to walking!" Ava said, pointing towards the steps. Angel stuck her bottom lip out, but did as she was told. Ava followed behind her. When Elle opened the door with Baby Kaylen on her hip, she frowned.

"Gel, what's wrong?" she asked while moving to let them in.

"Mommy thumped me!" Angel said. As soon as she saw Sunny on the couch, the show began. Angel stuck her lip out further and began pushing out tears. Sunny opened his arms and Angel ran into them.

"What she do?" Elle asked, laughing a little at how extra Angel acted around Sunny. "Swear she acts like Jay!"

"She almost killed us throwing her headband past my face."

"And you definitely can't drive anyway," Kaylen said, from his stretched out position on the love seat. Ava rolled her eyes before sitting next to Sunny.

"I'll get her, baby girl," Sunny said to Angel. "Go play with Jayla."

Angel nodded and ran off around the corner.

"She's been trying me all day. Romero wants her for the week. I might go on and let her go!" Ava vented.

"Go where?" Elle asked in shock.

"Yeah right."

"I'm serious," Ava said, defending herself.

"Well, why don't you just wait until we go out of town?" Elle suggested, rocking Baby Kaylen. "It's already the first."

"I want to go to Atlanta," Sunny said. Ava thought about her ghost writing deal. "Or St. Louis."

"Well pick!" Elle said.

"Ava, when you went down to the A did you have fun?" Kaylen asked. Ava looked at him for a second before shrugging.

"I was in meetings most of the time," she said. Sunny eyed her for a second before nodding.

"We all been there," Elle whined. "Let's go to St. Louis."

"I'm glad it's your birthday," Sunny said, sarcastically. Elle smiled.

"St. Louis it is!"

Baby Kaylen began to cry and Elle told Kaylen to feed him. Ava reached for him.

"Let me do it," she said. Elle handed him over. "Boys are so much easier."

"You want one?" Kaylen asked in amusement while handing her the bottle. She opened her mouth, but Sunny cut her off.

"Your bro is celibate," he told Kaylen. Elle looked at him and laughed. Ava's jaw dropped.

"What's that have to do with it?"

"You ain't getting none?" Kaylen asked. Sunny shook his head.

"Ava saved now," Elle said smiling, proud of her best friend. Ava nodded as if it were a question.

"You need to be going to church with her," Kaylen said. Elle frowned. "You a heathen."

Sunny laughed. Ava shook her head and continued to feed the baby. Elle swung and hit Kaylen in his chest. "See!"

"Shut up! We all about to go, how about that?"

"Bro, how long you doing that for?" Kaylen asked.

"Until someone decides to marry her!" Elle said, glaring at Sunny.

"Don't rush him!"

"See what you started," Ava asked Sunny. All he could do was smirk and shrug his shoulders. "That's why you about to be old!"

"So 26 is old?" he asked, laughing.

"Yep! Over one-fourth of a century." Ava laughed at her own joke before burping Baby Kaylen. Sunny slid a little closer to her on the couch.

"We going out of town with them, but it's my weekend with you," he whispered. "You know that right?"

Ava looked at the seriousness in his expression and her insides warmed. She nodded in understanding. They hadn't spent much time together lately and it was all her fault again. She swore to herself that when they got back together she would never lie to him again. Their break-up after he found out about the rape had been hard on her. She wasn't happy that he ran, but she understood.

And here she was, lying to him again.

The rape had been different. Back then, Ava was lying out of habit. She thought no one would believe her because of her past decisions with men. She hadn't even believed it when it happened. In fact, she'd already had sex previously with three of the four who raped her. She first lied in disbelief, but once she found out about Angel, she lied for survival.

Sunny believed her story about being jumped over some girl's boyfriend. He walked away from Ava for months when he found out the truth. If he walked away again, Ava feared it would be for good.

And it would be all her fault…again.

Ava thought it was very cliché that the first thing she saw in St. Louis when she woke up was the Arch. She had only been to St. Louis once before. She and Bri were around seven. Rico had to come for 'business' and Kita heard that the shopping was amazing. Granny Ran wouldn't watch Ava and Bri so they had to tag along. They spent most of the time in the mall with Kita.

"How far are we from the hotel?" Sunny asked. Ava looked to see Elle next to her and Sunny driving.

"Hey there, sleeping beauty," Elle said when she noticed Ava was finally up. "Angel called you."

"Already?" Ava asked. Elle laughed and nodded. Ava sent Romero a text and asked was everything okay. He replied that Angel got upset because she couldn't have her ice cream before dinner. Ava sucked her teeth. She called Romero instead of replying.

"She's getting out of control. Did you whoop her?"

"Bye Ava," he said, before hanging up. She was about to call him back, but they pulled up to Hotel Lumiere.

"Why we not going over there?" Elle asked as they passed the Four Seasons Hotel that was connected to the casino.

"Because you don't have a job," Sunny joked. Kaylen glared at him and tried hard not to laugh.

"Too soon, bro," Elle said, looking out of the window. Once Sunny parked in the gated lot, they all got out. Ava and Elle walked ahead while Sunny and Kaylen got their things.

"I thought it would be colder," Ava said, pulling her coat closed but not zipping it up. Elle looped their arms together and grinned. Ava looked at her sideways and laughed. "What?"

"Just excited to get a little break," Elle replied. Ava nodded. She was too.

After they checked in, they headed up to the third floor where their conjoining rooms were. Kaylen grabbed Elle's arm.

"We'll catch y'all in a couple of hours," he said. Elle laughed, but Ava covered her ears.

"Ew."

"Mind your business, bro. We married over here."

Ava rolled her eyes before following Sunny into their room. After she looked around, Ava sprayed the bathroom and put Fabreeze on the bed and couch. Sunny shook his head.

"Really babe?"

"You saw that show on hotel maids just like I did!"

Sunny licked his lips before pulling Ava to him. Ava stood still as Sunny ran his hand down her cheek and across her collar bone. She smiled when he kissed her shoulder.

"What you get me?" he asked. Ava smiled.

"You'll see tomorrow."

"All weekend is my birthday," Sunny said. "You ain't know."

Ava laughed while caressing his cheek. "Sunny, you know I love you right?" she asked, looking into his eyes. He nodded.

"I know you do," he said. "And because I love you, I'm going to act like I don't know you're hiding something."

Whatever Ava planned to say went right back down and fell into the pit of her stomach. She opened her mouth, but closed it as Sunny leaned in and buried his face in her neck and inhaled deeply. Ava swallowed any thoughts of crying when he pulled her tighter to him. She sighed and hugged him back.

"Sunny…"

"Don't," he said, the bass in his voice vibrating against her skin. "Just let me enjoy my birthday."

Ava nodded, rubbing his back as she did so. "What you want to do now? We don't have to wait on them."

"I know you want to get in the pool."

"Only if you do," she said. Sunny nodded, leaving Ava to dig through her bag to find her swim suit. She kept thinking to just tell him and get it over with. She'd grant his birthday wish and hold it in until they got home.

Ava laughed as Sunny picked her up once she had her suit on. She grabbed a towel on their way past the bed. Sunny didn't put her down until they got by the elevator. They walked around for ten minutes before going to the front desk.

"Where is the pool?" Sunny asked.

"It's actually in the Four Seasons, but we can give you access cards to it."

"What?" Ava asked. "We have to go across the street to the pool? In the cold?"

"Yes ma'am."

"What type of foolery is this?" Ava mumbled, turning around. Sunny laughed.

"Would you like an access card?"

"No thanks," Sunny said. He grabbed Ava's hand and headed back to the elevator. "Stop being so mean."

"How do they not have a pool?" she questioned. Sunny shrugged and kissed her shoulder. "I can cool it and take a nap. I'm straight." Sunny said when they entered the room again.

"You sound like Daddy," Ava said, before mocking him.

"Yeah?" he asked. Ava laid on the bed next to him. She nodded.

"Old man."

"You lucky we being good or I'd show you how old I am."

Ava just laughed before going to take her swim suit off. When she came out, Sunny told her to call Elle back before he went to sleep.

"What's up?"

"This dude sleep!" Elle said with an attitude. Ava laughed and told her Sunny was too. "Let's take the whip and find a mall."

"I'm down, I'll meet you in the hallway," Ava said, looking around for her brown boots. She pulled them from her bag, but one fell and hit the ground.

"Stop making so much noise!" Elle said. "Hurry up!"

Ava laughed before hanging up on Elle and sliding her phone in her back pocket. She slipped her boots on, grabbed her coat and wallet and went out the hotel door to meet Elle. Once they got out to the car, they realized they had no idea where a mall was. Ava shook her head as Elle laughed.

"Go to the map on your phone and type in malls," Elle instructed her as she turned the key in the ignition. "Hurry up before they wake up."

"Calm down, G," Ava said. "Go out the parking lot and turn left."

"Am I getting on this highway?" Elle asked. "70 West?"

"You gotta get up there first!"

"Shut up and don't get us lost!"

Once the pair made it to the St. Louis Galleria, they parked in the Macy's parking lot. Ava hated shopping in her coat, so she took it off and threw it in the backseat.

"You're going to freeze, bro."

"The door is two steps away, Kaylen," Ava said, calling Elle that for using the annoying nickname he had given her. Elle laughed while getting out of the car and telling Ava that she was going to be sick. Ava told her that she'd be fine before running towards the door. She could hear Elle laughing behind her. Ava smiled, suddenly glad to get some alone time with her best friend so that she could talk to her about what Sunny said in the hotel room earlier. Ava had enough sense to at least tell Elle what was going on. She hesitated in filling her in, though. She didn't want Elle to be in the middle when Sunny found out, but like the best friend she is, Elle always kept Ava's secrets.

"Look! Momma just sent a pic of Jayla trying to feed Baby Kay," Elle said, cooking over her children. "She thinks she's his momma."

"At least she likes him," Ava said. "I don't think Gel will do well if I had another one."

"You want more?"

"I wouldn't be mad," Ava said. Elle nodded as they continued to shop. Ava wandered into a book store and made her way to the religious section. She wanted to get Bri a New Living Translation Bible. Ava knew if she bought Bri a King James Version, she would get frustrated and never read it. While she was looking, she noticed a book called, "I Declare," by Joel Osteen. The name sounded familiar, like she'd heard it at church before. Ava got that and a book by T.D. Jakes.

While she was checking out, Elle walked into the store with a frown on her face.

"They're up," she said, pointing to her phone. "We haven't been gone that long, chill out…you shouldn't have gone to sleep, Kay!" Elle whined. Ava smirked as she walked past Elle out of the store. Elle followed her and they left out to head back to the hotel.

The rest of the trip was pretty flawless. Sunny got everything he wanted for his birthday. Ava bought him a gift certificate to get the automatic starter for his car and an outfit. Elle and Kaylen bought him shoes and the girls attempted to make him cards. Most of it was scribble, but they did manage an "A" for Angel and a "J" for Jayla.

Ava knew it was time to come clean to Sunny that following Sunday of the week after they got home. He had gone to church with her again and Angel had just come back from Romero's house from staying the night before.

Angel had been real clingy when Ava tried to leave her in children's church, she gripped Ava's neck and began to cry. Ava didn't like keeping Angel in the sanctuary because she got antsy, but today she just lay on Ava's chest and went to sleep. Ava just figured that Angel must have been coming down with something.

The sermon that day was about resolutions. Since it was February, people usually began to lose motivation with their New Year's Resolutions. The pastor equated that to lack of spiritual strength. Ava felt her heart twist when he mentioned that lying was something that weakened the spirit. He said it was why so many relationships were broken and why no one truly let go of sin. Even little white lies counted.

 Ava couldn't help but cry while the congregation praised God. She could feel Sunny's eyes on her and it made her cry more. She knew that she had to tell Sunny today, but in her heart she feared the worst. Ava could still feel the pain from when he left once she told him about the rape and Angel four years ago. How could she go through that again?

 Ava exhaled slowly before she tried to clear her mind with a prayer. She never really knew how to pray, but there was no way she could get through her emotions on her own.

 "Lord, I know I caused this and I pray that You can forgive me. I was sure it was the right thing to do and now I see what my lies have done in my life. I want this to work out to my desire, but I'm learning that Your will is better." Ava kept her head down after her silent prayer.

 After church, Sunny carried Angel to the car and Ava followed behind them slowly. She watched him put Angel in her seat and her little head fell sideways against it.

 "You hungry?" Sunny asked after they were in the car. Ava shook her head. Sunny looked at her for a moment before starting the car. He drove for a few minutes before he sucked his teeth. "Start talking."

 "Now?" Ava asked, looking in the backseat to see if Angel was still sleep. When she turned around, she caught Sunny's glare. Ava sighed. "I need to apologize to you first," she said, willing herself to not even think about crying.

"What for?"

"For not being the girlfriend you deserve," she replied.

"I don't deserve you."

"Ava," Sunny said, gripping the steering wheel. "Don't give me a reason to hate you."

Ava's eyes grew wide, but she kept her cool. "I've been lying to you."

"You been creeping?"

"I said lying, not cheating. You know better."

"Obviously, I don't."

"Can you just let me talk?" Ava asked. Sunny's jaw tightened, but he nodded slowly. "Last year, Dre set up this ghost writing deal for me to be able to write for artists without my name being attached, which is more money."

"And?" Sunny asked when Ava took too long to continue.

"Well, I was actually out of town with Dre for assignments when I went to Atlanta and New York," she blurted out. "Not for work."

"So you been out of town with another dude and told your man it was for work?" Sunny asked.

"It wasn't like that."

"I'm saying, you couldn't tell me the truth in the first place it must have been something you needed to hide."

"Santana, I wouldn't do that," she sighed, pushing her head back into the head rest.

"I don't know what you would do. Apparently, you like to lie a lot. You keep doing this and its making me wonder why I'm making all these changes for you and you KEEP lying!"

"What changes?" Ava asked.

"I'm not even about to keep talking to you right now. I don't know what the hell you on."

"I didn't sleep with him!" Ava yelled. Sunny just shook his head. "I know you don't trust me right now, but I wouldn't do that."

"You had no reason to lie," he mumbled, still shaking his head. He pulled in front of the house and parked. Ava sighed.

"Sunny, I lied because I wasn't sure how the deal would go. I didn't want to travel much, but it seemed like the only thing I could do to get my foot in the door."

"None of this shit adds up to why you should be lying to me!"

"Can you please calm down?"

"Nah, we through talking." Ava leaned back, his words hitting her chest. Something inside of her said just go in the house. She quickly got out, pulled Angel from the backseat and made her way up to the lawn. She let Angel walk in first after she unlocked the door, happy that Bri was gone and she beat Rico and Charity home. Angel went into her room to play and Ava went in her room.

Instead of taking her church clothes off, Ava lay on top of her bed and opened up the book by T.D. Jakes that she bought on their trip to St. Louis.

Charity smiled before spooning ham fried rice into her mouth. Rico was lying at her side, talking to the baby. Ever since they found out that the baby was his junior, Rico began talking to her belly a lot more.

"He's going to be a boxer," Rico said. Charity frowned.

"A boxer! Why?"

"You know how much they make?"

"Everybody ain't Mayweather, Papi," she said, laughing. Rico just smiled.

"He'll be better."

Charity saw the change in Rico immediately and she could do nothing but thank God. After he got shot she felt so helpless, but after attending weekly prayer service for a month, she began to feel peace.

When they found out they were having a boy, Charity knew that Rico accepted Jesus. That night, Charity heard him whisper that God had given him everything he ever wanted. She could hear the surrender and appreciation. For that, she was grateful.

"I need some hot sauce on this," she said, looking down into her box of rice. Rico sucked his teeth.

"You had hot sauce on your eggs this morning."

Before Charity could respond, Angel slowly walked around the corner.

"Papi, I'm scared of the monster."

"What?"

"She's been having bad dreams the last few days," Charity explained while putting her food down. "Come here, baby girl. You wanna talk to Uncle?"

Angel nodded with her bottom lip poked up. Rico picked her up and put her in between him and Charity. She curled into Charity's side and placed her small, right hand in the middle of Charity's belly and her head on the side of her chest.

"Will Uncle be your favorite?" she asked Rico. He leaned over and kissed her cheek.

"He'll be my favorite boy. You'll always be my favorite girl."

That made Angel smile.

Rico watched Angel for a second, noticing that her behavior was off. Even though she had just gotten up from her nap, she was more quiet than usual. Rico made a mental note to ask Ava when she got in from work.

It had been a few days since Sunday and Sunny had made no efforts to talk with Ava. She felt like she was having déjà vu, except this time she wasn't pregnant.

She and Sunny had gone through too much, but she had to respect his space. Ava realized she didn't have to lie. She hadn't trusted her man to *be* her man. She hadn't even told him the whole truth about Dre's confession. The only thing she could do now was try to fix it.

"Bro, you want to know how he's doing?" Elle asked. Ava sighed as she drove towards Dre's house. She talked to her lawyer and since she hadn't gotten any advances, only money for the work she'd done at home and New York, she wouldn't be penalized for breaking her contract. Ending this with Dre definitely wouldn't be easy, but his confession left her no choice.

"No, I don't," Ava finally answered. Elle sucked her teeth.

"I wish y'all would just get married already," she said.

"He don't want to marry me."

"Ava, shut up! That's stupid."

Ava sighed as she pulled up to Dre's. She told Elle that she would call her back and hung up before she could respond. When Dre let her in, all he said was, "what's up," and walked into the kitchen. Ava closed his front door and followed him. He was stirring something at the stove.

"What you cooking?"

"Beef steak. You eat?"

"Yeah."

"What's in the envelope."

Ava dropped it on his table. "You know what it is."

Dre put the spoon down and turned around. "You really about to lose this opportunity over something petty?"

"How are we supposed to move on from this?" Ava yelled back.

"Man, why you gotta be so emotional?"

"You serious right now!?" Ava asked, almost laughing. "You come at me with some secret feelings you kept for years and I'm the emotional one?"

"It hasn't been years," he mumbled. Ava sucked her teeth.

"Dre!"

"What will it take for you to reconsider," he said, stepping close to her. Ava backed up a little.

"The deal, or you?" she whispered. Dre looked her up and down before stepping closer. Ava froze.

"Can I just kiss you once?" he asked. "Please?"

Ava shook her head, but no words came out. Her heart rate rose as she tried to think of what to do. Just as Dre's lips touched hers, Ava's cell phone interrupted the moment and gave her a welcomed distraction.

She frowned at the unknown number, but answered anyway to get Dre out of her face.

"Ava…can you hear me?"

"Ro, what's wrong?" she asked, but he didn't respond. "Romero!"

"You gotta get to the hospital, man," he slurred. Ava could tell by his tone and the pounding of her heart that something was wrong with her baby.

"What's wrong with Angel?" she asked, picking up her keys and rushing out of Dre's house.

"They…Ma took her to the hospital," Romero said, his voice cracking. "I don't know."

Ava's throat tightened as she got in the car. "Why don't you know?" she asked. "Why aren't you with her?"

"I'm at County."

"You're at County," Ava repeated. "What did you do to my baby?" she screamed as she began to drive a little faster. Romero tried to talk, but Ava heard someone in the background tell him that his time was up before the call was disconnected. Ava screamed before calling Rico.

"Daddy, Ro did something to my baby!" Ava cried into the phone.

"Calm down, I can't understand you."

"My baby in the hospital. I have to get to her," Ava said. "I have to get to her."

"I'm on my way!"

Ava threw her phone down and made a quick right into the emergency entrance. She pulled up in the front of the building, pulled her keys out and jumped out of the car.

Ava felt like her legs would give out any moment and she could feel herself shaking. When she neared the reception desk, she all but fell into it.

"Angel Na'mya Daniels."

"And you are?"

"Her mother, please just tell me where my baby is."

"Right through that door in Trauma One."

Ava pushed the door open and looked around until she saw Romero's mom, Sarah.

"Ava," she started, but Ava shook her head before pushing past her and into the room.

"No, no, no! This is not happening!"

Angel had a bandage around her head and her tiny left arm. She was hooked up to a breathing machine and it looked like she had a cut under her eyes. Ava's feet felt like bricks as she pushed her hands together in front of her to try and stop the shaking but to no avail.

"Gel," she whispered, finally making it to her side. "Mommy's here. Gelly, get up please?"

Ava put her head on the bed as the nurse came in to speak with her. "We had to sedate her. She was in so much pain." Ava felt her knees buckle. "Her arms is broke and she took some pretty bad blows to the face."

"Oh my God!" Ava said, leaning over Angel carefully. "Baby, Mommy is so sorry, love… I'm… God please!"

"We'll know more when she wakes up."

Ava heard the door open. She glanced at Sarah before wiping her face and looking back down at her helpless four-year-old.

"Why would he do this?" she asked. She heard Sarah gasped.

"Ava, Romero didn't hurt her. He loves her to death and he would never do this! He doesn't even whoop her!" Ava looked up at Sarah in confusion. "Melody did this."

Thirteen

It had been two hours since Ava made it to the hospital. Everyone was there and Angel wasn't up yet.

Elle and Kaylen dropped the kids off with Miss Janet and Bri cut her study date short.

"Twin, you been shaking since I got here. Let me get a nurse."

"No!" Ava snapped, looking through the window into Angel's room. She was waiting for them to finish her tests so she could go back in. She glanced at Sunny, but then turned back. She was glad he was there for support, but also glad that he hadn't tried to talk to her yet.

Sarah stood up and walked over to Ava. Ava looked at her as she handed her the phone. Ava sighed before taking it.

"What happened, Ro?"

"How's she doing? Is she up yet?"

"Tell me what happened!" Ava yelled. Romero sighed.

"Angel was sleep and we were chilling in my room. Angel had been fussy all day, but I knew she was getting over that cold. Ma came in and asked me to go with her to pick up the new grill. Since Angel was sleep, I asked Mel to watch her. Man, we were only gone thirty minutes!" Ava could hear the rage in his voice. She stayed silent. "When we got back…I could hear my baby screaming from outside. When I saw Mel swing back and hit her and Gel was bleeding…I lost it."

Ava started crying again and since Elle was the closest to her, she moved closer to hug her. She gave the phone back and just cried while she heard Sarah clear Ro's name to everyone else. The doctor announced Ava could go back in. She quickly wiped her face and jumped out her seat.

When she entered the room, Angel's eyes were open and Ava could see the fear in them. She rushed to keep her from moving so that she wouldn't pull any of her IVs out.

"Mommy," Angel cried. Ava carefully got in the bed and held Angel as best as she could.

"I'm here baby."

Ava knew that her family wanted to see Angel and make sure she was okay, but she needed a little time with her alone. She had never been so scared in her life. Her fear had quickly turned into hate for Romero's girlfriend. Once she made sure that her baby will be okay, she wanted to finish what Romero started.

Every time a story about a little child being molested or beaten to death came on the news it made Ava cringe and they often talked about what would happen to the suspect once they got to jail. Ava would never understand what would possess someone to hurt a child, especially *her* child.

She wondered what Angel did that caused Melody to snap. If Angel was asleep when Ro and Sarah left, it couldn't have been much. Ava wondered how often Ro left Angel with Melody and if this was even the first time that Melody put her hands on Angel. Ava was seeing red by now. Her body heat rose as she carefully laid Angel back in the bed since she had fallen asleep. She slipped out of the bed and by the time she got to the room door, Ava thought of ten different ways to kill Melody. Then it clicked....

There was only one hospital in Hamilton. Melody had to be there.

Ava walked out of the room and everyone looked at her. "Charity, can you go sit with her? She's sleep now, but I have to check on something."

Charity frowned, but nodded. Ava took off down the hall, looking at the name tag on each door in the trauma department. She heard Rico behind her, asking her what she was doing. Ava's shoes made a squeaking noise when she finally found what she was looking for. She turned the knob and pushed the door open with force.

Melody tried to scream as soon as she saw Ava, but it was too late. Ava already had her fingers pressed to Melody's throat.

"I'll kill you for hurting my baby!" she yelled, looking directly in her eyes. "Huh? You thought you would get away with it?"

Melody's machines began beeping, but Ava didn't let up until she felt arms around her and a voice behind her demanding her to stop.

"Let her go, Ava!" Rico said. "Angel doesn't need both her parents in jail!"

That made Ava's loosen her grip and allow Rico to pull her out of the room. Ava kicked and screamed, trying to get back in.

"She tried to kill my baby!" Ava cried. Rico pulled her into his chest and held her close.

"She's fine," he assured her. "Angel's fine."

"I want her dead!" she cried. Ava began to struggle a little more, but Rico held her tight until he got back in front of Angel's room. He pulled Ava in front of the window as everyone else looked on in silence. Rico reached around and roughly grabbed Ava's chin.

"Look!" he said. Ava watched Charity slip Angel's hand into her own as she bowed her head in a praying position. "That's what you focus on! She is the only thing you think about right now, you hear me? You thank God that your daughter is alive and focus on making sure she knows she is loved unconditionally and that this isn't her fault!" Ava slumped over and cried, shaking her head.

"I can't," Ava mumbled.

"You don't have a choice!"

Ava whimpered. "Why did this happen to my baby? I was the one lying!" she said. Sunny looked up, but didn't say anything. "She wasn't supposed to be hurt."

No one knew what to say. Bri was shaking with anger and was almost contemplating running to Melody's room while Rico was holding Ava.

Elle looked at Sunny and nodded towards Ava. He frowned.

"What?"

"You ain't that mad!" she said.

"Babe, stay out of it," Kaylen said. Elle shook her head.

"You ain't," she repeated. "And even if you are, now ain't the time."

Sunny sighed heavily while running both hands down his face and trying to push his own feelings aside to focus. Even though he wasn't talking to Ava, Rico was right. Everyone's focus needed to be on Angel and Sunny knew he was the one who could get Ava to pull herself together. He got up and walked over to Ava and Rico.

"Come walk with me, shorty." Rico let Ava go and she followed Sunny around the nearest corner. When he pulled her in for a hug, Sunny had to admit that he missed her. He was just tired of Ava not opening up to him with all of her trust.

"I'm not strong enough for this," Ava mumbled into his chest. Her body was still shaking.

"Then who is?" he asked. Ava didn't reply. "Love, you're the strongest person I know."

"My baby didn't deserve this."

Sunny rubbed her back before he began to pray. It wasn't a long prayer, but Ava's heart rate slowed down and she began to breathe regularly. Sunny let Ava get her thoughts together before moving her from his embrace to look at her face.

"You good?" he asked. She nodded before turning to get back to Angel's room.

It had been three days since Angel had been in the hospital. Ava took off from work and hadn't left her side. Melody was still in ICU and Romero was facing attempted murder charges. Ava had to focus on Angel.

"Did you bring Doc?" Angel asked, trying to scratch her arm through her cast. "If not, we gotta go."

Ava laughed. "Yes, Ti-ti B packed Doc and you'll leave when your real doctor says you can."

Angel sighed dramatically while Ava got off the bed to get the bag of toys that Charity brought over on her way to work. She got the Dr. McStuffins toy out and handed it to Angel. Someone knocked on the door and Ava smiled to see Jayla stick her little head in.

"Gel, look who's here!"

"Hi Jay!" Angel said, waving. Jayla smiled. Ava looked up at Sunny before bending down to pick Jayla up and put her on the bed with Angel.

"Remember like yesterday, not too rough okay?" the girls nodded. Ava sat in the chair next to them and Sunny sat in one by the door.

"When can she leave?" he asked.

"Tomorrow," Ava said, scratching her scalp through her messy bun. Sunny nodded. The awkward silence that followed made Ava uncomfortable, so she moved her chair closer to the bed and played with the girls.

WHEN ALL ELSE FAILS

The last few days had been horrible. Ava thought her nightmares were bad, but her heart broke every time Angel woke up from a bad dream or cried out in pain. She had been praying non-stop and now that Angel was recovering, things were looking a little better. Sunny came every day after work to bring Jayla to see Angel, but he and Ava didn't really talk.

The girls played until it was time for Angel to take her medicine. She was sleep within minutes after that. Once everyone was gone, Ava read her Bible until Romero called.

"How you doing?" she asked.

"I'm not even thinking about this place," he admitted. "How's my baby?"

"Medicine has her tired a lot," Ava said, watching Angel toss a little in her sleep. Romero sighed. "What?"

"The lawyer wants to talk to Angel. Said it would help my case."

"She's too young to testify."

"I know. They just want a statement. I don't want her going through that."

"You're her dad," Ava stated. "You were trying to protect her."

"I should have known something was up," he went on. "She got so quiet around Melody, but I figured she just wasn't feeling her."

"I don't want to talk about her anymore."

"I heard they moved her."

"They needed to."

Ava knew she would have tried to go back down the hall if they hadn't. Romero chuckled.

"I'll call in a couple of hours to see if she's up."

"Okay."

Ava made a mental note to call Ro's lawyer in the morning before she stretched out on the couch.

Even in her sleep, Ava couldn't rest. Knowing she was lying on a couch in her baby's hospital room was not helping at all. Ava sat straight up on the couch and narrowed her eyes to get a good look at Angel in the dim light of the room. Her eyebrows were low and scrunched together and her lips were moving. It took Ava to see Angel gripping her cast for her to realize that Angel was having another nightmare.

Ava removed the thin blanket from her legs and rushed over to the bed just as Angel cried out for her and Romero. Angel even cried out for Sunny.

"I'm here, Gelly," Ava said, scooting into the bed with her. "It's just a bad dream, baby."

Angel pushed her face into Ava's chest and cried. Ava rocked her and rubbed her back, all while holding back tears of her own. Their night went on that way until Angel woke up for breakfast.

Ava was exhausted when Pastor Davidson and Zemira walked through the door, but she forced out a proper greeting. She hugged them both before helping Angel with her food. Since she was left-handed, Angel got frustrated that her cast was keeping her from doing things as she normally would.

"How is everything?" Pastor Davidson asked. Ava sighed, ready to vent and comforted by the fact that she felt close enough to him to share her thoughts with no filter.

"She's frustrated, I'm exhausted and I don't even want to think about her D-A-D's situation right now."

"I know that spells daddy," Angel said, picking at her food. Pastor Davidson chuckled and Zemira shook her head with a smile.

"Stay out of grown folks conversations, little girl."

Angel rolled her eyes and went back to eating. Pastor Davidson laughed before putting his hand on Angel's cast and holding his other hand out for Ava to take. Zemira placed one hand on Ava's shoulder and the other on her uncle's. Zemira hummed a little before Pastor Davidson began to pray. He started off with a softer voice, but was soon speaking in tongues as his boisterous voice launched off the walls. Ava felt a little awkward. She had never "had church" outside of church, but she began to hum as well and after Pastor Davison said, "Amen," she and Zemira sang together.

Ava hadn't realized her eyes were closed until she opened them and saw the two staring at her and smiling.

"What?" Ava asked. Angel went back to playing with her food.

"Girl, you just blessed me with that voice!" Zemira said, obviously hype to finally hear Ava sing for real. She laughed in embarrassment.

Pastor Davidson looked at Zemira and nodded with a smile. "She's good."

"What are you two up too?" Ava asked. Zemira gave her uncle a look and she nodded.

"There's a mother down the hall," he said. "I'll be back."

Ava kept her eyes on Zemira.

"So, I need your help."

"On what?"

"I know you told me that you've never written gospel before, but we harmonize well together, so I could really use your help flushing out this song I'm writing for someone. It's a duet, so I need another voice." Ava just looked at her, so Zemira took a breath and continued. "I can come to your place so you won't have to drag Angel out."

"…What about the track?" Ava asked. Zemira slowly smiled.

"It's on my phone."

"Okay, fine!" Ava laughed as Zemira squealed and hugged her.

"Thanks Ava! I promise that I owe you big!"

Once Angel was released from the hospital, things went back to as normal as they could. Ava wasn't used to dealing with Angel without Sunny and Ro and it made her appreciate them both. However, since she had been clinging to Angel, Ava didn't mind much.

She was getting updates on Melody's condition from one of Charity's co-workers, only because Ava knew that once she was released, all the mess would start. Ava was pressing charges on Melody, but Melody's family was pressing charges on Ro.

Ava thought since Ro was only reacting to Melody hitting Angel that he should be okay. Her lawyer informed her that a crime was still a crime. With the severity of Melody's injuries and Ava's rape case on his record, it wasn't looking good. Ava became upset with Bri all over again. She was the one who forced the issue of the rape back when it happened and nothing came out of the ordeal. It wasn't even Ava's idea and even though she dropped the charges, her lawyer assured her that the defense would bring it up to prove Ro's violent behavior is repetitive.

Ava kept praying, trying not to get stressed about that or Sunny. Her focus had to be Angel.

A few days after Angel's release, Zemira kept true to her word and came over to work on the song.

"Angel, I brought you something," she said, handing Angel a bag. Angel used her right hand to separate the flaps and peek into it. She smiled to see a coloring book inside.

"What you say?" Ava asked.

"Thank you, Miss Z!" Angel said, slowing pulling it out as if it were fragile. Ava made sure she was good in her room before taking Zemira into her own room.

"So I know you've never written a gospel song, but this is more of like a love song to God. I'll play the track and sing what I have so far until you catch it okay?"

Ava nodded as Zemira tapped away on her phone before a smooth tune came through its speaker. Ava immediately felt it and began to bob her head. Zemira smiled victoriously while passing Ava a piece of paper. She hummed a little before actually singing.

"What we have, they can't call superficial. 'Cause this love, is only unconditionally. I'm not scared, don't have nothing to fear. Because I got God, and He'll get me through it all, it all."

Ava could feel each word twist at her heart. The words were so simple, but it moved her in a way that made Ava believe that this was what she was supposed to do with her talent. She was scared, but something inside of her pushed her to harmonize with Zemira once she repeated the words.

Ava noticed that Zemira was giving her the same look from the hospital the other day.

"What is that look for?" Ava asked. Zemira sighed.

"Do you know what having an anointed talent means?" she asked. Ava shook her head. "Our job as Christians is to win lost souls for the kingdom of God right?" Ava nodded, remembering having heard that at church. "Well, He gives us all talents that we can use to win souls if we allow Him to anoint that talent."

"I get it," Ava said, slowing nodding. Zemira smiled.

"You my friend, have an anointed voice."

Ava frowned a little, wondering why Zemira would say that. Ava felt so disconnected to God at times, how would anyone be won over by her voice? Ava put her head down and sighed.

"Hey, what's wrong?" Zemira asked.

"I just don't think I'm worth that much," Ava mumbled. Zemira looked at her and then sighed.

"Can I tell you something?" she asked. Ava nodded. "You were there when I first came back to church right? Well, Pastor was so happy because he knew how hard it was for me to come back. My mother and I have a very damaged relationship. Once I left for school I had no intentions of ever coming back. Not only was I forced in that private school, but I had to deal with her alcohol problems and her boyfriends and girlfriends."

"Dang," Ava blurted out. Zemira nodded.

"She distanced herself from the church because of her preferences and her brother being the pastor. She wouldn't even let me go. Her and her boyfriends constantly beat me up until I was 18."

"Nobody helped you?"

"What could they do?" Zemira asked. "I blamed myself for speaking up the first few times and nothing happened and I got it worse. After a while I just never said anything. I just made my plan to leave."

"Why?"

"I didn't speak up when I had the chance. After a while, I thought that was love. I didn't think differently until college."

"We all deserve real love," Ava mumbled, thinking of Sunny. Zemira nodded and smiled.

"I didn't know real love until I started singing gospel music. At first I didn't get it. Why were these people crying and carrying on just because I was singing? Then one day, I felt it."

Ava sat up straight. "Felt what?"

"I was singing and all of the sudden I couldn't hear anything and then God spoke to me. It was so clear and I'll never forget it."

"What did He say? Do you really hear His voice like people say?"

"Yeah," Zemira said. "He said He loved me."

"That's it?" Ava asked. Zemira giggled and nodded. Ava looked up when Angel crept into the room, trying not to be seen. Ava smiled and motioned her over. Angel moved slowly to her side.

"You want to hear a song, mini?" Angel nodded. Ava pulled her into her lap, but frowned when Angel tensed up.

Ava and Zemira sang the song while Ava rocked Angel to sleep. Ava cried while looking down at Angel. Zemira put her hand on Ava's arm.

"I just don't know what to do to help her though this!"

"Pray about it and love her like you do. I'm here if you need me," Zemira assured her. Ava nodded, realizing that she'd found her second true friend.

Fourteen

Romero was being held at the same jail Rico had been held. It hadn't changed much since the last time Ava was there. That was five years ago when she told Rico that she was pregnant and didn't know who the father was.

There weren't many people in the visiting area, but she waited nearly thirty minutes for them to yell, "Colby!" and bring Romero out. Ava laughed at his scruffy facial hair and the wild curls growing. He rolled his eyes while picking up the phone.

"Shut up," he said. "Where's my baby?"

"I'm not bringing her in here."

"Well, I don't want to see you."

"Cute," Ava said, sucking her teeth. "I just left your lawyer's office. They asked for the emergency reports on Gel's hospital stay. They say it might help reduce your bail."

Ro looked at her for a second and then nodded. Ava thought he looked kind of cute with the curls, almost like the little boy that used to annoy her in school.

"Did he say anything else?"

"Wouldn't tell me anything since I'm not related." Ro swiveled on the stool and sighed.

"Best case scenario is aggravated assault."

"Worst case?" Ava asked after he was silent for a moment too long.

"Attempted murder."

Ava sighed and tried to get her emotions in check, but it seemed like all she had been doing the last few weeks was crying.

"This just ain't happening."

"Ava, stop it."

"I can't raise her without you," she admitted. Ro's eye widened in shock.

"You ain't about to raise her without me, stop talking crazy. Melody is out of the hospital. She just bruised up! Ain't no jury going to send me to jail for what happened. We see it on the news all the time. A man killed his daughter's rapist and got off free. What did they expect me to do?" Ava looked at him, trying to take his words as assurance. "I'm not stressing, don't you stress."

"She's acting different," Ava said. "Not listening and being extra stubborn. Zemira said that's normal for kids in Gel's position, but I don't know what to do."

"Who is Zemira?"

"A friend from church."

"How she know what's normal for a kid in Gel's position?"

"Just does."

"Yeah okay," he said as the officer on duty told him that his visit was over. "I know you don't want her in here, but I really need to see her soon."

Ava nodded. "I'll think about it." Ro rolled his eyes before getting up. Ava smiled, glad that Ro seemed okay despite the circumstances. She sighed when she glanced at her phone and saw she was going to be rushing to get to work on time. She had been getting migraines at work lately. She would be fine all day until she clocked in. Charity said that was how she felt right before she decided to go to nursing school. Ava didn't know what that meant.

For the next couple of hours she had to deal with customers with broken phones. Her and her co-worker hadn't been able to take any breaks. When she heard the bell ding again, Ava looked up and sighed when she saw Kaylen and Sunny walk in.

"I need a new phone, bro."

"You just got one."

"I broke it."

Ava shook her head while pulling up his account on her sales rep's computer to give her the sale.

"You want the same one?" she asked. Kaylen nodded. "Told you to get insurance. Give her your ID." Ava went to the back to get a new phone out of inventory. She opened the box and pulled it out while walking back out front. She noticed Sunny was gone.

"Where he go?" she asked, putting the battery in the phone and sliding the back on.

"To the car so y'all can talk."

"What?" Ava sucked her teeth. "I'm at work."

"Oh, Katie already said it was cool," Kaylen said. Katie laughed when Ava side eyed her.

"Girl take your break, you know you miss your man."

Ava rolled her eyes, but walked out to Sunny's car anyway. She walked slowly, going over her responses to what she assumed he would say in her head. Ava reached for the passenger door and sucked her teeth to see that it was locked. She heard it click and then she tried again. Sunny was laughing when she got in.

"That's not funny."

"Chill shorty, I was just messing with you," he said coolly.

"You think that's appropriate right now?"

"I miss you, man," he admitted. Ava sucked her teeth harder. "I can't miss you?"

"I been three places the last two weeks; home, church and work. Can't miss me that much if you know where I been and haven't seen me or Gel."

"I seen her."

"What? When?"

"When I'm off and you here."

"That's foul."

"You jealous?"

"So what you plan on doing about us, Santana?" Ava asked, ignoring his question.

"You forget you the one that messed up?" he asked, side eying her. Ava huffed.

"Please don't do this," Ava said.

"You did it to yourself."

"So we aren't going to discuss it 'cause you want to be petty?" Ava asked, narrowing her eyelids and glaring at him.

"We ain't talking about it because your little ass doesn't know how to tell the truth!"

"Don't cuss at me." Sunny's nose flared, but he apologized and sighed. "Sunny, I said I was sorry, what do you want from me?"

"I want you to grow up! I want you to fully trust me. I want you to believe that if I'm your man that I got you and you don't need to trip."

Ava put her head down and groaned. "You're right," she admitted.

"Have I given you reason to doubt me?" he asked. Ava sighed, but shook her head. She looked out the window and she could see Kaylen rushing to the car. "Go on back to work."

Ava just looked at him for a moment. Part of her wanted to stay, argue, and punch him in the face. He barely talked to her in weeks. Even though she had been busy making sure Angel was okay, it still hurt. She huffed before swinging the passenger door and hopping out of the car. Kaylen stopped the door with his hand.

"Guess that didn't go well."

"Bye!" Ava snapped before jogging back into the store front. "Don't let them in anymore." Katie laughed.

"Diveno is kind of cute," she said.

"And married to my best friend," Ava replied, sitting down at her desk. Katie giggled and threw her hands up.

"Chill girl. I saw the ring."

Ava shook her head before getting back to work.

When Ava got home that evening, Granny Ran was there.

"Long time, no see," she said. Ava tried hard not to roll her eyes, but spoke before heading to the kitchen. Bri was leaning against the counter eating dry cereal in a bowl with a frown on her face.

"Why your face like that?"

"'Cause, man!" Bri said, rolling her eyes. "She been getting on my nerves since she got here. Ain't came the whole time Gel was hurt, now she wants to show up talking mess!"

Ava smirked in times like these when she and Bri had twin thoughts.

"I'm not even worried about her," Ava said, taking a handful of Bri's cereal. "Where's Gel?"

"Time out," Bri said. "She broke her remote."

"How?" Ava asked, frustrated that they couldn't really discipline her now without feeling guilty.

"She said she got mad because some show went off," Bri said. Ava sighed. "You need to talk to her."

"Alright."

Ava went up to her room to change into a pair of shorts and an old tee of Sunny's before going into Angel's room. The first thing Ava noticed was a massive head of curls. It had taken her an hour to do Angel's hair in braided ponytails the night before. Ava shook her head, noting Angel's position in the middle of her bed. She had her feet tucked under her little body as she tapped on a small toy in her lap.

"You supposed to play with toys in time out?" Ava asked, stretching across the foot of the bed in front of Angel. Angle poked her lip out.

"Ti-ti said one toy only."

"Tell Mommy what happened."

Ava frowned when Angel shook her head. "Why not?"

"I don't want to see Melody."

"Why do you think you have to see her?"

"When you get mad and take me to Daddy's, she always there." Ava sighed before lifting Angel's chin.

"Listen to Mommy, okay?" Angel nodded. "You will never have to worry about Melody hurting you again. Me and Daddy are very sorry that we let that happen."

"It's okay."

"You still love me?" Ava asked. Angel smiled.

"Always." Angel giggled when Ava gave her a bear hug.

"Thanks baby. That made Mommy feel a lot better."

"So I can get off time out now?" Angel asked. Ava looked towards the ceiling and rubbed her chin.

"No," Ava said. Angel pouted and fell back against her pillow. "You can watch your movie though." Ava laughed before getting up and leaving the room.

"*I should go pray,*" Ava thought. She stopped in the middle of the hallway, turned back around, and went back into Angel's room. She had started watching a movie, so she didn't pay attention to Ava when she kneeled next to the bed to pray. She was only praying for a few minutes before she heard Charity yelling downstairs. Ava sighed before getting up to see what was going on, closing Angel's bedroom door behind her.

"Get out!" Ava heard Charity yell again before she made it downstairs.

"Charity, that's my mom!" Rico said. Charity shook her head while pacing.

"I don't care, she will not disrespect my family in my house anymore," Charity began to cry. "I'm sorry, I can't."

"Baby, why are you crying?" Rico asked. "Ma, what did you say to her?"

"I didn't say anything that wasn't true!" Granny Ran said. "She shouldn't be so sensitive. It wasn't even really about her."

"Lord!" Charity cried out.

"Charity come in the kitchen with me," Ava said, gently grabbing her arm. Rico and Bri continued to argue with Granny Ran, but Ava was more concerned with Charity and her baby brother.

Ava helped Charity sit down at the kitchen table. Charity was shaking, Ava could see her hands as she flexed them against the table. Ava hurried to the fridge and got Charity a bottle of water. She sat next to her as she got her breathing together. They listened in silence as the muffled voices from the living room came into the kitchen. It was far enough away that they couldn't make out the words.

"You okay?" Ava asked. Charity wiped her nose with the back of her hand and shook her head.

"Son is kicking like crazy right now," Charity mumbled. Ava laughed before reaching out to touch the top of Charity's belly.

"Bro, you gotta chill," Ava said. Charity laughed while wiping her tears. "We good out here, I got this."

"He really listened to you," Charity said, laughing. Ava nodded.

"We see each other," Ava said. Charity swatted her hand away and drank from the bottle of water. Ava allowed her a few more moments before talking now that she wasn't crying. She caught a few words from Bri in the background. If it sounded like Granny Ran said what she thought, Ava was going to be just as mad as Charity was two seconds ago. Probably more so.

"What she say?"

"She said you never should have been a mother," Charity said. Ava's blood immediately began to boil. Her leg began to shake and her left hand fisted. "And the same thing she always says about me not being able to take care of her son and now there would be another kid she'd need to raise."

"She didn't raise us!" Ava yelled. Charity shook her head. "I'm so tired of her! She been talking mess since Papi went to jail. My mother never did anything to her! My baby never did anything to her!" Ava began crying from being so upset.

"Ava, I'm sorry. I shouldn't have told you," Charity said. "Please calm down."

"Why does she even come around here?" Ava asked, feeling herself getting emotional. Granny Ran had been criticizing them since day one. She never liked Kita, never cared for Charity. No one was good enough for her son; even after all the dirt he did.

"It's not our battle to fight," Charity said. Ava sucked her teeth.

"Charity what are we supposed to do? Just let her keep getting away with it. He lets her do this mess all the time!"

Charity grabbed Ava's hand and put her head down. She took a few breaths before looking back up at Ava.

"When we made a choice to be saved, we made a decision to let God handle everything in our lives. A lot of times, when we first start out, we don't really know what that means. It took me a while, and as you can see I still don't always get it right, but this is a perfect time to witness."

"Witness to what?" Ava asked, a little frustrated because she felt like Charity was talking in circles. "You want to let her win this argument?"

"It's not about her winning, but in a way, I have to let it go and probably apologize to her."

"Now you're crazy," Ava said, shaking her head. Charity smiled and threw up her hands.

"Hear me out," she said. Ava crossed her arms and sat back in her seat. "Your grandmother is bitter. She's bitter because the only man she could keep around was her son and when he got his own family she felt like she lost him. She tries to run off the women he loves that aren't her. In the end, because she's so bitter and unforgiving, he'll chose us whether we push that or not and she'll still be bitter. She'll be upset and angry and harbor that in her heart until she decides to let it go."

"That's the truth," Ava mumbled.

"But if we develop a hatred for her and don't forgive her for acting out of her bitterness, what more will that say about our character than hers?"

"Wow," Ava said, more to herself than Charity. She never wanted to be compared to Granny Ran and Charity's comment made her realize how much like her grandmother she was acting.

"When all else fails," Charity started. "When everything we tried to do on our own ends up broken and irreparable and every avenue of self trust we have is completely gone, God shows us that He would have gotten it right in the beginning. That He could fix all of this, but

He's just waiting for us to say, 'Okay God, I give up!' People like Granny Ran are not even looking for a way out of bitterness because they are just so used to it or they are tired of trying to find a way out and failing. We have to show them that we know what works the first time."

Ava sat in the kitchen while Charity went back into the living room and apologized to Granny Ran for telling her to get out. Ava could hear a pin drop in the living room.

The next couple of days, since Sunny still wasn't talking to her, Ava helped Zemira work on songs for the choir. Some of the new members of the church were complaining about the music being boring, so Zemira was trying to find ways to liven it up, but still keep those who wanted the old hymns sung every Sunday happy.

"Z, I don't think you'll be able to make everybody happy," Ava said, as she tried to remember the cord Zemira taught her on the keyboard. They were in the sanctuary and since it was empty, it was easy to hear Ava's mistakes. She cringed when Zemira laughed.

"You right about that," Zemira said. "But I think that duet we worked on would be a good start."

"I thought that was for someone else?" Ava asked. Zemira sighed.

"It is, but they want to hear a recorded version with a choir behind it," Zemira said. "You'll sing it with me?"

"At church? On a Sunday?" Ava asked. Zemira laughed at Ava's facial expression.

"Where else?"

"Z, I don't really sing no more."

"You don't sing secular music anymore," Zemira corrected her. "You never did this."

"Is it really that different?" Ava asked. Zemira bit her lip while looking around the church.

"When we were writing the song, how did you feel?" Zemira asked. "Honestly."

"I felt peace mostly," Ava said. "It made me feel like I could zone out and just be."

"Did it feel like that before, when you were singing R&B?"

"Yeah I guess, but it wasn't as deep," Ava admitted. Zemira smiled.

"There's the difference."

Ava laughed. "I'll think about it."

Truth was, a part of Ava was excited to sing again. She'd felt nothing but love and acceptance since she started going to the church. There were a few girls who seemed to eye her sideways and that even doubled when Sunny started attending with her, but that was definitely something that didn't bother her at this point in her life. They'd even taken up a collection for her when Angel's hospital bills got out of hand last month, so Ava was sure she'd sing the song with Zemira.

She'd just let her sweat a little before telling her that much.

"Girl, did I even teach you this?" Zemira said, playfully pushing Ava's hand off the keyboard. Ava laughed when her cell phone began to ring. She looked at it, and upon seeing Elle's name, immediately realized she was late for her dress fitting. She jumped up and threw her phone in her purse. "What's wrong?"

"Elle is going to kill me," she said, running out. "I'll call you later!"

"She's here, calm down," Miss Janet said as Ava ran through the door of the bridal shop. She prayed all the way on the twenty minute drive, that she made it ten, that she wouldn't get pulled over. Elle crossed her arms and huffed in Ava's direction.

"I'm so sorry, G," Ava said, holding her hands up in a praying motion. "I love you. That dress is cute."

"I don't like this one and it's the second one I've tried on without you!" Elle said. Ava bit her lip.

"Well, I'm here now. Let's find one you like."

Trishelle and Kaylen were set to renew their vows early summer. Since she didn't get to wear a wedding dress the first time around, finding the right one was very important. Ava felt guilty that she had forgotten the appointment and knew she'd have to make it up to her best friend.

They were at a little bridal shop over in Jasper because Elle didn't like the one in town. They weren't going to do this traditionally. The only thing Elle was worried about was getting married in a church with a dress on. Miss Janet's pastor had agreed to it and they would have dinner at Miss Janet's afterwards.

Ava could tell that Elle was upset that she was late, so instead of trying to talk her anger down, Ava figured she would find Elle the perfect dress to make her forget about it.

"Elle, you still a six?" Ava called from behind a rack of mermaid style gowns.

"After two kids? Try a ten!"

"Don't say it like that."

"Like what? Like I'm fat?"

"Girl hush and try this dress on," Miss Janet said, pushing Elle back into the dressing room. Ava picked out three dresses and went to sit next to Miss Janet on the couch near the mirrors.

"How you been kid? I haven't seen you."

Ava sighed. "Just trying to get back in the swing of things."

"How's Angel doing?"

"She's good. All of her bruises have healed so I'm grateful for that."

Miss Janet smiled and agreed. "I'm proud of you for handling it so well," she admitted. Ava frowned in surprise.

"I ain't much to be proud of."

Elle came out of the dressing room with a straight face. She stopped short of the platform as she got a peak of the dress in the mirror.

"Nah," Elle said, shaking her head violently. "This is the worst!"

Miss Janet gasped as Ava laughed.

"Let me look at it," Miss Janet pleaded. Elle crossed her arms and pouted. Miss Janet sucked her teeth. Ava grabbed her three picks and stood up, following Elle back into the dressing room.

"Let me unzip it first," Ava said, moving Elle's hands away as she tried to take the dress off in a hurry. Ava laughed, but Elle rolled her eyes.

"You look just like Jayla doing that," Ava said, unzipping the next dress. Elle's face softened.

"How's Angel doing?"

Ava looked up before focusing on getting the dress undone. "She's adjusting."

"Still acting up?" Elle asked as she stepped into the dress Ava was holding.

"This one is better," Ava said. Elle nodded, saying they were getting closer before taking it off. "She's trying us a little, but Zemira says that is normal."

Elle cut her eyes at Ava in the mirror. "Umph."

"What was that?"

"How does Zemira know how Gelly should be acting?" Elle asked.

"Cause she been through similar stuff," Ava said. "Why you say her name like that?"

"Zip this dress up. How did I say her name?"

"Za-mere-ah, like you got an issue or something."

"I don't even know the girl."

Ava watched Elle as she scrunched up her face at the dress she had on and immediately began to unzip it. Miss Janet yelled for them to come out and Ava said they'd be out in a second.

"G, tell me your problem before I make you my ex best friend."

"Seems like you already did that," Elle mumbled.

Ava stopped helping her put the dress on and made her turn around. Elle stepped back and crossed her arms.

"You serious?" Ava asked. Elle just looked at her. "So I gotta tell you why you can't be replaced in the middle of a dressing room?" Elle looked Ava up and down . Ava sighed. "Trishelle Marie, you been my ride or die when no one else even thought to love me. You saved my life and you are stubborn just like me, but having KJ has made you soft. It is funny that you acting jealous right now though," Ava said, trying not to laugh. When a tear fell from Elle's eye, Ava felt bad. "Boo, why you crying?"

"G, you the only friend I got. Like seriously the only friend that's mine. I don't want to lose you to Sunny and especially not to another chick!"

"Ain't nobody ever going to take me from you. I put that on my life."

"I know," Elle sniffed. "I'm just emotional."

"Well, cry baby," Ava smiled. "Turn around and you'll have something to cry about."

Ava made Elle turn and face the mirror. She laughed when Elle covered her face and cried harder, this time it was more of a joyous cry.

"Momma," Elle said, picking the dress up and shuffling out of the dressing room to show Miss Janet the dress.

A week later, Ava woke up with good news for Angel. She took the day off and went shopping with Elle, Angel and Jayla. It was a couple of weeks before Ava and Bri's birthday, so she needed something to wear.

"Sunny taking you out?"

"Elle, you know as well as I do we aren't on good terms," Ava said. Elle sucked her teeth.

"Well, what are we doing?"

"I'm just going to church and probably out to eat."

"Cool, sounds like a plan," Elle said. "What time church start?"

Ava tried not to smile. "10:30." she looked down and saw two pair of feet sticking out from the circle rack of clothes. Ava held her hand out to get Elle's attention.

"Elle, have you seen those two little munchkins?" Ava asked loud enough for them to hear.

"I don't know, they were right behind me, but I don't see them anywhere." Angel and Jayla giggled.

"Well, we better leave then," Ava said. The rack began to move as both of them ran from under it screaming not to leave them. Each began to hug their mom's legs.

"Oh, there's my mini me," Elle said.

"You promised not to leave!" Angel said. Ava picked her up.

"I was joking baby, but guess what?" Ava asked.

"What?"

"Somebody wants to see you."

"Daddy!" Angel yelled, running up the yard as Ro ran out towards her. He dropped on his knees in the grass to meet Angel with a hug. Ava smiled to hear Angel giggle as Ro kissed all over her face.

His lawyer had gotten his bond reduced and Sarah posted it by selling his car per his request. Ro would still have to go to trial, but he wouldn't be stuck in jail while waiting.

"Daddy, you stay!" Angel demanded.

"I am, love," he said. "I promise."

Ro kept kissing all over Angel's face until Ava walked over with Angel's backpack.

"I'll be back in the morning."

"Take your time," Ro said. Ava laughed while getting back into her car.

Ava went home to an empty house. Bri was on campus studying for finals and both Rico and Charity were at work. Ava put her things down, grabbed a notebook, and went to sit on the front porch. She hummed a tune that Zemira composed a few days ago while writing some words down. She flushed out a verse before Sunny's car pulled up. Ava kept her position on the porch swing.

She watched him walk up, but looked back down at her notebook when he made it past the steps. He held back a grin as he sat next to her and pushed the swing with his feet.

"Ro got out yesterday," she said. "Angel's with him."

"I came to see my shorty."

"Your shorty, huh?" Ava asked. Sunny nodded. "Here I am. Where you been?"

"Working straight sixteens," he said, moving closer. "You miss me?"

"You still mad?" she asked. He shook his head. "Well, I am."

Sunny laughed. "I know."

"Nothing's funny," Ava said, cutting her eyes at him. He just kept smiling.

"I love you."

Ava closed her notebook and sighed. "I don't know what you on right now, but its not cute."

"You're cute."

Ava sucked her teeth. "Sunny!"

"Alright," he laughed. "I quit. Gimme a hug!" Against her will, Sunny pulled Ava to his side and kissed her forehead.

"You learn your lesson?" he asked. Ava nodded. "You gotta trust that I'm with you."

"And you have to stop running when stuff happens that you don't like," Ava countered. Sunny smiled when Ava held her left pinkie finger up to him. He wrapped his around hers before kissing their fingers that were intertwined.

"Deal."

Ava smiled before opening her notebook.

"You want to hear this love song I'm working on?"

"Love song?"

"To God." Sunny chuckled before nodding.

"Better be to God," he mumbled. Ava rolled her eyes and kicked his foot.

"I missed you a little bit," Ava admitted. Sunny licked his lip.

"I know."

"Really? I can take it back." Sunny laughed and Ava felt right in her world.

"Let me hear the song, goofy girl."

Ava sang her first verse and part of the chorus. The rest of her day was spent with Sunny while she worked on her song.

May 22, 2011

Ava held her laugh as she pretended to still be sleeping. She and Bri had fallen asleep in Bri's bed the night before. They were eating ice cream and reminiscing about past birthdays from elementary school. Ava woke up to the hushed voices of Angel and Charity.

"Slow down and don't make so much noise," Charity said.

"That's no fun," Angel said. Charity chuckled.

"Go on and wake them up."

Angel beamed with joy before jumping on the bed. She yelled, "Happy birthday!" before jumping on Bri first, waking her up. Ava laughed before grabbing Angel off of Bri and tickling her.

"Gel, you were supposed to get them first," Charity said, laughing.

"I tried!"

"And failed!" Bri said.

"Don't jump her," Charity said. "Come eat. Papi made breakfast."

"Can you believe we are 22?" Bri asked, cutting her pancakes. Ava shook her head, definitely not believing it herself.

"You look old," Ava joked to Bri. Rico and Charity laughed. Bri sucked her teeth.

"I look better than you!"

They all joked around and ate as Bri told Ava all the people that commented on her Facebook page, telling them both happy birthday. Bri had changed her profile picture to a one of them on their eighth birthday with Kita and Rico kissing their cheeks and smashing cake in their faces.

"Where you get that?" Ava asked.

"Daddy had it."

"Send it to my phone. You going to church with us?" Ava asked. Bri looked around the table and shrugged. Ava sucked her teeth.

"I need to go get my nails done."

"You can do that after church," Charity added. "Our service doesn't last long."

Bri bit her lip in hesitation and Ava knew she needed to bring out the big guns.

"Gelly, don't you want Ti-ti B to go to church with you?" Ava asked with a sly grin. Bri gasped in shock at Ava's sneak move when Angel's eyes lit up.

"Oh yes! Ti-ti can see my pictures on the wall!" she yelled.

"She'd love to see your pictures, mini!" Ava said before turning to Bri. "Wouldn't you, Briann?"

Bri narrowed her eyes at Ava before smiling at Angel. "Come help Ti-ti find something to wear." Bri hit Ava in her arm while getting up from the table and Angel followed her. Ava, Rico and Charity laughed.

"You ain't slick," Rico said. Ava shrugged.

"It worked."

The doorbell rang and Ava smiled.

"Must be Santana," Charity teased. Ava playfully rolled her eyes and got up to answer the door. Ava laughed when she saw two big teddy bears instead of Sunny's face. Ava grabbed one and let him in.

"Happy birthday," he said. Ava leaned over and kissed him.

"Thank you, baby," she turned towards the stairs. "Bri, Sunny bought you something!"

"Yay, presents!" Bri yelled back. Ava shook her head.

"Why aren't you dressed?" Sunny asked, putting Bri's bear down on the couch and handing Ava another bag with her gift in it. She already knew it was the two pair of shoes they picked out earlier that week.

"Charity and Rico cooked breakfast," Ava said. "Go eat while I get dressed."

They got to church a little late, and to Ava's surprise, Elle, Kaylen, Jayla and KJ were already there. Ava and Bri took Jayla and Angel down to children's church while everyone else went into the sanctuary. Ava could tell that Bri was uncomfortable, but kept smiling to save face in front of Angel.

Ava was elated that all the people she loved were there. During praise and worship, she couldn't do anything but thank God, especially for Angel's recovery. Angel saved Ava's life the day she found out about her. She had no clue what she would have done if Melody would have accomplished the unthinkable.

Ava's lawyer told her that Melody's trial had been expedited. They weren't required to be there due to Angel being a minor, but pictures of her injuries, Sarah's testimony and the doctor's reports were enough to charge her with battery and two counts of child endangerment.

Ava wasn't satisfied, but her lawyer said considering the fact that Melody wasn't pressing charges for the little stunt Ava pulled at the hospital, that she should be.

Ava smiled when the choir was introduced and Zemira got up. She could clearly remember that day in high school when she strutted into the auditorium with Elle to try out for the school musical. She was nervous and exited all at the same time. Ava's heart skipped a little when the choir's first selection was over.

"Before this next selection, I want to say a few words," Zemira said. "Today is a very special day for a new, close friend of mine and her twin. Let's all say happy birthday to Ava and Bri." the church clapped. "Ava has helped me a lot over the last few months and a lot of you don't know this about her, but her voice is crazy anointed."

"We know!" Elle and Bri said. Everyone laughed.

"So I'm going to ask her to come join me in this next song that we wrote together."

Ava exhaled as she stood up and everyone clapped encouragingly. When Ava got close enough, the musicians began playing the song and Zemira handed her a microphone. On her 22nd birthday, Ava closed her eyes, lifted the microphone and totally fell in love with Christ.

"You know you have to warn me when you sing!" Charity said, sniffling and wiping her tears away when Ava sat down. Ava giggled and told her that she was sorry. The deacons called for offering, so Ava reached for her purse that was between her and Elle. She looked at her and frowned.

"You good, G?" Elle kept looking straight ahead. "Trishelle."

"Huh?"

"You good."

"Yeah...I'm good."

Ava looked at her for a moment before getting her offering ready. Ava felt Sunny tap her thigh. He pointed up at the small sign behind the pulpit.

"Oh Lord!" Ava mumbled. Sunny chuckled as the sign called for the parents of Angel Daniels to report to the nursery. Bri stopped Ava from getting up and told her that she would get her. Ava knew Bri just wanted to leave out of the service, but she let her go anyway.

There was a guest pastor that day who spoke about outward appearance versus inward appearance. He even used a prop of an inside-out jacket. Stores display the outside because its pretty, but in reality, it serves no purpose to the functionality of the jacket. The real beauty is in the inside. The stitching is the hard work and the tag is a symbol of who made it. His metaphor was symbolic of the believer. A believer's tag should reveal they were 100 percent made by God. The stitching should show His good works. Everyone loved the metaphor and the display, especially Trishelle.

"G," she whispered to Ava. "Go up there with me."

"Huh?"

"I want to go up there."

'Up there,' was altar call and Elle didn't give her time to think. She grabbed Ava's hand and stood up. Ava followed her out of the pew and everyone began to clap. They got up to the altar and the pastor smiled.

"Ava, who do we have here?"

"This is my best friend, Trishelle."

"I saw you drag her up here, Trishelle." They laughed. "What brings you?"

Elle sighed. "Ever since I met this girl, she's been going through it. I've seen her go through so much and I love her like blood. I've never seen her this happy," Elle said, looking at Ava who was now crying. "I don't know much about God, but I know I want whatever it is that she has now."

A few people in the congregation clapped and said, "Amen," as the pastor began to pray for Elle and had her recite the sinner's prayer. Ava thanked God that she was able to be a testimony to the person who had helped her get through so much. She couldn't explain the feeling, but Ava knew that it felt right.

Fifteen

"I picked the wrong time to stop drinking," Ava mumbled, leaning back on Elle's couch. Miss Janet laughed as Elle sucked her teeth.

"Be serious, this is important!"

"Would you calm down, you act like you aren't already married," Miss Janet said.

"This is different and you know it."

It was the middle of June and Kaylen and Elle's ceremony was two weeks away. They were still having dinner at Miss Janet's, but since Elle joined the church on Ava's birthday and Kaylen joined a few weeks later, they were going to have the ceremony there. The girls were going over details and the menu when Ava realized that Elle was a crazy bride.

"I'm not going to play with you, Trish! I know how to cook!"

"Mommy, some of Kay's family is coming and you know your food is too spicy for them."

"Skip them!" Miss Janet said. Ava fell over laughing. "They shouldn't have so many health problems."

"Don't laugh at her," Elle said when Miss Janet went to the bathroom. Ava shook her head.

"She's funny, man."

"She's nuts, that's what she is."

Just like so many times before, the front door opened and Kaylen and Sunny walked in. Angel and Jayla were napping, so their welcome wasn't as exciting as usual, but that didn't halt the matching, goofy smiles on Ava and Elle's face.

"Little man knows how to wave bye!" Kaylen said, putting KJ's car seat down and unstrapping him. Elle sucked her teeth.

"No, he don't!" Elle said. With an annoyed look on his face from his wife not believing him, Kaylen turned his junior towards her.

"Wave at him."

Elle sighed. "Bye son!" She waved with her left hand. KJ looked at her and slowly lifted his hand. It stayed sideways as if he was saying come here instead of bye, but Kaylen smiled victoriously when Elle gasped and got teary eyed. Everyone else laughed at her reaction.

"Told you!"

"Y'all been gone two hours!" she said, reaching to take him from Kaylen. "Stop growing up so fast, son!"

"He's grown."

"He's only six months!"

"Stop crying," Sunny said. Ava moved closer to him when he sat down. When Sunny finally forgave Ava, she vowed not to keep anything from him. He had proven his loyalty to her and Angel and he deserved that much.

Elle and Kaylen began to argue about who taught Jayla how to talk.

"She said momma first," Elle argued.

"That don't mean you taught her to say it, babe," Kaylen said.

"Ugh, why would you teach her to say momma and not daddy?" Elle asked, her eyebrow raised.

Kaylen smirked. "I taught you how to say daddy."

Ava frowned. "Ew!"

"I'm done," Elle said, laughing. Miss Janet walked back in with her purse. "Where you going?"

"Away from you," she said. Everyone laughed. "Call me in two weeks!"

"I'll see you tomorrow!" Elle called after her.

"I'm just ready for the honeymoon," Kaylen said.

"Sis coming back pregnant," Ava said. Elle glared at her. "What?"

"I'll act like you don't see this baby in my lap!"

"Y'all agreed to three when we were younger," Sunny said. Kaylen nodded.

"Can I get son out of diapers first?" Elle asked. "Dang!"

Kaylen nodded. "I can deal with that." Elle looked at him and rolled her eyes. Ava's phone rang. Romero was calling.

"Hey, can I get Angel tonight?"

"Yeah, why you sound like that?"

"My lawyer got my sentencing moved up to tomorrow."

"What? Why didn't you tell me?"

"Didn't want you to trip."

"Ro, this is serious," Ava said.

"Don't trip. I just want to chill with her tonight… just in case."

Ava closed her eyes tight, not wanting to digest the weight of those last three words. "I'll bring her when she wakes up from her nap. I'm at Elle's."

"Okay. I got clothes over here."

"What's up?" Sunny asked.

"Ro's sentencing got moved up to tomorrow."

"You going?"

"Should I?"

"Might look better if you and Gel there," he said.

Ava nodded.

"Guess I'm going then."

Ava didn't really want Angel in court, but since she didn't have to see Melody and it benefitted Romero's case, she agreed.

Ava met Romero, Angel and Sarah outside of the courthouse. When they all walked in, Ro's lawyer smiled.

"You all are here!" he said. "Good."

"How's it looking?" Ro asked.

"Good," he said. "Them being here definitely helps. I will warn you all that Melody's family is here."

Ava rolled her eyes and pulled Angel closer to her side.

"It don't matter," Ro said, giving Ava a reassuring nod.

292

Sarah sighed. "We better head in."

They all followed the lawyer into the court room quietly since other cases were being heard in the open court. Romero bent down and picked Angel up as they walked in.

"You gonna be good and quiet for Daddy while we in here?" Angel nodded and Ro kissed her temple.

"I haven't been in here since Daddy got arrested." Ava whispered when they finally sat down.

"Was it bad?"

"To me it was."

Thirty minutes went by while they waited for Romero's case to be called. Angel got restless and ended up falling asleep.

"She looks more innocent sleep, anyway," Ro joked. Ava laughed and agreed. He finally got called and Ava was sure her heart stopped when Romero and his lawyer got up. She wondered if Angel was up, would she feel like Ava felt all those years ago when she saw them take Rico away in cuffs. Sarah moved closer to Ava and held her hand. It was a little awkward, but Ava said a silent prayer and tried to relax.

"Case 17641; Romero Colby versus Melody Shaw," the judge said. "Defendant has already been charged with one count of domestic battery and we are here for sentencing. Based on evidence of case and the victim's prior conviction against the defendant's child, I have made my decision. I am sentencing the defendant to 52 weeks probation, taking into account the six weeks served in temporary custody, which leaves a remaining 46 weeks, checking in every four. The defendant is also ordered to stay at least 100 feet away from the victim. Case dismissed."

"Lord, I was so worried," Sarah said, hugging Romero once they left the court room. He smiled and laughed in relief.

"I told y'all not to trip," he said, taking Angel from Ava. He gently poked her nose to see if she would wake up but all she did was swat his hand away and snuggle into his chest. "Let's go celebrate!"

"Y'all can go," Ava said. "I'll pick her up later."

"What? No!" Sarah frowned. Romero sucked his teeth.

"You going!" he said. "I'm buying."

"Fine."

Ava noticed within the next few weeks that Angel became a compete daddy's girl. Whenever Ava was off work, she had to practically beg Angel to come home. Although she missed her being around all the time, it did give her time to write and help Elle with the ceremony.

Ava was glad when the day came because Elle had gotten crazier as time passed. She had to admit that it was nice and intimate. Elle and Kaylen looked flawless. Ava felt a little guilty though, because all she could think about was taking pictures with Sunny and Angel. They hadn't been formally dressed and matching since her prom and Angel looked too cute for Ava to pass up the opportunity.

The pastor was very excited about them taking vows in front of God, especially since they accepted Christ as their Savior. Ava could tell their bond had deepened if that was at all possible.

Ava thought about her own wedding. Zemira and Elle were her only friends outside of family, but Sunny had a lot of family back home. How would their wedding go? Was Sunny ever going to ask? Ava looked at him standing across the isle behind Kaylen. He winked at her and Ava blushed. They were good, so she wouldn't press the issue. Not now, anyway.

Ava gigged at how Kaylen pulled Elle to him to kiss her. Elle squealed before jumping in his arms. Miss Janet told them to calm down. Kaylen came up for air and told her that he could do what he wanted. Ava laughed before linking arms with Sunny and walking out behind Kaylen and Elle. Angel pulled on the leg of Sunny's suit and he leaned over to pick her up.

"I told you, you getting too big for that!" Ava said, fixing Angel's headband. Angel shook her head violently. Ava nodded. "Yes you are. You'll be in school soon."

"I'll still pick you up," Sunny said. Angel stuck her tongue out at Ava. Ava flicked Angel's nose. Sunny laughed before grabbing Ava's hand and kissing the back of it. Ava smiled, looked up at him, and said, "Love you, shorty."

Sunny laughed.

The whole time Ava was at Miss Janet's, Dre kept calling her. She sighed, wondering why but not wanting to answer to find out. She groaned when she saw he was now texting her. Sunny leaned over and looked down at her phone.

"What's up with Dre?" he asked. Ava sighed.

"I don't know. I haven't talked to him since I deaded our deal."

"You ain't tell me that!" Sunny said. "Why? Thought it was good money."

Ava sighed again, knowing that her vow of honestly was imperative. She ran her hand down her face before looking at Sunny. "Um, because he told me, in so many words, that he had feelings for me."

She bit her lip at Sunny's silence. Ava could practically see the gears in his head turning. She waited to speak, letting him get his thoughts together.

"He ever try you?" he asked. Ava shook her head. "See what he wants."

"Huh?"

"Call him back."

Ava looked at him for a second. He did not flinch, blink or chuckle. She unlocked her phone and called Dre.

"Ignoring me is not necessary."

"Didn't think we had anything else to discuss."

"Don't be so dramatic. You need to meet me at my lawyer's office on Monday."

"What? Why?"

"Omar and Solace are buying out your rights to the songs you wrote for them."

"Those are my songs though!" Ava frowned, looking at Sunny.

"What?" he whispered, but Ava held her finger up.

"You want out right? Her producer is about to single it and the other is going Omar's album. They don't want to pay you royalties every month if you no longer on the team."

"Fine," Ava said. She didn't like his tone. "What time?"

"11."

Ava hung up without warning and told Sunny what Dre said.

"I have to work Monday," he said. Ava frowned.

"So do I, but I'll just take my lunch early."

"I can't."

"Sunny, I can go by myself," Ava said, laughing at his audacity. Sunny eyed her.

"Can you?" he asked, sarcastically.

"Yes, I can."

Dre's lawyer's office was in the only corporate building in Hamilton. The only reason it was even there was to attract recent college graduates from Jasper and get them to relocate. Ava had Katie cover for her just in case this meeting ran over her lunch hour. She wanted to get everything done so that she could be free of Dre's attitude. It wasn't her fault he played himself by catching feelings.

Ava found Mr. Coffman's office on the second floor and Dre was sitting outside of it.

"You're on time," he said.

"Let's get this over with."

Dre sighed. "Ava wait. I need to apologize to you. I didn't mean to make all this weird," he said. Ava frowned, not even wanting to have this conversation. However, she knew this wasn't something that needed to drag on.

"Don't even worry about it," she said, waving it off. Dre opened the door for her and she walked in.

Ava couldn't believe that Solace and Omar were giving her $3500 for the rights of two songs. Granted, she knew that if Solace made it big, they would make a lot more off of it, but that wasn't her concern. That money could definitely help her pay off some bills that had stacked up due to Angel's hospital stay.

"Thank you, Jesus," she thought to herself as she signed the paper work. The lawyer read over the contract and made sure Dre and Ava were both in agreement. She still had half an hour left of lunch when she walked out.

"You know, I appreciate everything you did music wise," Dre said. "I learned a lot working with you and I would really marry you if I had the chance," he said, laughing as if he was joking. For some reason, Ava knew he wasn't.

"I definitely learned a lot from you," she said. "All good things come to an end. Besides, I'm writing gospel music now."

"Really?" he said, wide eyed. Ava nodded and smiled. "Good for you."

"Yeah, see ya around."

Ava was ready to get back to work, finish her day, and head to Sunny's for date night. She rounded the corner to see a crew working on the elevator. One of the men saw her and smiled.

"Sorry darling, gotta use the stairs."

Ava sighed before turning around and walking back down the hall towards the stairs. Just as she was about to go past the men's restroom, she heard a loud voice coming through the door.

"You can't be serious, Dad? You expect me to stay here after all these years! I made a mistake, you can't fire me!"

Ava recognized the voice and leaned against the wall to hear better. She was grateful that Angel wasn't with her because something deep inside of her wanted to confront him at that moment. It had been nine months since Angel's birthday and she hadn't been equipped to speak to LaDanian Taylor then, but now she knew exactly what she wanted to say to him.

"Dad," he said, his voice broken. "I can't stay in Hamilton...yes sir."

Ava straightened up when she heard his footsteps nearing the door. She crossed her arms and smiled when he opened it. LaDanian stopped and looked up at her with wide eyes. The door to the bathroom closed as they watched and waited for each other's next move. Ava didn't move or step back, knowing it would leave him to believe she was scared like last time.

"What?" he snapped. Ava smiled.

"Work troubles?" she asked, pointing the phone in his hand. LaDanian glared at her.

"Stay out of my business."

"Gladly, as long as you know while you are here to stay away from mine."

"I have no interest in your life, Ava," he said. "You're irrelevant."

"Keep telling yourself that," she said. "If my child even breathes wrong while you're in town, I'll blame you. You don't want that type of hurt," she said. LaDanian smirked.

"So now you run Hamilton or something?"

Ava gave him a look that she was sure rocked him to the core. She wasn't playing and he knew it. LaDanian was all talk and the only way he was ever about action was if he had his flunkies behind him. Not only was he alone, but he had failed at his own game. Ava felt a little sorry for him, but she still wouldn't take back her promise.

"Nice seeing you," she lied, while walking off. "Have a nice day."

"That's all you said?" Bri asked. Ava nodded. "I guess."

"He got my point."

"I thought Christians were against violence?"

"The Bible says to turn the other cheek and let God handle things," Ava said. "But I had to let him know how I felt."

"I'm telling your pastor on you," Bri said, laughing. Ava rolled her eyes.

"Why do you care anyway? You haven't been to church since our birthday."

"Just ain't got time."

"Whatever, liar."

"I just don't see the point," Bri said. Ava nodded, not wanting to have the same conversation with her that they'd been having since she began to invite Bri to church regularly. Charity told Ava to just pray that Bri came around and she would. Ava had to take her advice and have faith that God would deliver Bri just as he had done Elle. She couldn't rush her, everyone had to go on their own time.

Ava sighed as Bri walked out of the kitchen. She went back to reading over her Bible study lesson when her phone rang.

"No peace," she said, pulling it from her purse. "Hey Z."

"What's up!"

"Nothing."

"Unc asked me to call in a favor from you," Z said.

"What's up?" Ava asked, wondering what the pastor needed.

"He has this friend who is a singer and they are looking for some new material. He said she is wanting to do an upbeat song that appeals to our generation. She's a little older."

Ava laughed. "How old?"

"Girl, I don't know, but I picked up too many hours volunteering for this degree so I didn't want to commit to it. He asked for you anyway."

"Cool," Ava said. "Is there a deadline."

"Yeah, about that…"

"Z."

"He said she wanted it by his anniversary celebration."

"Z, that's next month!"

"You got it."

Ava sighed. "I guess."

"So, I'll tell him your down?" Z asked.

"Tell him I'm down."

Ava couldn't really tell Pastor no, and she felt like he and Zemira were starting to realize that. She didn't mind though. She still hadn't joined the choir, but she sang with Z every now and then and helped her with the music. She had to admit that she had been writing songs left and right. Writing gospel music came easier to her than anything she'd done in her life. It also helped her dig more into scripture and pull songs out of what she studied.

Reading her Bible made Ava question what she wanted to do with her life. This time last year, she was so set on being a ghost writer and building a career in music and now she wasn't so sure. Ava knew she didn't want to sell phones for the rest of her life and she wanted something that would be stable enough to provide for her and Angel, even if Sunny got up the nerve to propose. Seeing what Kita went through when Rico was gone made Ava realize she had to be prepared for the worst, even if the best was just around the corner. She just didn't know it.

Sixteen

In six years, Rico had gone from a prison cell to a church. Charity sat next to Ava shaking while tears fell from her eyes. Angel, who was seated quietly on Ava's lap, leaned over and tapped Charity's hand before telling her to stop crying. Charity gave her a weak smile before a quick explanation of what "happy tears" meant. There were only a handful of times that Ava could remember having happy tears.

Bri sat on the other side of Ava with a pair of knock off Gucci glasses on. Her legs were crossed and her hands were tucked in between her thighs and the cushioned pew.

Harmonies lifted from the choir stand as a line of four men wearing all white descended down the aisle. Angel spotted Rico and stood up in the pew, waving her arms.

"Papa!" she yelled for his attention. He only glanced at her and smiled. Ava pulled her down and held her, knowing that telling Angel she was wrong for yelling would do no good.

Pastor Davidson stood in the pulpit and ushered the four men down to the first pew on the left side. Ava's heart raced as he talked, but not from his words, from what today would mean.

Seconds seemed to pass when Rico stood up and walked over to the small pool of cold water that ordinarily wasn't there. Because there wasn't one build in, every first

Sunday they brought in a temporary pool to baptize those willing.

Glimpses of the sad tears that fell the day Ava found Kita's vacant body in her bed got stuck behind her eyelids. When she opened her eyes, Rico swung his leg over and stepped into the pool alongside Deacon. His lip twitched as they placed his arms across each other on his chest.

"He's nervous," Charity whispered.

"I now baptize you, Brother Daniels, in the name of the Father, in the name of the Son and in the name of the Holy Ghost."

Ava's heart thumped as she stood up and clapped for Rico as he was brought up out of the water. He let out a little yell and threw both of his hands up and waved them. The congregation began to do the same, some more radical than others.

Charity rushed out of the pew as best as she could with her belly and towards the front, wrapped a towel around Rico and helped him towards the back to change.

Bri got up and followed but Ava knew she was leaving the church now that Rico's baptism was done. Ava stayed through prayer. Angel had fallen asleep, slumped over while sitting up.

"Lord I'm begging you to save my sister."

It was almost as if Bri took what happened to Ava all those years ago as personal attacks from God. It made perfect sense to the old Ava, but she wanted everyone she loved to feel what what she felt now. The love of God was truly transforming her heart. Hopefully Ava's heart could change theirs. She just had to be patient like Charity said. So far, Ava had to believe that. Charity hadn't pressured Rico into joining or getting baptized. After the shooting, he did it on his own. He went though the new members class and was very excited about his new life.

After church, Ava waited for Rico to come and carry Angel to the car and they went out to eat to celebrate. Days like this made Ava feel like the struggle was worth it.

"We going shopping tomorrow right, since you're off?" Charity asked while they waited on their food. Ava nodded.

"I'm warning you that I'm not ready for her to go to school," Ava said. "So I might just cry."

Rico laughed, but Charity frowned. "You aren't serious."

"She probably is."

"If you cry in this store, I'm leaving you."

Ava laughed before pulling the list of school supplies that was required for Angel's particular school out of the slot in the middle of Target. Charity rubbed her belly before putting her bag in the top of the cart. They were shopping for last minute baby things and Angel's school supplies.

Ava couldn't believe that Angel was going to pre-school in three weeks. She'd be five in a little over a month, but since her birthday was after the school year started, she'd have to go to pre-school first.

"Why does a pre-schooler need a twenty-five pack of high lighters?" Charity asked, looking over Ava's shoulder at the list. She shrugged.

"I don't know, but can you get my brother off my back please?" Ava asked. Charity sucked her teeth and moved to the side of Ava.

"Shut up! I can't wait to have him, I feel like I'm going to explode."

"Yeah, you are way bigger than I was," Ava said. Charity glared at her.

"Thanks a lot."

Ava laughed. "What do you need?"

"Burp cloths and onesies. That baby shower my co-workers threw was right on time."

"Rico bought some Jordan's the other day."

"He better hope those expensive things fit," Charity said, rolling her eyes. "I'm so glad I only have to go through this once."

"Mine wasn't that bad, but I think God just had mercy on me since everything else was going nuts," Ava said. Charity laughed and nodded.

They went through the school isle first and got everything on the list. Angel wanted a Dr. McStuffins backpack so Ava made sure to get the cutest one. She'd go clothes shopping with Sunny next week and Romero said him and his mom were going, too. Angel was going to be the flyest little pre-schooler ever.

"I'm excited for the anniversary, I hope I don't have the baby before then because I really want to do the welcome."

"Who will do it, just in case?" Ava asked, knowing that Charity probably wasn't going to make it to the beginning of September.

"Sister Karen," Charity said. "You finish that song?"

"Yes, I sent it to Pastor yesterday. He still won't tell me who it's for," Ava said.

"Maybe he wants it to be a surprise."

While they were looking through the baby stuff, Charity began to complain about her lower back hurting, so they checked out and headed home. Bri and Angel were watching a movie in the living room. Charity went to lay down and Bri and Ava helped Angel put her things in her backpack.

"You ready to go to school, Gelly?"

"No."

"Why not?"

"Daddy said I had to sit still and learn when I got there," she said, pouting.

"You will have to behave, but you'll have fun," Ava said.

"I want to stay here with you."

"You'll only be gone for a few hours and Jayla will be there."

"You promise?" Angel asked. Ava nodded. "Well, I guess."

Bri laughed. "This kid's a mess!"

"No mess, Ti-ti…I'm an angel!"

"Oh Lord," Ava said, handing Angel the backpack. "Go put this in your room."

Angel grinned and took off for the steps. A few minutes later, she was yelling.

"What is going on?" Ava asked, running up the stairs. Angel was pointing in the bathroom and the door was open. Bri looked in and saw Charity sitting up against the tub, gripping her belly.

"My water broke!" she yelled. Bri backed up and Ava laughed at Bri's face.

"Go call Daddy," Ava said. "Angel go put your shoes on."

"Is my uncle coming?" she asked. Ava smiled before looking for a towel to wipe Charity's face.

"Yep, looks like he is."

Rico couldn't stop smiling since he got to the hospital about twenty minutes after Charity was admitted. She found it very annoying but he kept a smile on his face, overjoyed that he finally had a son and he was on his way. Granny Ran had opted not to come, but nobody was upset about it. Some things just weren't going to change over night and Rico knew it, but that wasn't his concern.

Romero came and got Angel, against her will. She fought tooth and nail before Romero had to promise to bring her back first thing in the morning. The beginning of Charity's labor wasn't pretty, but it seemed as if not long after her epidural that Rico was cutting the cord and holding their son, Jonah Eli Daniels.

"He's fat!" Bri said, leaning over Charity to see her brother after Rico finally passed him to her. Charity looked up at Bri and frowned.

"He's healthy," Charity said. "He's perfect."

"Hey brother," Ava said, leaning behind Bri to touch the baby. He sucked on his bottom lip before it trembled a bit. "Yeah, we're going to be the ones getting on your nerves."

"Tell me about it," Rico said. Charity laughed.

"No, you need to worry about your niece," Bri said. They all agreed while looking over Jonah, everyone falling deeper in love with him by the second. Rico smiled before taking a picture of his family.

Ava was tired after work, but she'd promised Zemira she would come to the last choir rehearsal before the anniversary. She was also supposed to be going out with Sunny and needed to go home and get ready. Jonah had been home for three weeks and he had completely turned the house upside down. He was spoiled rotten and often needed to be held for anyone to get some peace. Charity was already dreading the thought of going back to work and Rico had picked up hours so she wouldn't have to. Charity, Ava and Bri had a little shift worked out with

Jonah. Rico said they were just making him more spoiled, but nobody could handle him crying for more than two minutes without picking him up. Even Angel was always entertaining him when she could.

Ava rubbed her exhausted eyes as she walked into the church. She greeted everyone there and sat down next to Zemira.

"Hey, what's up?"

"Girl, tired," Ava said. "What we working on?"

"Last song before the guest speaker preaches. You up for singing?" Z asked. Ava nodded. "That's why I like you girl!"

"Um hum," Ava joked. Z and a few other choir members laughed.

"Let's get this song together, we all tired."

Two hours later, Ava was putting on her tan wedges to match her shirt when Sunny walked into her room. Her curls were just about dry and all she was putting on her face was lip gloss. She looked up at Sunny and smiled. He had a button down on and some jeans with a fresh hair cut.

"Hey handsome," she said, standing up to hug him.

"You look tired, babe," he said, kissing her. "You want to just chill tonight?"

"No, I know you been planning this. I'm good."

Ava took a five hour energy shot before she took a shower. She just hoped it would last long enough to get her through date night.

"You'll have fun," he said. "I promise."

Ava bit her lip before following Sunny out of the room, telling everyone bye when she passed them in the living room. Sunny held the door open for her before getting in the car. They made small talk about their day until Sunny pulled up at the diner he and Ava went the first time they hung out together.

Ava laughed. "What is it with you and this diner?" she asked. Sunny chuckled and licked his bottom lip.

"Best day of my life," he said.

"Aw, baby!" Ava said, pulling him by his collar to kiss him. "You're too smooth."

"I know."

Ava laughed before they got out the car. Ava wrapped her arms around Sunny's arm and hugged him. She inhaled deeply, glad to be spending time with him. He kissed her forehead before opening the door to the diner. They sat at their booth and both ordered chicken and waffles.

"I think I'm getting fat."

"You did gain a few pounds," Sunny said. Ava threw her straw wrapper at him and he laughed. "Just in your hips though baby."

"You could have led with that, Santana!"

Sunny looked at her and smirked. "I love when you say my name like that."

"Don't try to come back all sweet, Mr. Smith."

"That's even better." They laughed.

"Angel ready for school?" Ava groaned.

"I'm not ready and she keeps saying she doesn't want to go. It's taking all of me not to be like, okay baby you can stay home with me forever!"

"Does Ro know I'm going on the first day, too?" Sunny asked. Ava nodded. "We are going to embarrass her."

"She'll be good."

Ava, Romero and Sunny were taking Angel to preschool the first day. They had agreed that Ava would drop her off in the morning before work and Romero or Sarah would pick her up and keep her until Ava got off. She was having anxiety about her going to school after the whole thing with Melody, but she knew she couldn't shelter her from the world. Ava would have to grow up and let Angel live.

Sunny got out of his side of the booth and came and sat next to Ava. She smiled when he wrapped his arm around her.

"I think I'm going to take a few days off next month," he said. "Head home for the weekend. Thinking you and Gel should come with me?" he said. Ava nodded, knowing she hadn't been since Sunny's mom's funeral.

"I'm down," she said. "Just let me know when."

"You down, huh?" he asked. Ava looked at him sideways and nodded.

"Always."

Sunny smiled before kissing Ava slowly. "That's what I like to hear."

The pastor's anniversary was the same day as the church's anniversary. Pastor Davidson was celebrating his 20th anniversary, but it was the church's 49th. Everyone was running around the church, decorating and doing last minute preparations for it all. First Lady Davidson had worked with the children to do a speech for the pastor, so Ava had been helping Angel learn her line by heart. She wasn't sure if she would actually go through with it or not, but she was excited while rehearsing.

Sunny picked them up for church. Rico said he would stay with Charity and help her get ready. This would be Jonah's first trip to church. Other than going to the doctor, he hadn't been out the house in the two months since he'd been born.

"Oh snap," Sunny said, running his hand down Ava's flat ironed hair. "Haven't seen my other girlfriend in a minute!"

"Sunny, that's Momma!" Angel said in the back seat. Ava laughed before putting her seat belt on. Sunny always made jokes when she flat ironed her hair.

"You look extra good today," Ava said, noticing that Sunny had on a vest and tie.

"I know," Sunny said. "Figured you would appreciate it."

"I do," she said, kissing his cheek. She turned on his radio to the gospel station and sang along with Angel while they made their way to church.

When they got to church, Zemira was walking in.

"Ava, I'm glad you're early. I couldn't hold this in until the end of service!" Zemira said, jumping a little and pulling on Ava's arm.

Ava frowned and laughed a little. "What's going on girl?"

"I can't even tell you, you just have to come see!"

"See what?"

"Someone is in my uncle's office to see you!"

"We going to sit down," Sunny said, grabbing Angel's hand. Ava nodded and followed Zemira.

"You are creeping me out," Ava said.

"It's going to be awesome," Zemira said. They got to Pastor Davidson's office and Zemira knocked.

"Come on in," he said. Ava walked in behind Zemira.

"Oh Jesus…"

"Ava, how are you?" Pastor Davidson said. Ava stood there stunned.

"You know you're Yolanda Adams right?" Ava asked. Zemira, Yolanda and Pastor Davidson laughed.

"Yes dear and I just wanted to meet you personally and thank you for that beautiful song you wrote for me."

"Huh?" Ava asked. Pastor Davison smiled. "That song was for Yolanda Adams!?"

"Yes!" Zemira chimed in. "Isn't that incredible?"

"You all set me up?" Ava asked.

"I wouldn't call it that," Pastor Davidson said.

"I knew how you were feeling about your deal you told me about, and you were so inspiring with the songs you helped me with. When this opportunity came up, I told Unc to make it happen. Are you mad?"

"No! This is Yolanda Adams!" Ava said. They all laughed again.

"The song is wonderful, we're recording it soon and I would love for you to come check our studio out and possibly write me some more."

"Are you serious?"

"Yes."

"Well, I'm in," Ava said, holding her chest. "My God, this is amazing."

"You deserve it," Zemira said. Ava bit her lip and nodded. "Now come on."

"You will not believe what just happened," Ava said as she sat down next to Sunny.

"Hey, ain't that Yolanda Adams?" he asked, pointing towards the door. Ava smiled and nodded.

"And she wants me to write for her!"

"That's what's up baby," Sunny said, holding up his hand for a high-five. Ava giggled and high-fived him. "It all worked out then."

"Yeah," Ava said, sighing in relief. "It did."

Rico and Charity came in with Jonah and soon after Kaylen, Elle, Jayla and KJ came in. They sat in the row behind them as Ava took Jonah out of his car seat and kissed over his face. She couldn't wait to tell everyone the good news after church, but right now she just wanted to enjoy the service.

Everything was great. The praise and worship team took the service to another level and the spirit moved all over the building. Yolanda said a few words and even sang. Ava didn't know that Pastor Davidson went to college with her and that's how they knew each other. After she sang with Zemira and the guest speaker preached, Ava was exhausted but full from the day's events.

She was about to slip out and go get a drink of water during altar call, but before she moved, Sunny did. Ava watched him get up and hold his hand out to her. Ava smiled hard as she grabbed his hand and walked up to the front of the church with him. Everyone clapped as a few other people walked up as well. Pastor Davidson got up and smiled.

"Now, I wasn't supposed to do anything today, but this young man came to me a few days ago and he wants to be a member of the church!"

Everyone clapped and cheered, including Ava, who was beyond happy that Sunny wanted to join. He had been going with her faithfully, so she knew it was only a matter of time before he did.

"He also has a few words to say," Pastor Davidson said, before handing Sunny the microphone. Ava looked at him, noticing he hadn't let go of her hand.

"Ava, I thought about how I would say this to you over the last few days and everything I wanted to say just don't make sense now."

"What are you doing?" Ava whispered. Sunny winked at her.

"I can't even imagine doing anything else for the rest of my life besides living to make you happy," he said. Everyone 'awed' as he handed Pastor Davidson back the microphone. He pulled a box out of his pocket and got down on one knee. Ava screamed when he opened the box. "Will you marry me, shorty?"

Everyone laughed at Sunny's choice of words as Ava nodded and held her left hand out eagerly. Sunny slid the ring on her finger and stood up. He hugged her close to him.

"I'll kiss you later," he whispered in her ear as everyone clapped for them. Ava nodded before crying into his shoulder.

"Why would you do this in front of everybody?" she cried. He laughed.

"So someone can take a picture of your ugly, crying face."

Ava hit him in his arm as they walked hand in hand back to their seat. Everybody was standing up to hug them. Ava couldn't even talk she was so overwhelmed.

"This is unreal," she thought. "God, you have amazed me on so many levels. I cannot begin to thank You for blessing me this much, but I promise I will forever be grateful. You have shown me that I can't do anything on my own and I don't even want to. Everything I tried to do within myself bombed and now I know that when all else fails…You won't."

Amen.

Made in the USA
Middletown, DE
04 December 2022